Love in TRAINING

EMILIA REED

FOX DEN PRESS

Trade Paperback ISBN: 979-8-9870785-8-7
eBook ISBN: 979-8-9934953-0-9

Cover design by Staci Hart
Editing by Comma Sutra Editorial

*Content note: this story was written for mature audiences and discusses topics regarding PTSD, depression, suicide, grief, stalking, assault, and emotionally abusive parents. Reader discretion is advised.

For the imposters

PROLOGUE
TWO YEARS EARLIER

My name is scrawled in a familiar script on the envelope I discover at the bottom of my purse. I retrieve it and the decorative comb for my hair with a curious smile. That would be just like Kyle, hiding a little love note even when it breaks the no-contact tradition. But I drop it back into my bag as Lydia scurries back into the room.

"Oh, good. You've got your something old." She takes the comb, placing it carefully in my upswept hair. "And your something new—this gorgeous dress. Something borrowed— your mom's earrings. All we need is—" Lydia hands me the bouquet of white roses and blue forget-me-nots, then steps back, beaming. "Oh, Caprice. You're perfect."

I close my eyes, letting out a contented sigh. I *feel* perfect. Everything is finally coming together. The church, the dress, the planning, the people—well, most of them. I could never have guessed ten years ago, after that first awkward date in high school, that this is where Kyle and I would wind up. But we'd stayed enamored with each other through college and even figured out the long-distance thing once he enlisted. Now, after managing to exist separately for so long, we're finally tying the knot and will spend the rest of our lives together.

My mom comes over, not-so-subtly wiping tears from her eyes, fussing with the lace on my gown. My one enormous splurge in an otherwise modest wedding. It's a champagne color that makes my brown skin glow, with a plunging back and a skirt that hugs my curves before giving way to a three-foot train of silk and lace. I'll still be paying for it several years from now, but it'll be worth it. I've waited so long for this moment. I feel more beautiful than I have in my entire life. I've kept the dress a secret from Kyle just so I can see his expression for the first time today as I walk toward him down the aisle.

"Is everyone here?" I ask Lydia, my one and only bridesmaid, matron of honor, and best friend.

"I think so." She glances over her shoulder. "Anton just went to make sure everyone's in place."

A flutter passes through my chest, and I reach out to squeeze my mom's hand.

"Wedding jitters?" she says with a smile.

"Maybe a little. I don't know why." I let out a small laugh. "Kyle and I have wanted to get married for years, but it's still . . ."

"A big day?" My mom winks. "Even my wedding felt like it at the time."

My cheeks heat when she mentions this. Her own marriage ended four years in, after my dad confessed he preferred to sleep with men. While this was a difficult revelation, things *might* have worked out if he hadn't decided to skip out on being a father. She hardly ever talks about him, and when she does, it's usually under duress. But right now, there's nothing but mirth in her eyes.

"Everything about my *wedding day* was perfect," she says with a wistful smile. "And you're an even more beautiful bride."

Anton ducks back into the room, looking like a Ken doll in his dark blue suit, his brown hair perfectly styled. Which wouldn't be funny if Lydia didn't very much resemble Margot Robbie from the *Barbie* movie. They're the most stereotypically beautiful couple. They're also two of my favorite people.

"Looks like a full house out there," Anton says. "The minister is all set . . ." He looks at me, Lydia, and my mom, but his gaze skates past us to an empty chair in the corner of the room. "Where'd Theo go?"

"He stepped out earlier to take a call." Lydia shrugs.

My twin brother is pulling double duty in the ceremony, walking me down the aisle and serving as best man. Theo and my fiancé had been friends way before Kyle and I fell in love with each other, but he'd taken our romance in stride. The two of them were already practically brothers.

"Right . . ." Anton says. "I'll just go see if I can find him."

My stomach does a little flip as he leaves, and I imagine the rows of people who drove out here to see Kyle and me get married in this beautiful mountain chapel. It's mostly my mom's family and our friends from high school and college. Kyle's parents and brother were invited, but declined the invitation. I have told myself a hundred times it wasn't because of me, and he's told me the same thing. But deep in my heart, I know he's hurt by their absence. Especially his brother's.

After this is over—after the reception, the cake, and a week together on the beach—Kyle will report back to North Carolina, and I'll fly back to Denver to pack up the rest of my things.

Then I'll be all the family he needs.

"Mom, one of your pins is loose," I say, grateful for something simple to focus on while we wait. She steps closer, and I take a minute to fix her updo. My mother is a tall, elegant white woman whose nearly black hair has only one thin streak of gray to betray her age. We share bone structure and the same smile, and one day I kind of hope I get that gray streak too. "There," I say, tucking her updo back into place. "All fixed."

We smile at each other. Then we both look at Lydia, whose face betrays a glimmer of anxiety the longer we stand here in silence. Theo and Anton have been gone a while.

"Not to worry," my mom says, taking my hand again. "Theo will be back in a minute. I'm sure he just had to get Kyle situated with the minister."

I nod, trying to ignore the twisting in my middle.

"Yeah, exactly." Lydia clears her throat and picks up her phone. "I'll just go—"

At that moment, my twin brother blusters into the room, all spiffed up and elegant in his service dress blues, his shaved brown head gleaming in the light. Almost as good-looking as the groom. Except when I look up, his handsome face is not at all excited. It's serious and drawn.

"What's wrong?" I ask before he can even open his mouth.

Theo hesitates, and for a second, it's clear he's attempting a smile. My brother is well known for blowing sunshine where it doesn't belong, but the sinking feeling in my gut is not going to hear that. Not on my wedding day.

"Uh . . . Reece? Can I talk to you alone?"

My fist tightens around my bouquet. "No."

He tugs at his collar, looking past me to Lydia and my mom. Behind him, Anton fills the doorway, a pair of small lines pushed together between his brows.

My heart jumps from a low thud to a stuttering gallop as I realize I'm about to hear something awful. I slept at my mom's last night. Kyle and I agreed not to call or text in case it was bad luck . . . but he left a note in my purse. What if he was in an accident? What if he's hurt? What if—I sway on my feet and close my eyes as the unthinkable crosses my mind.

"Theo, is Kyle—"

"He's not coming, Reece," my brother says quietly. He steps forward, his normally playful demeanor soft and somber.

"*Why?*" I bring my hand to my chest, trying to breathe, but my lungs are a vacuum. Grief pricks the corners of my eyes. Because the only reason Kyle wouldn't be here, wouldn't already be at the altar waiting for me, ready to say *I do*—is the very worst reason. The one that, until this moment, had only existed as a distant nightmare in the darkness that sometimes consumes him.

Next to me, my mother whimpers. But then Theo awkwardly shatters my whole conception of worst things.

"Um . . . I just spoke to him. He was getting on a plane to head back east."

Air sucks back into my lungs at the realization that Kyle's alive. But only for a moment before an empty ache squeezes in like a fist.

"He *what?*" Lydia's indignation is a shadow of what's going on inside me. She's just one hundred percent more capable of speaking.

Theo bows his head. "I'm sorry—I didn't know, or I would've dragged his ass here myself. Maybe I can still—"

"You think she still wants to marry a guy who abandoned her at the church?" Lydia snaps. Then her face flickers, and she whips her head toward me. "Do you?"

My knees give out. I sink to the floor, champagne silk and lace pooling around me. Aside from some restless noises filtering down the hall from the sanctuary, the room is dead silent. No one around me moves.

I stare at the bouquet still clutched in my hands, the forget-me-nots somehow already more gray than blue as the emptiness in my chest expands, working down into my limbs.

"Did he say why?" I whisper in a voice that doesn't sound at all like me.

"He just, uh—" My big, fearless Navy SEAL brother chokes. "He said he was trying to protect you? I don't know. Reece, I'm sorry."

I look up into Theo's sorrowful brown eyes. Our mom has moved next to him, clutching her hand to her chest, and as she does, some deeper part of my heart breaks. Kyle hasn't just hurt me; he's hurt everyone he loves.

"Trying to protect me?" I murmur.

Theo's mouth presses into a line. "Look, Caprice, maybe he just got cold feet—"

"Staff Sergeant Kyle Forbes?" I snarl. "You think a Silver Star-decorated Army Ranger got cold feet about saying *I do*?"

"Well, no." He frowns. "You're right. But you know, since his injury—"

"Fuck his injury," I say, starting to sound more like myself. "He made a full recovery. We worked through his grief over the dog. He helped me *plan* this wedding. If he had reservations, he had months to let me know."

"I'm not defending him." Theo's eyes flash. "But I think he's struggling—"

"And what am I doing right now?" I smash my bouquet onto the floor, grinding it into the carpet. "Am I supposed to feel bad and forgive him? I'm the one who has to face the people out there." I gesture toward the sanctuary with my decimated flowers.

"Um, I can handle that . . ." Anton offers behind me.

"Thank God for a competent man," I hiss, dragging myself to my feet. I face my tiny wedding party and lift my chin. "Lydia, could you please get me the leggings, sneakers, and hoodie I was wearing this morning? I need out of this dress *now*."

My matron of honor hustles off to find my clothes. Her husband follows her out, on his way to inform my friends and family that I've been dumped.

I turn back to my brother, ready to let loose another

torrent about Kyle, but when I see his face, I lose my resolve. He looks wrecked. Like he's been abandoned by a beloved brother, much as I've been left by the love of my life.

"Go get changed, Theo. We're finding the nearest mountain, and I'm not stopping till we've climbed to the top."

"Quandary Peak isn't far from here," our mother cuts in, sounding shell-shocked. "You can reach the summit without any gear."

I look at her gratefully and nod.

Theo follows her out as Lydia reenters and hands me my bag—the one I was supposed to take this evening on a flight to Cancun. She turns me around without a word and starts unlacing the back of my dress.

"If Kyle thinks he can do this to me . . ." My voice quakes as she works. "He's the one who's going to need to be *protected.*"

Lydia places a gentle hand on my shoulder, and when I turn to look at her face, I burst into tears.

"I love him, Lydia." She guides me to a nearby couch where I collapse, sobbing into her arms. "Goddammit, I hate him. But I *still* love him so much."

Once Lydia frees me from my prison of fine fabrics, Theo and I sneak toward a side door, intent on making a break for his car while Anton does damage control with the guests left behind in the church. My hair is still picture perfect, but I washed off my ruined makeup. At least in my hoodie and sneakers, I can pretend I feel like myself.

"Let's get out of here," Theo says, squeezing my hand as he opens the exit door.

But the moment we step outside, we nearly collide with a tall figure in a suit. I gasp in confusion at the familiar large frame, the dark hair—but the glasses, those are wrong. My brother steps forward with his chest puffed up.

"What are *you* doing here?"

Air reenters my lungs, and my brain catches up. If not for the uncanny resemblance to my former fiancé, I would never have recognized his estranged brother.

Drew Forbes looks from my brother to me, taking in our casual attire, brows drawn together. "I . . . came for the wedding."

And with this, my heart has had quite enough.

"There is no wedding," I sneer. "There never will be."

I brush past him, making a beeline for my brother's car. I don't notice until we're pulling out of the parking lot that I'm still wearing Kyle's ring.

Theo and I spend my wedding day hiking the arduous trail to the top of Quandary Peak. We hug each other, crying, at the fourteen-thousand-foot summit and hardly say a word on the way back down.

I don't remember Kyle's envelope until the next day, when I dump out my purse.

Maybe he thought I'd see it and be able to call off the ceremony before anyone arrived at the church in fine dresses and suits. But if his intentions were good, I don't feel like giving him any credit. He could have spared me a lot of pain by just saying something to my face.

My name is on the envelope in simple black script. On the back, it says *I'm Sorry.*

I can't bring myself to open it. My inclination is to rip it to shreds. Burn the pieces. Maybe mail him the ashes. My mom stops me before I get the chance.

"You're not ready to read whatever's in this right now," she says. "You might not ever be. But in case that ever changes, let me hold on to it."

I don't say anything. Don't nod. But I let her take it out of my hands. Put it away somewhere in her house. I don't ask where—I don't want to know. I just zip my beautiful wedding gown into its garment bag, take it home, and shove it to the back of my closet.

Sunday, June 6, 20__, 10:58 PM

To: Kyle.Forbes@mail.com

From: Caprice_Phipps@mail.com

Subject: no subject

Dear Kyle,

Since you weren't brave enough to say goodbye to my face, I'll say it here, in a bland fucking email. Maybe I ought to say thanks for "protecting" me from a lifetime of love. All you've really done is deny yourself something you clearly didn't deserve.

I'm blocking you now, so don't reply. Nothing you write could ever fix this. For someone so valiant, you are such a coward. I thought we had everything. I can't believe you did this to me.

C

CHAPTER
ONE

It's fifteen minutes until the Monday meeting and time to regret all my choices.

"Hi, is this Chloe? This is Caprice Phipps with the *Mile High Observer*." I flip through hangers in my closet, land on an olive blouse I don't hate, and yank it over my head.

"Oh," the woman on the line says as I readjust my earbud. "Hi."

I zip my skirt and clear my throat, zeroing in on my lucky pair of Louboutins. I used to be better at this. I'd show up to the office early, dressed to the nines and armed with five or six leads on a spreadsheet. Spend some time bantering with my colleagues about the previous week's stories before we'd settle into a friendly pitch competition. Randall gets the final say, of course, but I always had a selection of solid features to choose from.

But here I am rushing around at home, smoothing my hair into a ponytail and still trying to scrape together one pathetic idea.

"Listen, I know it hasn't been long since we last talked, but we had so many comments about you and Greg after our feature, I thought a follow-up might be—"

"Yeah, don't bother," she says, flicking the words off her tongue like they taste bad.

I pause, ears perking up as I sit on the bed to fasten my shoe straps.

"Oh . . . did something happen?"

"You bet it did."

The corner of my mouth tugs, but I don't rub my hands together quite yet. I glance at my smartwatch and wince at the thought of running in these heels. If this story goes the way it sounds like it's going, though, it'll be worth it.

"I'm so sorry to hear that," I say. "I'd been hoping to write a part two about you guys after the wedding."

She snorts. Greg and Chloe had been the darlings of my Valentine's Day feature last month. They were supposed to get married at Loveland Ski Area's annual Mountaintop Matrimony ceremony after literally running into one another on the slopes the year before. She had a concussion—he scooped her up and skied down the mountain for help, then lied to the ski patrol about being her boyfriend just to stay with her and get her number.

Honestly, Valentine's Day is not my thing, and I'd kind of phoned in the feature. But apparently they were the meet-cute story everyone else wanted to hear. I've had more comments and emails asking for an update on their nuptials over the last few weeks than anything else I've written for months.

"Yeah, I found Greg in bed with *two* other women the morning of the wedding," Chloe snarls.

I try not to squeal. This just keeps getting better. I might be late for this morning's meeting, but I'm going to dash in there with a story that'll make Randall salivate. Scandal, sensation, a happily-ever-after in ruins because of a degenerate man. This is the kind of thing I live for—and it also sells ad space.

"Oh, Chloe," I say. "I'm . . . so sorry."

"Not as sorry as I am," she huffs. "He actually had the balls to invite me to join them."

My eyebrows shoot up. Oh hell *yes*. I'm already writing the feature in my head—a Valentine's Day postmortem with a twist no one saw coming. Our readers will be scandalized, and my editor will love it. I've been searching for the right lead to position myself for a raise, and I think I might have just found it—right until the moment Chloe bursts into tears.

"I thought he was everything. I just wish I'd never even met him!"

Her words echo through my head and sink into my chest, slowing the world down. Suddenly, I'm aware of each breath moving in and out, each thud of my heart. My gaze flickers involuntarily toward my closet. To the garment bag barely visible in the back, holding a beautiful champagne-colored dress. Quietly, I rise from the bed, closing the doors on the wedding gown and the ache in my heart. I grab my keys and glance at my smartwatch.

"Girl, believe me . . ." I say to the woman sobbing quietly in my ear. "I get that."

By the time I blow through the front doors of the *Observer*, I'm a full ten minutes late. I ignore the judgy look Tracy shoots me from reception, hurrying past her for the conference room, though the temptation to slink into a ball under my desk is strong.

On the speed-walk from my apartment, I tried to manifest some other leads. Yesterday, I had three in the running, but they fizzled one by one. Love—or love gone wrong—became kind of my brand last spring after I published a series of controversial articles about Unmatched, a dating app for married cheaters. Lately, though, it's started to feel less like a brand and more like a pigeonhole.

I slip into the conference room in the middle of Randall's review of last week's hits and misses, grateful to find an empty chair at the end of the table. We make eye contact as I sit, but his gaze is neutral, so I let myself breathe. He's going over the stories that got pushed because of the primary elections. An opinion piece on downtown taco shops, an update on local population growth, and a feature of the local band Cognitive Distortion.

"All right, so I've got a stack of assignments up for grabs," he says, pushing back in his chair at the head of the table. "But before I get into those, let me hear what you've come up with."

I place my laptop in front of me, opening up the spreadsheet where I organize my pitches, trying hard to swallow despite my throat being bone dry.

"I've got a lead on nefarious funding for downtown construction projects," my colleague Brian says, taking the stage. Randall nods, giving him an instant green light. Of course. Ever since Brian broke a story about a member of the Colorado House of Representatives blackmailing interns at the state capitol, he's been Randall's golden boy.

"E-scooters being used by crime rings," Adrienne offers. "And I got a tip this morning about a brand of cannabis being recalled at thirty-plus dispensaries."

Randall pauses, then nods again. You can't go wrong covering the marijuana industry in Denver. "Fine. Just be sure you've got actual police reports for the scooter thing."

Jana sits forward in her seat next to me. "I want to do a feature on the cats of Coors Field."

There's a twitch in Randall's right cheek. Otherwise his face reveals nothing. "Didn't you already do that last spring?"

"Yes . . . But I want to do a follow-up on the fan-led spay and neuter campaign."

He runs a hand over his face. Jana might be our interim sports reporter, but she'd dedicate an entire section to animal welfare if she could. "Fine. Whatever. But how about you *also* give us a perspective on the Rockies' prospects after spring training." He shifts slightly, turning toward me. "How about you, Caprice? What's cooking this week?"

It kills me how optimistic he sounds. So far, no one's hit on the type of story Randall really craves—a thrilling insta-headline like the one I practically held in my hands half an hour ago. Unfortunately, I'm not about to either.

I look again at my spreadsheet with its three dead-end ideas, then raise my chin and attempt to pull something out of thin air.

"Um, I was thinking of doing a piece on how much dating sucks in Denver . . . maybe try to turn it into some kind of series?" As soon as the words are out of my mouth, I *feel* how uninspired I sound.

Randall's face falls. He glances around the table, then pinches the bridge of his nose without looking at me. "Is that really the best you can do?"

The way he says it, I'm not sure if he's speaking to me or the entire room. But my cheeks are already on fire, and I'm too mortified to look up from my screen. I work harder than anyone else at the *Observer*—I have to as the only Black woman on staff. And I hate how much this stings.

He closes his laptop. "All right, we'll lead with Brian's construction story unless Adrienne's cannabis turns into something bigger. But I also want one of you to cover the public school board meeting this week. Two of the board members nearly got into a fistfight last month, which should have already been on everyone's radar. Adrienne, take Jeremy with you when you're looking into the e-scooters thing and see if you can get some photos to go with it. The rest of you, I want follow-ups and reader opinions on every piece we've printed for the last month. If we have to rehash the Sylvester murder again, go ahead, but we're not going to fill these pages with fluff." He turns directly to me. "Caprice, I want you on the assignment desk. Also, I'm going to need you to cover the Denver PetExpo this weekend."

"*What?*" Jana and I echo in unison. The assignment desk is a low-level punishment typically reserved for interns and new hires. You slog through every *Observer* voicemail, email, and social media account, sifting through the complainers and conspiracy theorists looking for real tips. That alone tells me where I stand with my boss. But it's an unspoken rule in our newsroom that Jana always covers anything dog or cat related. She's literally obsessed, and I'd rather clean the office toilets.

Randall turns to Jana, barely blinking. "You said you'd be gone this weekend for your grandfather's funeral?"

She shoots me a look, sucking in her bottom lip, and all I can think is her grandpa better really be dead because my weekend plans did *not* include tromping around an event complex that smells like dog pee.

"Great," Randall says, rising from his chair and looking around the table. "If anyone needs help drumming up ideas for next week, you can check with Caprice."

Brian shoots me a smug look, and I close my eyes. His dumb construction story isn't even interesting—it just sucked less than everyone else's. I force myself to wait a beat as Randall exits, then fly out of my chair and follow him down the hall.

"Okay, look," I say before I'm even through the door of his office. "I know I can do better—"

"I'd get cracking on those reader emails if I were you," he says, breezing behind his desk. "Tracy said we were about seventy-five deep after this weekend."

I close the door behind me, ignoring his directive. "I *had* a much better pitch this morning—"

"Then next time, I suggest you share it." He sets down his laptop and gives me a hard look. "The *Observer* has done the dating column thing. We stopped for good reason."

I bite the inside of my cheek. "All right, that's fair. I'm just —I'm trying to stay on brand."

He studies me across the desk and softens a little. Randall looks like a slightly heavy Colonel Sanders, with snow-white hair and a matching goatee, though I doubt he's even sixty. Sometimes he can be a real hardass, but in this moment, he's looking at me more thoughtfully.

He sinks into his chair. "What *is* your brand, exactly?"

"I beg your pardon?"

He leans back, steepling his fingers. "What kind of journalism do readers expect from Caprice Phipps?"

I falter a moment. I've been struggling with this question for months now. Which is probably why he asked. And for a heartbeat, I even consider sharing an idea I've been sitting on for almost a year. But instead I say, "Um . . . sex and dating?"

"Why?"

My skin flushes hot. "Because I've had success with that topic in the past?"

He doesn't say anything, and I become preoccupied with a smudge on the wall behind him that looks a little like a skull. And the fact that my left shoe feels too tight. And I should probably get on those emails like he suggested—

"Caprice."

I meet his gray-blue eyes and let out a long, shallow breath. There's a reason Randall is an excellent editor. Not only does he have keen intuition, but he also has a delicate way of pointing out the most suffocating elephants in any room.

I clear my throat. "You know, I think I might be missing my calling as a barista," I say, sinking into one of the chairs across from him.

He chuckles and smooths his mustache. "You might be. Though after a successful, viral takedown of Denver's married cheaters, writing people's names on paper cups seems like a waste of your talent."

"But covering a *pet expo* definitely isn't."

He shrugs. "Guess if you're fixing lattes, we'll never know."

I shoot him a glare.

"I'll take mine extra hot, with a double shot of espresso and two pumps of—"

I smack his desk. "Baristas probably get paid better."

"Better than a staff writer at a regional weekly," he says, calling out our mutual employer. "But maybe not a feature writer at, say . . . *Denver Editorial*."

My lip curls. "I wouldn't know."

"You still could."

He holds my gaze and I don't look away, even as I feel my insides shriveling. "Is it time to go over this again, Randall?" I say to the smudge behind him. "The last time I tried to improve my prospects, I received an inbox full of death threats. I'm a woman of color, and I live alone. I'm not interested in putting career ahead of personal safety."

"I'm not saying you should."

"Great, we're on the same page. Now, if you'll excuse me, I'm going to sift through reader emails and write up a nice selection of copy you can print without a byline."

"Is that really what you want?" he asks, watching me rise from the chair.

I force myself to meet his eyes, but I don't answer.

"I'm not putting you on the assignment desk as a punishment," he says, folding his hands. "Sometimes being on the front lines can help. There are so many leads, it can break you out of a rut."

"You think I'm in a rut?"

"I think you can do better than sex and dating." He pauses, glancing at the closed door. "And unlike some of your colleagues, I know you can do better than the *Observer*."

I raise my brows and lower my voice. "Careful, Randall. If your office is bugged, you'll be working an espresso machine with me."

He chuckles, but his eyes are serious. "Caprice, we both know you're destined for bigger things."

My voice shakes as I turn away. "See, that's where you're wrong. I like it here. The pace is good, my coworkers are tolerable. Even if the pay does suck."

"Bring me the right story and you've got yourself a raise," he says as I open the door. "It doesn't need to be sex or dating. Your strength is human interest."

"Sure." I snort. "I'll get right on that after I cover Denver's puppies and kittens."

CHAPTER
TWO

LYDIA

My mom and sister are FINALLY on a plane
back to Ohio.

> YAY. Can I print T-shirts now? I survived the
> Baby Shower of 20__

LYDIA

LOL. Thanks again for coming. And for the
adorable layette set.

> I hope Anton rubbed your feet afterward.

THIS IS THE NICEST THING I CAN THINK TO SAY, AND I'M GLAD
when Lydia doesn't answer. I have my best friend's no-good
husband to thank for my biggest journalistic success. And the
fact that I haven't had another one since. I was doing casual
research for an article on dating sites about a year ago when I
stumbled across Anton Richie's profile on the Unmatched app
—a site that exists solely for married hookups.

I one hundred percent expected to be reintroducing Lydia
to the dating scene by now, after she nailed Anton's balls to
the wall in divorce court. Instead, after a tumultuous few

months during which she catfished and confronted him, and he put her through an obscene amount of pain, I just attended a baby shower for their firstborn.

She's explained it to me in more detail than even my stomach could handle. TMI about the dynamics of their marriage and sex life, and not nearly enough about Anton laying down a good grovel. If you ask me, the man doesn't know how.

But he claims he'll never try to cheat again. And Lydia seems . . . happy.

So I keep my mouth shut. And mostly only scowl at him when she isn't looking. But watching that all go down was reaffirming. Lydia can keep her marriage, if that's what she wants. And I'll just keep writing about all the reasons men can't be counted on.

Or at least, that seemed like a solid plan until November.

When I arrive outside my apartment door, I let out a relieved sigh, looking up and down the empty hall. No unexpected deliveries. No envelopes taped or tucked into the cracks of the door. And I haven't received a legitimately threatening email for at least a month. But once you get in the habit of being paranoid, it's hard to let go.

I checked my peephole camera app before leaving the gym after work, and it hadn't recorded anything of note. So I let myself in, flipping the lights on and dropping my bag onto one of the stools at my little breakfast bar.

I live in a studio apartment, which is easy enough to scan and clear mostly in one glance. Everything's exactly the way I left it this morning. On the far side of the room, my bed is made with the fluffy purple duvet and green pillows I splurged on when I moved in. My green midcentury microfiber couch, an incredible find from an online second-hand market, divides the "bedroom" space from the living area. A TV is mounted to the wall by the door, because the opposite wall—the entire reason I originally moved in—is one long counter with a stretch of windows to the ceiling. When the sun is up, I have the most incredible view of the Rocky Mountains to the west of Denver.

I flip the deadbolt, but don't set down my keys or kick off my shoes until I've peeked into the bathroom and inside the closet. Once I'm satisfied I am well and truly alone, I let go of my pepper spray canister and strip off my clothes to shower.

A day in the life of a lady journalist.

After I've rinsed away the forty minutes of squats and deadlifts I put in after work at the gym, I condition and wrap my hair, heat up a frozen ramen bowl, and settle on the couch to catch up on email. Randall wasn't kidding about staying on top of the *Observer* inbox. Keeping it at zero has been so time-consuming, I haven't had time to check my own—which isn't the worst thing. Sometimes wading into my work email is more precarious than stepping into my apartment. But I need to deal with both before bed or I won't sleep.

Monday, March 8, 20__, 6:09 PM

To: Info@MHObserver.com

From: GESmith@mail.com

Subject: feedback

Does the *Observer* not use a proofreader? There was a typo in your article on the new club on Lincoln Street. I'll let you find it yourself.

Monday, March 8, 20__, 3:59 PM

To: Info@MHObserver.com

From: iluvcox@mail.com

Subject: Garbage

I am never reading the political waste featured in this publication again. Pleese fire Adrienne P and hire someone more attractive.

Monday, March 8, 20__, 3:16 PM

To: Caprice_Phipps@MHObserver.com

From: Mrs.R@mail.com

Subject: A proposal

Ms. Phipps,

Randall Jones suggested I email you directly. I have a story you might be interested in—information you have not yet covered related to the Unmatched app. Please reply to this message, or you can call or text: 303-555-4462.

Mrs. R.

I close my laptop and wander to the fridge for a bottle of water, scrolling through my phone for music to break up the thoughts in my head. If there's anything worse than reading your own hate mail, it has to be also sifting through everyone else's. I was not, however, expecting to find an actual lead.

I want the raise my boss offered today. *Need* it, if I'm honest—my credit card balance has crept into the lie-awake-at-night range. But I'll have to find something else to write about. I don't know where Randall dug up "Mrs. R.," but I'd still rather lose sleep worrying about money than ever write another word about Unmatched.

Before I can turn on my favorite guilty pleasure Broadway score, the theme from *Scooby Doo* cuts through the air, and my brother's face fills my screen. I let out a resigned sigh.

"Shouldn't you be out causing trouble?" I ask. "Thought you were deploying soon."

"Yeah, soon," Theo confirms. "Just trying to tie up some loose ends."

Something in his voice sounds off. He hasn't mentioned being sick recently, but I find myself scanning his handsome face, looking for signs he's been under the weather. Nothing stands out. His eyes are clear; his skin flawless, as always. There's stubble across his square jaw, but his head is shaved so close he might as well be bald. Otherwise, he'd have a full head of thick, curly hair like mine. In the looks department, we're a fifty-fifty mix of our Italian mother and Black dad. I guess despite all his faults, no one can dispute that Anthony Phipps was attractive.

"What loose ends? You literally don't even own a houseplant."

Theo's a Navy SEAL and has been for the last eight years. It had been his goal since we were at least ten, but I didn't really understand the phrase "living the dream" until I attended his graduation ceremony. After I watched him receive his trident with the rest of his class, it was clear he lived and breathed for those guys, and they felt the same way about him.

I thought I'd had something like that too.

"Actually, I'm going to drop in on you one last time before I head out."

"Theo. I have managed to maintain my existence the last six months, even with you back in Virginia."

"I know. I've been monitoring your front door footage."

I huff and wrinkle my nose. "You won't be able to do that from wherever it is you're going this time."

"True. Which is why I'm bringing you something before I leave."

"Oh no. You've done more than enough in the way of gifts. I already have pepper spray, a Taser, and a personal safety alarm—*which*, by the way, went off by accident in the grocery store last week. I couldn't figure out how to shut it off for like two minutes."

Theo bites his lip in amusement. Since we were old

enough to walk, he's swung back and forth between serving as my protector and enjoying my torment. "Just looking out for my little sister."

"I am still, and always will be, three minutes older than you."

His joking tone fades abruptly. "Anyway, I might need you to come get me at the airport Friday . . . with a car."

I furrow my brow, setting my water aside. "I might be able to borrow Lydia's. Why?"

He grunts. "I really think you should have one of your own . . ."

"Maybe when they start giving them out for free. My Vespa gets me anywhere I can't ride my bike. Or I take the light rail."

He frowns. This is an old argument. "Whatever. Sure, borrow Lydia's."

My mood—and the appeal of his visit—is dropping by the moment. I glance at my calendar, remembering the stupid pet expo Randall's making me cover. "Actually, I'll be busy that day. Call Mom or get an Uber."

"Reece. Can you just not make everything an argument for once?"

I set the phone against my fruit bowl and fold my arms. "Okay. I won't argue. If you tell me why I need to phone in a favor with my best friend just to give my grown-ass special ops-trained little brother a ride home from the airport."

He looks up at the ceiling. "It'll be much easier to explain once I get there."

"Great. Then get yourself to my apartment and explain it to me then." I reach forward to end the call, no longer in the mood for Theo's games.

"*Wait,*" he says. And the ragged edge of his tone, paired with the haunted look on his face, keeps me from hanging up.

"The thing I'm bringing . . . it's . . . it's important."

"Come on, Theo. This is stupid. If you won't tell me what it is, just tell me *why* all this is necessary."

"Because." He swallows, and then his jaw hardens as he stares at me through the camera. "I'm bringing you something of Kyle's."

My lips part as I sink onto one of my barstools, trying to process what he just said. Why Theo would do this to me.

Because Kyle is dead.

CHAPTER
THREE

There must be hundreds of dog and cat-related vendors crammed into the National Western complex for the opening of Denver PetExpo on Friday evening. By five o'clock, we've walked by everything from five-hundred-dollar dog beds to rhinestone collars and leashes, to jewelry made of cremated pet ashes and specialty toys made to look like political figures. There is a stage holding a pet costume contest, an arena for "wiener races," and an enormous inflatable pool for something called "dock diving," where dogs launch themselves into the water to retrieve floating toys. On top of that, we've passed a poodle dyed six different colors, a sheepdog being pulled in a wagon, and a fleet of little fluffy dogs that could bark the tune for *Jingle Bells*.

We are in Lydia Richie paradise.

"What should we look at next?" she says, staring around the room with wide eyes, smiling like everyone here is offering her candy.

I glance over her shoulder at a demonstration of a machine that vacuums up dog hair while cutting it, and watch in disgust as a black lab lifts its leg on the end of a table.

No wonder this whole place reeks.

"Are you sure you don't need to sit down for a little while?" I ask. "We could go back to the Pooch Park booth and get you off your feet?"

Lydia crosses her arms over her nearly eight-months-pregnant belly and glares at me. "You sound just like Anton and Henry."

"Sorry." I grimace. "Didn't mean to emulate the patriarchy."

This makes her chuckle, but she *does* look tired. And the thought of spending even twenty more minutes here makes my skin itch. I glance at the folded-up program in my hand and the notes I've jotted down over the last hour.

"Really, though. I think I have enough for my write-up. Jeremy's still around somewhere, taking photos. I'm just going to do an overview of the demonstrations and make sure to name-drop The Pooch Park. Randall will dedicate most of the page to cute dog pics anyway."

We both pause, watching a fluffy white dog walk by in a rainbow tutu.

"If you think that's enough." Lydia looks at her smartwatch and shrugs. "What time is Theo's flight?"

"He doesn't get in till seven. But he's being really weird, insisting I can't just pick him up curbside. He wants to text me directions when I get there."

She narrows her eyes. "What's that about? Where do you need to go?"

I shrug. There's no way in hell I'd be jumping through hoops like this for anyone but my brother. "Probably he's just trying to bring Mom something exotic and this whole story about Kyle is a ruse."

It isn't totally far-fetched. My brother travels all over the world with the Navy, and he's made a habit of bringing back rare souvenirs. Once, he got tied up in customs for hours trying to bring home a fancy Japanese parasol. The agents thought the handle was carved ivory. Turned out it was high-quality plastic.

Except I'm certain Theo would never use Kyle's memory for a stunt like that.

Lydia regards me. "And you have no idea what it could be?"

"No clue." I turn up my palms. "He didn't even own enough stuff to fill his apartment. And his family took what he did have."

"Maybe it's something Kyle wanted you to have," she murmurs quietly. "Something that might help you . . . move on?"

I roll my eyes. "Are you serious right now? I moved on after the anti-wedding."

At that moment, a woman walks by with two enormous Akitas. Her T-shirt says *The more people I meet, the more I love my dog,* and Lydia loses all control. She knows a compatriot when she sees one.

"Oh my gosh, can I say hello? I have an Akita mix at home."

The woman stops and smiles at Lydia's pink maternity shirt, which reads, *Shh . . . we haven't told the dog yet.* I take the opportunity to step aside and check my email. As promised, the assignment desk has kept me on my toes this week. I'm putting the finishing touches on at least two more staff stories for next week's issue in addition to the PetExpo feature. But to Randall's annoyance, I have not followed up on the Unmatched lead. Nor do I intend to.

"Oh! You have got to check him out!" The woman with the Akitas is exclaiming to Lydia. "He's over in the next building. The obedience was amazing, but his agility trial was the best I've seen in years."

"Totally. We'll have to go see." Lydia's voice recaptures my attention. Her tone is no longer like a kid being given a puppy, but more like one being force-fed broccoli. She meets my gaze with such a pained expression, my senses sharpen immediately.

"You're not like, having contractions, are you?" I say under my breath.

"*What*? No." She shakes her head, but also takes my hand, tugging me in the opposite direction from where the woman is pointing. "Thanks for letting me pet Khaleesi and Drogo."

But *Game of Thrones* lady is not done yet. "You should go catch the end before he finishes. It's the best thing at the entire expo."

This piques my interest. I've already planned to turn this feel-good pet story into a promo piece for Lydia's doggie daycare, but I wouldn't mind adding some other highlights, just to make it look like I tried. "What should we see?"

"The agility demonstration!" the woman replies with fervor. "It's over in the next building. Drew Forbes is the best in the state. You should see him work a border collie. He'll be taking home *all* the ribbons this weekend."

The name hits my brain like a dusty book falling off a shelf. Sort of startling at first, and I find myself waiting for the air to clear before I can speak.

"Drew Forbes?" I look at Lydia. "She doesn't mean—"

"You know, I think you're right and I've been on my feet way too long." Lydia rubs her hand over her belly. "Let's go back to the booth so I can sit."

I follow her without protest, trying to kick my brain out of its sudden fog. It was bad enough trying to understand Theo bringing me something that supposedly belonged to my late ex. Finding myself at an event with his brother on the same day feels too much like the universe trying to screw with me. And I don't even believe in that kind of stuff.

It couldn't be *that* Drew Forbes. Kyle was legitimately obsessed with dogs, to the point that he became a military dog handler. But his brother had gone to medical school to be a doctor, like their parents. There was no way he was here today as a dog trainer.

Lydia plops into a folding chair once we get back to her booth, and her business partner, Henry, hands her a bottle of water, trying to mask his concern. "Feeling all right?" he asks.

"I'm fine. We just needed a break. How's it going here?"

The expression on Henry's face is priceless. He must be the only person attending the Denver PetExpo in a Ralph Lauren suit. With his perfectly coiffed hair and hint of British accent, he strikes me as a character from *Downton Abbey* who's been dropped into the *Puppy Bowl*. Not that I fit in any better—but at least I had the sense to wear jeans. I don't know what drove Henry Hill to invest in Lydia's grooming and doggie daycare businesses other than money, but it's been almost a year, and he's still rolling dog hair off his twill trousers like the most committed fish out of water. I admire his stuffy dedication.

"So far, no one is interested in my franchise projections," he complains. "They just want to know whether we have swimming pools and tennis balls."

Lydia laughs. "Why don't you walk around and scope out some of the competition? I can sit here and speak dog for a while."

Henry walks off, clearly relieved, and I take the seat next to Lydia.

"Hey, don't let me stop you if you want to go see the agility thing."

She pulls her blonde hair over one shoulder and turns to me. "Why would I do that?"

"The lady from Westeros made it sound like the main event." I shrug. "I wouldn't want you to miss out."

Her lip curls. "In my experience, Drew Forbes has the personality of a snapping turtle. He's been making a name for himself as some kind of dog-whispering guru. And thanks to a few recent viral videos, he's kind of having a moment. But I think it's mostly hype."

I press my mouth into a line. "Is it—is he really—"

"Kyle's brother?" Her forehead wrinkles in sympathy. "I'm afraid so."

I look down to find myself worrying my ring finger. It's been bare much longer than Kyle's been gone, but if there's anything I've learned about grief, it's that it always finds new ways to surprise you.

"Well, if you want to see what all the hype's about, I'll stay here and hand out your flyers," I say quietly.

"No, thanks," she says. "I tried to network with him last year. He called doggie daycares 'a useless fad to make people feel good about neglecting their pets.'"

I raise my brows. "You didn't tell me that."

Her face softens and she squeezes my hand. "At the time, there was no need to."

I sink back in my chair, trying to recall any of my own memories of Drew Forbes. Kyle's older brother had already left for college by the time we started dating. The absent golden child to Kyle's black sheep. Their physician parents had their futures all planned for them—but Kyle had other ideas. After he enlisted in the army instead of going to medical school, they barely spoke to him. Once we got engaged, I don't think I saw any Forbes again until his funeral.

But . . . that isn't true. Somewhere in my foggy brain, I dredge up the memory of an emotionless face in glasses and a dark suit outside the little mountain chapel. I'd almost forgotten. I've tried my hardest not to remember much about that day.

"I'm going to take off in a sec," I say, checking the time on my phone. "I need to . . ."

I trail off as a new email pops up from that woman Randall dug up, promising she'll make it worth my while if I talk to her about Unmatched. This is the third one she's sent this week.

"What's wrong?" Lydia watches my expression change and lowers her voice. "You didn't get another one of those emails, did you?"

"N-no." I breathe in slowly through my nose and out through my mouth. "Just Randall giving me more mind-numbing assignments."

She narrows her eyes. Lydia knows better than anyone what I've been through over the last year. My career's shooting star success when I wrote about Unmatched, and the rapid decline after it earned me an online stalker.

I let out a low breath, afraid what I say next could trigger her, but also desperate for reassurance. "Someone . . . um, someone wants me to write a new article about Unmatched."

She rests her hand on her bump, but if she's bothered by the subject, she does an excellent job of hiding it. "Well, that's too bad, isn't it?"

I stare at my lap. If I look up, she'll see exactly how seriously I've been considering giving in.

"How long has it been since the last message?" she asks quietly.

I don't even have to think. "Twenty-nine days."

"Must feel like such a relief. Are you sleeping better? How are the nightmares?"

My cheek twitches. I know she's trying to help—that's actually what I wanted. Only now that we're talking about it, I wish I hadn't brought it up. "Don't worry. I'm ignoring it."

Something flashes in her eyes, but she doesn't press further. She just leans back, looking tired. I squeeze her hand.

"What time did you get here?" I ask, changing the subject.

"I don't know. We set up sometime after lunch?"

I purse my lips. "And let me guess, you were at one of the Pooches the whole morning before that?"

Lydia cuts me a look. "I own three businesses, Caprice. They don't run themselves."

"Fair," I say gently. "But why don't I drop you at home on my way to the airport? Henry will survive the last couple hours here on his own."

She lets out a long breath. "Did my husband put you up to this?"

"I try not to talk to Anton if I can help it." I sniff. "I'm just looking out for my best friend. You know, when you're eight months pregnant, you're allowed to take a nap."

This gets under her skin. "You know, society treats pregnant women like they have a *condition* when it's a totally normal part of life."

I bite my lip, wanting to rant with her about discrimination and the unfairness of it all. But the fact is, Lydia's a workaholic. And after a scare we all endured early in her pregnancy, I *did* conspire with the men in her life to try and make her take it easy.

"Okay, how about this?" I ask. "You overwork yourself, the little bundle of joy comes early, and you don't get the chance to complete the remaining eight hundred or so things still on your pre-birth to-do list?"

This quiets her down. Satisfied, I wave at Henry, who's been covertly circling the booth like Lydia's a ticking time bomb.

"Thank you *again* for letting me borrow your new car," I say when she hands me her keys. "I'll return it as soon as I've dealt with Theo."

She rises from her chair with some effort, waving me off with one hand. "Don't rush. Since everyone apparently wants to coddle me, I don't need it back right away. But you better text me when you're home. I'm dying to find out what Theo's been up to."

CHAPTER
FOUR

I have to drive the airport loop three times before I find the exit for the American Airlines cargo terminal. Which means by the time I get there and find it's basically an industrial loading dock, I'm fifteen minutes late with a headache coming on. The sun has already set, and the building looks mostly deserted, so when *Scooby Doo* starts playing in my pocket, it just adds to the overall aesthetic.

"I hope you didn't really expect me to take an Uber," Theo says.

"Bro, relax. I'm here in the parking lot. Can you find me, or do you need me to come in there and retrieve you?"

He pauses. "Can you come in, actually?"

That weird tone is back in his voice. The uncertain one that has no business coming out of my military-trained twin brother. I want to question him on it but decide it'll be easier face-to-face. "You're so buying me dinner."

A jet roars overhead, vibrating down my spine as I exit Lydia's SUV. I check over my shoulders, waiting for normal sound to return. A few other people are going to and from cars, but I don't know how busy this place gets. Once I climb the steps and open the door of the cargo pickup, however, everything is chaos. Vaguely, I register a few people in line and a person behind a counter with a great pile of cardboard packages. Beyond that, toward the back, I spot the familiar, muscular shape of my brother. He's arguing with an employee in front of two large dog crates, and the animals inside sound like they're losing their minds, barking, whining, and scratching to get out. The noise intensifies as I draw closer, and now I wish I had something to take for my headache.

"Look, my supervisor called asking me to hold this shipment. I'm just following orders."

My brother looms large. "Sir, I know all about following orders. However, I am the guy who shipped it, so I'm not sure why you're giving me trouble about this."

"Well, for one, your name isn't on the shipping order—I have the recipient down as a Caprice Phipps."

"That's me," I yell over the fray, shooting my brother a withering glare. My head is fully pounding now, and with all the noise, I'm struggling to figure out what he's trying to do.

"Okay, yes. That's my sister—who is right there—but *I* am the guy who shipped him. Anyway, it doesn't matter. She's here now. Can we please claim him?"

Wait. Claim *him*?

All at once, my senses sharpen. I watch my brother gesture at one of the two crates beside him. The ones with the green LIVE ANIMALS stickers on the side, where all the whining, barking, and crying is coming from. Suddenly, all the pieces of this scenario fuse in my stupid, lagging brain. The last-minute trip. Theo's caginess. His request that I borrow a car for the "important" item of Kyle's.

"Theo, what is this about?"

My brother's deep brown eyes fix on mine. I watch his Adam's apple bob, the way it does every time he explains that it's easier to ask forgiveness than permission. But before he can speak, his gaze strays to a commotion behind me.

My ponytail rustles like someone's come in the door on a breeze. But my head hurts and the barking hasn't stopped, and I am so acutely tuned in to Theo's face, I don't turn right away. Not until a booming voice breaks through the cacophony.

"Excuse me, I am here to claim that dog."

My heart skips at least a couple of beats. I know it couldn't be who it sounds like at first. The person I'm always desperate for it to be.

But that voice.

I turn, and at once my brain struggles to sift through an onslaught of shock and disappointment. At first, I'm sure the man standing there is a ghost. Tall and broad, with a face I've often longed to glimpse just one more time. A long, straight nose. Tan, determined jaw. And green eyes that used to look at me with such tender affection . . . except right now they're glaring.

I blink.

Reality catches up to me. Because this is most definitely *not* the person I wish it was. There's something different about his posture. His hair is darker, longer, with a little curl. This man wears glasses. And while the eyes behind them still seem haunted, they aren't troubled the same way Kyle's always were.

"Drew Forbes," my brother says flatly. "Imagine meeting you here."

The ghost walks toward us, and as he does, the last of the spell breaks. He doesn't grace my brother with a reply. He doesn't even *look* at me. Just approaches the man in the American Airlines shirt like they're the only two people here.

"Are you the guy who called earlier?" the employee asks.

"Yes," Drew says. "I got here as soon as I could. This dog belonged to my late brother."

From inside the crate on the right, there's a low whimper. But no more barking.

"Okay . . ." The airline guy looks at my brother and me. "Well, they say it's theirs."

"Uh, no—I don't," I say quickly, waving my hand. "I want nothing to do with this."

"*Caprice*," Theo hisses.

For the first time, Drew Forbes glances my way. And in the instant our eyes meet, we both flinch as if it stings. He stares at first like he has no idea who I am or why I'm even here. Honestly, that makes two of us. But after a long pause, recognition settles on his features. His jaw tightens. Then his lip curls.

"As you heard," he says, turning back to the airline employee. "They don't want him."

"That is *not* what she said," my brother growls. He'd been hanging back, clearly taking stock of the situation before deciding how to act, but now he steps right up in Drew's face.

I reach for him. "Theo—"

"I've been trying to track down this dog for a year." Drew snarls. "Did you have something to do with that, Phipps?"

"Military red tape." My brother shrugs. "You know how it goes—oh no, wait, you never bothered to care before."

Something flickers across Drew's face, but it quickly disappears. He folds his arms, unflinching in front of Theo—which, I have to admit, takes nerve. Drew *is* slightly taller and, from the look of it, comparably muscled. But Theo has the intimidating *don't fuck with me* vibe of the Navy SEALs. I'm not sure if it's trained in, or that's just the kind of guys they recruit.

Airline dude wisely steps away to help other customers.

"Thanks for your trouble," Drew says in a tone that does not suggest gratitude. "I'll take Rufus from here."

"No, you won't. He belongs to Caprice."

Drew doesn't turn his head, but we both say, "*What?*"

Theo raises his chin and looks at me. "Kyle wrote a will

before—" He swallows. "He explicitly stated he wanted you to have his dog."

"He . . . *why*?" I ask. Kyle and I had only spoken once after our ill-fated wedding day, and it hadn't gone well. That was before his second injury—the one that forced him into medical retirement. Before he even cut Theo out of his life. But none of that matters—Kyle knew better than anyone how I feel about dogs. "Sorry, it makes zero sense that he would bequeath me a pet."

Behind me, Drew mutters, "That dog is *not* a pet."

My brother glares at Drew, but when he turns back to me, his eyes are clouded. I may have had a complex history with Kyle, but Theo's is longer and possibly more complicated. They'd been joined at the hip since they were five years old, played soccer, football, and eventually both enlisted—albeit into separate military branches. Theo hadn't been thrilled when Kyle and I started dating, but he couldn't argue with it either. Kyle was a good guy.

Which is why we both tried so hard to rein in his darkness when he came back broken from one of his tours. My brother might be a member of one of the toughest military units in existence, but I know he feels like he failed on that mission. Right along with me.

I soften. "Theo, I just think—"

"I promised. He made me swear if anything happened to him—"

His voice breaks, and my throat tightens. Because something *did* happen.

"It's what he wanted, Reece."

"But why *me*?" The words waver coming out of my mouth. "I've never even owned a dog. That was always his thing."

Theo shrugs. "Because Rufus meant more to him than anything."

I flinch. It still hurts knowing he didn't feel that way about me.

"Clearly he wasn't in his right mind," a sharp voice cuts in. We both turn to find Drew scowling at us. Does he *have* any other expressions? "She can't have this dog. It isn't some fluffy pet."

I like this guy about as much as a yeast infection. But when I glance into the kennel at the fur-covered face watching this exchange from inside, I'm inclined to agree with him. I don't have much experience with animals, but Kyle and I were together long enough that I don't need to be told this one isn't a normal house pet. I lean closer to my brother. "Maybe he's right?"

Theo curls his hands into fists. "I promised Kyle. We have to respect his wishes."

Drew pushes his glasses up his artful nose. "Can I see these 'wishes' in writing?"

I bite back an urge to say *Should his own brother have to ask?* But I'm Kyle's former fiancée, and I'm just as much in the dark.

"Yeah. It's right here." Theo sets down the bag slung over his shoulder and produces a plain-looking manila envelope. He hands it to me first, which earns us further dirty looks. But after I skim the document, I pass it to Drew with a heavy weight in my stomach.

He flips through the pages so roughly, I'm sure they'll tear. But when he finishes, he raises his head and addresses me for the first time.

"You're the last person who should have this dog."

My lips part.

"Now let me take him, and let's be done with this." Drew moves toward the kennel, but I manage to find my voice before he gets there.

"Why?" The question comes out dry and cracked. I don't even know why I'm asking. I don't care what he thinks of me.

I don't actually *want* a dog. But maybe deep down I harbor some faded loyalty to a man I wasn't enough for.

He gives me a sidelong look as he speaks, voice dripping with disdain. "You won't know how to handle him. You said yourself you've never had a dog."

I can't argue with that. But I get the sense there's more to it. And the condescension in his tone gets under my skin. So I push.

"I have a houseplant. How hard could it be?"

Drew snorts, eyeing me up and down. I can't tell what judgment he's making, but I have a feeling it has more to do with the past than anything happening right now. "*I* can give Rufus what he needs," he says.

I take a step forward, invading his space. "If Kyle thought you could do that, then why did he give him to me?"

Theo steps between us. "You know, I'd like to keep this simple." He turns to me, lowering his voice. "*Are* you gonna keep him?"

His deep tenor hits a less keyed-up, more rational part of my brain, bringing my kicking feet firmly back to the ground. I glance inside the kennel again, and a pair of golden-brown eyes stare back at me. The dog whines and paws at the door.

"Um . . ."

It's difficult to imagine bringing an *animal* home to my apartment. Permanently. Will he make the place smell? Where will he sleep? How much does he eat? How often will I have to walk him? Suddenly, I'm not sure I can handle this. I was lying to Drew—I don't actually have a plant.

"I bet Lydia would be a big help," Theo says, reading my face. His voice drops further. "And Reece, this dog is a protector. If you take him, he'll keep you *safe*."

I soften, looking at my brother. At my transparent, loyal, badass sibling, who clearly jumped through at least a hundred hoops to deliver this "gift" from my ex in the name of loyalty. And because he knows what I've been through this year.

I could kill him.

"Yeah, okay. Lydia will help," I say quietly, in part to convince myself. I glance at Drew, standing with his arms crossed and a haughty glare. I might have zero interest in the dog, but I really don't want to give him what he wants. I raise my voice. "Come on. Let's get him home, Theo."

My brother goes to find the airline guy who'd made himself scarce during our exchange. But as soon as he steps away, a firm hand wraps around my wrist. Suddenly, Kyle's older, sharper-edged, almost-clone is pulling me close to him. Too close. Our eyes meet, mere inches from each other, and I swear my skin burns where we touch. By the way his jaw drops and he abruptly lets go, I wonder if he felt it too.

"What is your problem?" I hiss, clutching my wrist to my chest.

He gestures to the dog watching with interest from the kennel. "That is a military dog. If you take him home and treat him like a pet, you'll be in over your head in less than twenty-four hours."

"Okay. That would be my problem, not yours." I turn away.

He growls. "God, what did Kyle even . . ."

I stop in my tracks, close enough to guess the words that disappeared under his breath. I steel myself and face him again.

"You know what I always thought was odd? No one in your family ever had an issue with Kyle and Theo spending all their time together. They were thick as thieves, got into all kinds of trouble . . ." I swallow. "Maybe Kyle should've fallen for Theo instead. Because as soon as he started kissing *me*, you'd think I'd fed him a poisoned apple."

I don't see so much as feel the ripple of agitation from the surviving Forbes brother. "I only care about the dog."

I give him a smile that's all teeth. "Well, I didn't ask for him, and I wouldn't have. But if Kyle wanted me to have him, I'm taking him home with me."

Something cold flashes in Drew's eyes. "You don't deserve him."

I look at him dead-eyed, ready to walk away and never breathe the same air as him again. But morbid curiosity makes me ask, "And why is that?"

A shadow falls over his face, his words hitting like shrapnel. "Because you're the reason my brother killed himself."

CHAPTER
FIVE

I wait in the car while Theo walks the dog—my dog—around the parking lot to pee. It's fully dark out now, and I stare into the blackness, letting my thoughts descend to a place I rarely let them visit. Some of my early memories of Kyle almost seem to have a soft filter, a hazy glow around them as if they were a dream and not something real.

Something I had.

If I close my eyes, I can almost trace my fingers along the line of his jaw. Feel him breathe into my hair. Hear the rumble of his voice, low and serene. *I love you, Caprice—I always will.*

My chest aches.

Theo opens the back of the car, which dips lightly as the dog jumps into his crate. He says something I can't hear before closing up and sliding into the passenger seat next to me.

"Sorry about the drama with Forbes," he says, hunting around like he's looking for something in his pockets. When I don't respond, he looks at my face, wincing when our eyes meet.

"Why didn't you just tell me about Kyle's will?" I ask. "Why the surprise?"

He sighs. "If I had called and said you inherited a sixty-pound ex-military canine, what would you have said?"

"I would've hung up and changed my number," I admit. Which, obviously, he knew.

I start the car and steer out of the parking lot, wary of the quiet beast at the back of Lydia's SUV. She's going to flip out when I tell her what the car was for.

"It took me a while to track Rufus down after Kyle died," Theo says as I merge onto the highway. "Someone had placed him with a foster, and then I couldn't locate Kyle's will. He was about to be adopted, but I managed to stop it. I still wasn't sure they were going to let me take him until I got there."

"You should've let him stay with whoever wanted him," I say, shaking my head.

"I thought about it. I honestly don't know why Kyle wanted you to have him." He grimaces. "But then you started getting those threats, and I don't know—it felt like something I could do." He looks at me. "For both of you."

"Well . . . thanks?"

In the back of the car, the dog lets out a low whine, punctuating how much I regret everything about this decision. What am I going to do with a dog? A *big* one. Maybe not as large as Lydia's Akita mix, Heartthrob, but I doubt I could lift him. Just his crate takes up the entire back of this SUV. And he smells.

When we reach my building on the north end of Washington Park, I find a parking spot and shoot Lydia a text asking if I can return her car in the morning. She's going to hound me for details, and I will call her with them, maybe after Theo leaves. But I don't think I'm ready to articulate what just happened. Not tonight.

"Caprice." Theo calls for me from the back of the car. I shut my door and wander to where he stands under the liftgate, surprised when a curious snout comes in contact with my knees. I dodge out of its range with a frown, but then I notice my brother is holding the end of a leather leash out to me. "Here. You walk him in, and I'll carry the crate up."

I swallow. "You want me to—"

But then the leash is in my hand, and I'm looking down the length of it at . . . my new pet. I curl my lip. Under the streetlight, he's sort of tall and skinny. His face and pointed ears are black, as is the tip of his tail, but the rest of his body is a sort of honey blond. I barely know anything about dog breeds, but I've spent enough time hanging out with Lydia that I would've guessed he was a German shepherd if Theo hadn't told me he was . . . something else from Western Europe? No more appealing either way.

The dog stands in front of me, assessing my hold on the leash like he's equally unsure about my virtues. I guess that's fair. We're off to a great start—I don't like him; he doesn't like me.

But then he steps forward and nudges my hand.

I step back, tightening my fist around the leash.

"Whoa, easy there." My brother chuckles when I knock into him. "I mean, I'd say he won't bite, but I'm actually not sure."

"Great." I hold the door of my building open for Theo and the crate the size of my queen bed. "What breed did you say this is?"

"He's a Belgian Malinois. The military trains a lot of them. They're smart and motivated. Highly trainable, loyal. But they can also be fierce."

Once my brother is through the door, I look back to where the dog stands, still waiting outside at the end of the leash. "Why is he just standing there?"

Theo glances back and shrugs. "Not sure. He might need a command? I don't remember all the ones Kyle used."

I give the leash a small tug, but he doesn't budge. Who freaking has time for this?

My brother digs into his pockets and hands me a small bag of bone-shaped dog treats. "Here. Try just calling him."

I look around as a few people pass by on the sidewalk. I've seen Lydia do this a million times, but I feel stupid trying to talk to an animal like it's a person.

"Um, come here, dog . . . um, Rufus?" I hold out one of the treats.

Immediately, the dog runs through the door and snaps the food out of my fingers.

"Ouch!" I shake my hand, inspecting the skin. It isn't broken anywhere, but I am smeared with saliva. "*Eww*. I'm not doing that again."

Together, Theo and I try to navigate the building's one small elevator, but it's clear we're not all fitting inside with the crate.

"Go ahead and take him up first," he says. "Unless you want to take the stairs."

I frown. Normally, I avoid the stairwell. It's creepy and deserted, and has always felt like a place I wouldn't want to be caught alone. But I feel different with my brother present. I know he'd come looking for me in less than two minutes if something came up.

I leave the elevator to Theo and open the stair door, glancing at the animal waiting on the other end of the leash. "Come . . . Rufus."

He follows. And I'm grateful it's not at the sacrifice of my fingers. Actually, the dog seems enthusiastic, sniffing all the way up to the fifth floor. He doesn't miss a single corner. We don't run into anyone else on the way, but as the powerful canine tugs me up the dim stairs, it occurs to me, they'd probably leave us alone if we did.

Theo's in front of my apartment door with the crate standing up on one end when we exit the stairwell. His posture tells me he's already cleared my entire floor like an enemy stronghold, and now he's peering into my peephole camera as if it's a captive in need of interrogation.

"I can't wait to review the footage of your nostrils," I say in the most bored voice I can muster. He watches closely as I pull out my keys, scanning the hall and apartment door.

"What's the current threat level?" he asks in a low voice.

I'd roll my eyes, but he's been talking about my life like a military operation for months now. "Pretty status quo. Nothing new for almost four weeks."

I'm grateful this isn't a lie. When he calls from thousands of miles away, I can get by with some omissions. When we're together, however, I can't keep the truth off my face.

Before he can reply, the door of the apartment next to mine swings open. "That you out there, darlin'?" asks a frail voice.

"Yeah, hi Arlene," I say, perking up. I try to wave at my elderly neighbor around the giant dog crate and giant SEAL between us. "You remember my brother, Theo?"

She nods at him, eyeballing the dog with skepticism. I'm sure she's going to comment on the building's pet policy, which I don't know off the top of my head. But she just smiles sweetly. "I've got another novel for you."

"Oh, is it book club week already?" I ask, unlocking my door so Theo can carry the crate inside.

Her eyes light up, and she cackles. "This one had some spice. Stop over sometime and I'll lend you my copy. I marked all the good pages."

"I'll have to think about it," I say, watching my brother plunk Kyle's dog's enormous crate in my living room. "You know love stories aren't really my thing."

Once we're both inside, I stand numbly, holding the leash while Theo checks my bathroom and closets for intruders.

I just watch, trying to figure out what to do next and wondering why it feels hard. I should set down my keys, hang up my coat. Find something for us to eat. But my burly houseguest, the leash in my hand, and the memories in my head disrupt any routine I might've had. Finally, a low whimper snaps me back into the present.

"Oh . . . guess I should take this off," I mutter, reaching to unclasp the leash like Lydia does with Heartthrob when she brings him over.

But this dog isn't my friend's chill Akita mix. Instead of turning a circle and settling down, he dashes all over my little studio as soon as he's loose, sniffing every inch of every corner the way he did in the stairwell. Almost like he's searching for something.

"What is he—hey, get down!" I yell when he puts his front paws on my kitchen counter. He doesn't seem to hear, or maybe doesn't care, sniffing around briefly before leaping across my bed, then making a second circuit of my living space. "*Not* cool, beast. Stay out of my bed."

"He's just checking out his new digs." Theo chuckles, pulling a metal bowl and a small bag of dog food out of his duffel. "Rufus? You hungry, dude?"

I raise a skeptical brow, watching the dog beeline for my brother and immediately sit while Theo empties kibble into the bowl. I move to the kitchen to wash the now-dried saliva off my hands.

"I don't know, Theo . . . I'm not sure I should keep him."

He crosses his arms over his burly chest. "Why's that?"

"Just . . ." I press my lips together. My brother and I are pretty brutally honest about our feelings most of the time, but for some reason, I hold back on the string of protests in my head. *I don't like dogs. I have never wanted a pet. I don't need this constant reminder of Kyle.* "Like, my apartment is small enough with just me."

Theo shrugs. "You could move."

I close my eyes and exhale. "I've told you, I love this place. I've only been here a year."

Also, I couldn't afford to move.

"You might be safer," he says.

I grit my teeth. "Look, I got a camera at your insistence. I take self-defense classes. I carry pepper spray. And now I have *this*." I gesture to the dog, who's nosing the now-empty bowl across the floor. "Which I doubt will really help anything."

Theo's expression darkens. "When was the last time you charged your front door camera? Because my app says your battery's dead."

Crap. I go to the door and unfasten the battery pack, then plug it in on the counter. Normally, I never let it run down. But the one time I forget, of course Theo is here to check.

"Look, I know you're as safe as you can be." His voice gentles. "But when I'm in another hemisphere of the globe next week, I'll feel better knowing your new roommate here is looking out for you."

I study the dog with a frown. "What makes you think he'll do that?"

"It's what he's trained to do."

I wrinkle my nose. My "roommate" has given up on more food appearing in his dish and now paces the apartment, making a low whining noise.

I drop onto the couch. "Is he going to do that all the time?"

"He probably needs to go out," Theo says, reaching for the leash I left on the counter. "I'll take him. But where do you want me to put this?"

I look up at the huge, ugly dog crate blocking my door. The one doing zero for my cozy aesthetic. "Do I have to keep it? Can't I just get a cute dog bed?" Even as I speak the words, I can't believe they're coming out of my mouth.

"You might want to decide about that later. He's used to sleeping in it."

"Whatever. Just put it over there." I gesture to the farthest corner by my bed so I won't have to look at it in the center of the room. "Are you sleeping on my couch tonight, or what?"

Theo glances at the clock on my microwave. "If that's okay? I have to head out tomorrow, but I should probably run down to see Mom first or she'll never forgive me."

"Truth." I sigh, knowing she'll grill him, wanting to know the next time I'll visit.

I watch Theo maneuver the crate where I directed, even pausing to arrange a few books on top of it in an attempt at decor, and something loosens in my chest. He might be a brawny, overprotective dude's dude, but I know how lucky I am to have him.

I hop up, crossing the room to fold him into a hug. He stiffens and squirms, acting like my arms are covered in stingers before relenting and hugging me back.

"Thanks for looking out for me, little bro. I know you went to a lot of trouble to arrange all this, and I appreciate it."

He snorts. "No, you don't."

I pull away, unable to look him in the eye. "Your *effort* is appreciated."

"What are you writing about this week?" he asks, changing the subject.

I bite my lip, thinking about the Unmatched lead in my inbox. How I might not be on the assignment desk *or* as short on cash if I write the article Randall's pushing for.

"Pets," I say firmly, gesturing to the dog.

"Good." He grunts his approval, and that's when I realize he thinks it's that simple.

"You know I could write about the water table and some asshole would still send me nasty messages eventually, right? That's the nature of modern journalism. People like to say mean shit from behind their computers."

"Yeah, but you don't have to go baiting them." When I roll my eyes, he just sets his jaw, then reaches down to clip the leash to Rufus's collar. "Anyway, that's why you're keeping this guy."

"I don't want a dog, Theo!" I grab a throw pillow off the couch and launch it at him.

Theo dodges, but when he straightens, his eyes soften. "Just give it a month, okay? If you really still don't want him then, I'll figure something out. But can we just . . ."

He doesn't finish, but from his tone, I can guess what he didn't say. *Can we do this for Kyle?* I press my lips together, not sure I have this in me after everything my ex put me through.

The dog whines again. I glance at him, and when he cocks his head, Drew Forbes's words echo through my mind: *You're the reason my brother killed himself.*

I swallow hard, blinking at Rufus through a sheen of tears. He might've meant a lot to Kyle Forbes, but clearly he didn't make him any happier than I did.

"I don't know what I'm going to do with a *Belgian Malinois*," I mutter. "But I'm glad I didn't have to give him to Kyle's asshole brother."

After Theo heads out to walk the dog, I put my back to the enormous kennel by the bed, trying to focus on the other two-thirds of the apartment: the green midcentury couch and throw pillows I love, the cute coffee table and vintage barstools I sourced at a yard sale. I spend a minute imagining my life and home as they were yesterday—exactly the way I wanted them.

But my apartment already smells like dog. There's fur on my couch. Drool on my jeans. And a giant lump in my throat. It doesn't seem fair. I've been doing my best to move on for the last two years, rebuilding my life alone. But Kyle gets to haunt me with his dog, and I can't even ask why.

I curl my hands into fists and close my eyes, but as soon as I do, he's there. Handsome and smiling, whispering how much he loves me. When I open them again, my vision blurs. I reach for my laptop. I can barely see the screen through a sheen of tears, but still manage to pound out an email and send it into the ether.

Friday, March 12, 20__, 10:12 PM

To: Kyle.Forbes@mail.com

From: Caprice_Phipps@mail.com

Subject: Re: no subject

Dear Kyle,

Why is it you get to destroy yourself and keep destroying my life? A *dog*, really? What made you think any of this was a good idea? Did you even know me?

C

I don't really feel better once it's sent, but at least I feel like I did something. Then my phone chimes with a text.

> LYDIA
>
> Hey! No rush on the car. Are you back? What was it for?

> You won't believe me until I show you.
>
> Do you have some time in the morning?

> LYDIA
>
> Yeah, Henry and I don't need to be back at PetExpo until ten.

Damn, I almost forgot PetExpo. I get up and set my laptop on the counter, opening a new document along with my notes to write up the article for Randall. I already know what it's going to say. I'll open with a glowing description of the expo as seen through Lydia's eyes—the dog and cat wonderland of her dreams. Then I'll highlight some of the businesses, give generous exposure to The Pooch Park, while never even alluding to the dog trainer from the black lagoon.

Perfect. Pick you up at eight.

LYDIA

On a Saturday??

Trust me when I say this is an emergency. I'll buy donuts.

LYDIA

You hate donuts, Caprice. What is going on?

DREW

Drew slammed the door as he entered the house. Exhausted. Defeated.

Again.

The universe pulled him toward bed. Toward blackness and oblivion, at least for a few hours. And he would have kicked off his shoes and succumbed to it if he wasn't met at the door by a troop of hungry faces.

"Sorry." He sighed. "I know I'm late."

The old shepherd gave him a long, assessing stare. He had wise, dark eyes that had seen too much of the world. Much like those golden-brown eyes in the crate. The ones Drew had failed.

He went through the motions, putting food in each of their bowls, adding the correct supplements and medications. Then he patted every one of their heads the way they liked.

The English bulldog was the one to break the tension, of course. She snuffed and snorted, wiggling at Drew's feet, more interested in getting her butt rubbed than dinner. He sighed and sank to the ground to give her what she begged for. Excitement radiated from her stocky tan and white body as she grabbed a squeaky duck off the floor and presented it to him.

"Pudding, if you don't eat your dinner, Blitz will," he muttered.

The border collie glanced up at his name, gave a light wag of his tail, and kept eating. Not a surprise. He burned so many calories just existing, he never missed a single scrap.

Pudding ignored him, turning to rub her burly body against his legs with several delighted snorts. The shepherd, Diesel, was more attuned to the moods of his handler. He came over and quietly lay his head in Drew's lap, calm and reassuring. Telling Drew he knew he'd tried his best.

Except he hadn't. He'd failed Rufus *and* Kyle.

Drew dropped his face into his hands.

Naturally, that's when his phone rang. He didn't need to see the screen to know who it was. He didn't want to answer, but his fingers worked against him.

"We missed you at family dinner," his mother said in her stolid voice.

"Sorry." Drew sighed. "Something came up I had to deal with."

"I'm sure." She dismissed his excuse with just two words, like she was picking a piece of lint off her sleeve. "Next week, then."

He closed his eyes and said nothing. He should have flown to North Carolina to get Rufus himself. If he had, he might've been able to convince the rescue to give him the dog.

If he'd gotten there before Theo Phipps, that is.

Except . . . he hadn't known about the will. It was so uncharacteristic of Kyle to cross his T's and dot his I's like that. But his brother was always full of surprises.

"And you *will* be attending the ceremony next weekend?" his mom said in his ear, not asking so much as laying the expectation.

"Uh, yeah. I'll be there."

He'd rather chisel Pudding's dried drool off the ceiling, but he would go.

This was so like his parents. It wasn't enough to just hold a memorial service for Kyle when he died, pretending he hadn't taken his own life. They had to broadcast their grief. Make sure no one important missed their suffering. And just to ensure they didn't, it would now take the form of an annual local event.

Drew's stomach churned. All at once, he was grateful the first actual anniversary of his brother's choice to leave this world would fall on a weekday. He would sit in the high school auditorium with his parents next weekend, listening to whatever the principal chose to say based on the award being given and the size of the donation his parents surely made to the PTA. But on Tuesday, the actual first anniversary, Drew could remove himself from everyone. Everything. Spend it alone with his thoughts.

His guilt.

Just not Rufus.

"Good. Principal Beck will be announcing the scholarship winner, and it's important you be there."

He tried not to snort. In memory of his brother, a US Army dog handler who'd clearly and firmly rejected his parents' desires for him to follow their paths into medicine, they were going to set up some deserving local kid for medical school.

"Right," Drew murmured. Affirming and acknowledging what she said, the way he'd learned to in childhood. It was easier if you played along.

He stood abruptly, grabbing a bottle of water from the fridge. Then he scooped up Pudding's bowl, putting her behind a gate to finish eating where Blitz couldn't sneak in and steal from her.

"I need to go now, Mom. See you next week."

He hung up before she could add anything else. It was

champagne cocktail hour anyway—a routine in place well before Kyle died in which his parents got acceptably inebriated every night before bed because their comfortable lives were so hard.

He wandered into the backyard. Blitz followed, having given up on Pudding's dinner. Seeing a new opportunity, he snatched up a ball and begged Drew for a task. The yard wasn't huge, but Drew had squeezed a set of agility equipment onto the grass. It was a bit like a hamster wheel for the border collie. Drew positioned himself in the middle of the makeshift ring and barked a few commands at the black-and-white dog. And even though he'd already performed a good chunk of the day at PetExpo, Blitz lit right up, racing over the ramps, weaving between poles, and diving through rings like they provided the air he breathed. The hardest part for him was stopping on the table and waiting a whole five seconds. This time, he made it about four. And kept going, even when Drew settled into a chair on the small deck and stopped telling him what to do.

The dog found it soothing, so he did too.

Diesel came to the back door, content to watch the younger dog expend his energy, with zero desire to participate. He glanced at Drew, and they settled in, looking on together. The old K9 officer had had a long, successful career with the Jefferson County Sheriff's Office and was just about to enter retirement when his handler's young son developed severe allergies. Hardey didn't know what to do when he couldn't keep his partner, so he approached Drew, who'd just opened K9 Academy in an effort to lure Kyle back home. Drew went to great lengths to give Diesel the retirement he deserved. He'd hoped to do the same for his brother's dog.

His chest tightened as he wondered briefly how Rufus was spending his night.

Drew had known Theo was involved as soon as the foster

contacted him to say his adoption application was denied. Kyle and Theo had been attached at the hip growing up. Although they'd entered different branches of the military, they clearly stayed close, and Theo was the only person who might have known or cared where Kyle's dog would end up.

But his sister . . . Drew had never figured in Caprice Phipps.

He'd only briefly encountered her a couple of times when he'd come home from college. Even as a teenager, she was strikingly beautiful, with her supple brown skin and wide, dark eyes. Drew couldn't deny his brother for being drawn in, though he suspected some of Kyle's infatuation had to do with their parents' disapproval. Drew had always watched out for his little brother, made sure he kept his head above water, especially around their mom and dad. But the moment Caprice came on the scene, she took that from him.

He was surprised when they announced their engagement. Distressed when his parents instructed him *not* to attend the wedding. And relieved when he went anyway and found the bride on her way out. Kyle was brokenhearted when they finally spoke about it. All he would say was, "She's better off without me." But when his brother took his life a year later, Drew knew who to blame. Caprice had played with Kyle, made him dependent, then pushed him away when he needed her most, leaving him to battle his demons alone.

And he lost.

Drew would've been content never laying eyes on her again. But so much stood between him and Kyle, maybe he shouldn't have been surprised to see her at the airport. Her hair a little different, posture more confident, but still more stunning than he remembered. Even holding the end of Rufus's leash, grinding her heel into the last good thing he was trying to do for his brother.

He sipped his water, leaning back in his chair and trying to figure out why Kyle would *ever* leave his beloved dog to the girl who broke his heart.

The date on the will was recent—within a few months of his death. Maybe Theo coerced him. Maybe *she* coerced Theo. Except he couldn't discern why either of them would be interested in a retired, traumatized Belgian Malinois.

She basically said she wasn't a dog person, though it couldn't have been more obvious. She had such a look of revulsion when he caught her staring into the crate. He watched Theo take the dog to relieve himself before they left, and she stepped away when Rufus sniffed her, clearly more concerned about her outfit than letting him get familiar with her scent.

And now Rufus had to live with her. He hoped he peed on her favorite purse.

Actually, there was a high likelihood he'd do worse than that. Drew knew little about Rufus's history aside from the military exercise that sent both him and Kyle to the hospital, and from there into early retirement. Kyle obviously never recovered, and Drew doubted the dog was doing much better. Especially after losing his handler.

But maybe all Drew needed to do was wait Caprice out. A day or so with an anxious, traumatized canine would have her rethinking her plan, whatever it was. He hated that Rufus would have to endure more stress, but after seeing his brother's signature on the will, it seemed like the only straightforward path to helping him.

Blitz finally broke his circuit, parking himself in front of Drew for his reward. He gave him what he was after—a few liver treats and a quick game of tug—then led all three dogs to the bedroom they shared.

He felt more at ease by the time he fell into bed. He left the airport lower than he'd been in a year. Like he failed Kyle—again. But this wasn't over. Denver wasn't that big. He could keep tabs on the situation, wait it out, and be ready when things got desperate. It would only be a matter of days, maybe hours, before Caprice Phipps had enough of Rufus. She'd be searching Drew out soon enough, begging him to take the dog.

And he'd be ready when she did.

CHAPTER
SIX

By the time I pull into Lydia's driveway, I've walked my *dog*, bid my brother an early farewell, done thirty minutes of circuits at the gym, and visited the donut drive-through for my best friend. I finished and submitted the PetExpo write-up last night. It wasn't edgy or groundbreaking, and won't win any awards, but I'd be surprised if I got hate mail from it. It'll earn my paycheck, and should serve as a nice endorsement for The Pooch Park.

"Oh my God, I love you," Lydia says, accepting six donuts and a coffee as she wiggles into the passenger seat. I swear she's rounder than she was at her shower a week ago. "I forwarded the article to Henry after you sent it to me, and he's already buzzing about it. Thank you so much! I like that you put in a good word for MaxFund too. They're an amazing rescue."

She brings the coffee to her lips, spots Anton coming out of the house in his running gear, and pauses.

I roll my eyes at their shared glance.

"Don't worry, it's decaf," I say, mouthing the words with extra emphasis at her husband through the windshield. Pregnancy does weird things to people. "Anyway, thank *you* for lending me your new Honda," I say, reversing out of the driveway.

"You are such a good friend." She sips her coffee and sighs, then peeks over her shoulder to inspect her SUV. "So, what did he bring you?"

I open my mouth. Close it again. "It's at my place . . . might be best to just show you."

Lydia catches me up on the latest drama between her mom and sister on the ride over. After Lydia's baby shower, Marion apparently recorded a video that went semi-viral about how under-appreciated she is as a grandma. Knowing their mom has never so much as changed a diaper for Celia's baby, I was shocked Lydia's sister didn't murder Marion in her sleep. Neither Lydia nor I really knew our dads growing up, but I've always secretly thought hers must've just run for the hills.

We're laughing over the comments on the video when the elevator opens on my floor. But as soon as we step into the hall, we both stop and look at each other.

"What is that?" Lydia asks, tilting her head at a high-pitched sound.

It stops as soon as she speaks, and I furrow my brow. "Huh. I don't—"

A clear wail echoes down the hall, and now I think I can guess what it is, or at least where it's coming from. My skin prickles. I fumble with my keys, pace quickening as I close in on my apartment door.

"Oh, poor thing," Lydia says, trailing behind me. "I didn't know any of your neighbors had a—"

"Holy. Shit."

My door swings open, and at first, I think it must've

snowed indoors. There is white fluff and feathers everywhere. The entire floor is covered. It's on the coffee table and the counter. One of my barstools lies on its side. A framed poster is askew on the wall. And my couch—my cute velvety green couch—is destroyed. Stripped of half its fabric *and* stuffing. In a daze, I reach down and retrieve one of my prized Louboutins from the debris.

"What the . . ." My hands shake as I pick up the ruined heel. For a split second, I wonder if someone actually broke in, did this to hurt me—is my stalker back in the game? Until I look more closely at the shoe. And realize it's been chewed. *"Fuck!"*

As if in reply, a bark issues from across the room. There, in the center of what *used* to be my bed, sits a panting Belgian Malinois. Lydia swings the door shut behind us, and he stands up, barking.

"Lydia, open the door." I panic, stepping between the obviously insane animal and my pregnant friend. "Don't let him get close to you!"

She places a warm hand on my arm, and I pause, looking at her.

"Caprice," she says calmly. "Theo brought you a dog?"

I look at her dumbly. I had imagined picking her up, coming back to my place to surprise her with this news, then sipping coffee while she offered friendly advice on pet ownership. Now my gaze drifts from her face, around my destroyed apartment, and back to the canine still barking and wagging his tail on my shredded purple duvet.

"He—he was Kyle's." My back hits the door, and the next thing I know, I'm gasping for air.

Nearly eight months pregnant, my friend sets down her coffee and donuts and holds my hands as I sink to the floor. When she seems assured I'm not going to totally pass out, she hefts herself back up and coos softly at the beast on my bed.

"Hey buddy, how are you?" she says.

Rufus spins in circles, barking, sending feathers into the air.

"*Lydia*—" I croak, worried he's lost his mind and could bite her, or worse. But she just waves me off, reaching into her pocket and holding out a handful of the dog treats she carries everywhere.

"What's his name?" she asks quietly.

I stare ahead, trying to focus on the animal watching her. "Rufus."

"Oh, *Rufus*." I hear the smile in her voice. "How very canine."

The edges of my vision darken, and I put my head between my knees, forcibly slowing down my breathing. I refuse to lose consciousness while Lydia's doing something potentially stupid.

When I'm able to look up again, she's almost to the bed. She moves slowly, treats out in front of her. The dog spins like a top as she approaches, creating a new whirlwind of feathers, but pauses when she speaks to him in a low, soothing voice.

"There you go. It's okay. You've had a rough morning, huh?"

I snort, regaining control of my heartbeat.

He lets out a low whimper.

"Do you like cheese treats?" she asks. I hold my breath as she extends her palm flat in front of his snout. Tentatively, he leans forward, glances at her, and pulls back. He finally reaches out again and takes the small orange square out of her hand. "Good boy," she says, still quiet, but there's relief in her tone.

She repeats the process until he's stopped panting, and it's clear he's watching for goodies every time she reaches into her pockets. I drag myself to my feet, righting my barstool on my way up.

"Where's his water dish?" Lydia asks.

"His . . . oh." I flush with guilt. How did I forget to give him water? I pull a mixing bowl I never use out of the cupboard, fill it at the sink, and set it on the floor at the edge of the kitchen without looking at either of them.

"Okay, has he been fed?" She sounds a little impatient, but that's not unfair.

"Yes."

"Walked?"

"I took him right before I left for the gym. Which was only like . . . ninety minutes ago." I shake my head, leaning against the counter and surveying my apartment. "Did he really do this?"

"Well, yeah," Lydia says. And this time her tone is clipped. "As I understand, he was flown across the country by a stranger yesterday, then left with another stranger. Who then left him alone in a strange place with no water."

"It wasn't that long." I hold up my desecrated shoe. "Look what he did!"

Lydia winces. "Consider this your first lesson in dog ownership," she says kindly but firmly. "They can't tell time."

"Heartthrob has never done anything like this!" I gesture around the room, queasy just looking at my living area. I loved that couch. I loved those pillows. "Why would *any* animal do this?"

"It's separation anxiety. You said he was Kyle's, right?"

I press my lips together and nod.

"So, he was a military dog and went through who knows what," she speculates. "He lost his owner a year ago—and what's happened to him since? This poor guy's got some baggage." She frowns, glancing in the corner behind him. "Why didn't you put him in the crate when you left?"

I stare at the giant box, with its blanket inside and secure metal door, seemingly the only undisturbed item in the room. I know I don't have the right answer, so I just shrug. "I honestly didn't even think of it."

Lydia reaches to scratch the dog's fuzzy black ears. "Lots of dogs with separation anxiety do better in a crate when they're left alone."

"Now you tell me."

She gives me a sidelong look. "I did ask for an update yesterday . . ."

I bite my lip. Maybe she's right, and this whole situation could've been avoided. Which makes me feel worse. I glare at the dog, turn, and throw the heel at what's left of my sitting area. "Look what you did to my couch!"

Rufus stiffens next to Lydia and barks.

"*Caprice,*" she admonishes. And I get a weird flash of what she'll sound like as a mother. "You're going to freak him out again."

I exhale, walking to the kitchen for a garbage bag while she pets him and offers more treats. I know she isn't trying to blame me, but it seems like I have a right to be upset when my home is literally ruined.

"Hand me one of those," she says, scooping feathers from my duvet into a pile on the bed.

I grab the entire box, then glance at the clock. "Don't you have to get going? When did you say you'd meet Henry?"

She rests her hands on her hips, then pulls out her phone. "I'll see if Tomás can join him for a while. It's Saturday. The Pooch Park shouldn't be as busy, and this . . . seems like kind of an emergency."

A lump rises in my throat as I watch her shoot off a text. "You'll stay? Are you sure?"

"I'm not going to leave you hanging with your apartment shredded," she says gently, then eyeballs Rufus. "But I think I should stay for him as much as for you."

I glance at the dog, who leans into her touch adoringly, tongue hanging out on one side.

My eyes burn when Lydia looks back at me. We've been through a lot over the course of our friendship, but I don't think I've ever been more grateful to have her in my life. "Thank you. I—I need all the help I can get."

You'll be in over your head in less than twenty-four hours.

Drew Forbes's words invade my mind like a sneering I-told-you-so, souring my stomach. Rufus hops down from the bed and starts slurping from the water bowl, and I let myself sink to the mattress.

"Hey. We'll figure this out." Lydia sits beside me, pulling me in for a hug. "But I am curious . . . why did Theo bring him to *you*?"

"It's complicated." I shake my head into her hair. "I should've let Kyle's brother have him."

"Wait." She straightens, pulling back to look at me. "You saw Drew?"

I work my jaw, trying not to think about those green eyes —Kyle's eyes—flashing with so much malice. "He showed up at the airport trying to claim him, and you weren't kidding about him being Mr. Personality. But get this—Kyle wrote a will and put *in writing* that he wanted me to have him."

Lydia's brow wrinkles, clearly perplexed. "I don't understand. Like, no offense, but . . . did he know you at all?"

I huff, drawing my knees to my chest. "Congratulations. You've asked the fifty thousand dollar question."

Her eyes drift away as she thinks back, processing memories, clearly trying to make this add up.

"I mean, Kyle was obsessed with dogs, like you." I fold my arms. "I don't know what it is about me that attracts you people." My nose burns. "But dogs were part of the package if you loved him, and I accepted that. I would've lived with *some* dog, maybe even this one, if he hadn't . . ."

My throat closes up, and Lydia squeezes my hand.

Rufus comes to sit in front of her, glancing at me, and my mood darkens. I cross the room to start bagging up pieces of my couch.

"Anyway, Drew seems to think I'm the last person who should have Rufus now, and he's probably right."

Neither of us says much for a while, so I assume she agrees. I fill my trash bag, then a second, and Lydia does the same. She sits quietly on the bed, scooping up pieces of fabric and destroyed pillow, while the dog just sits there, watching us clean up with the audacity to look curious.

"I think he's wrong," Lydia says after thirty minutes or so.

"Sorry, what?"

"Drew Forbes. He's wrong. He doesn't know you. But Kyle did."

I set my ruined Louboutins on the counter. "What do you mean?"

She crosses the room, sinking heavily onto what's left of my couch. It's not even ten a.m. and she already looks tired. I go to the fridge and grab her a bottle of water.

"Look, I know Kyle had his demons . . ." Lydia says, taking a long drink. "But this dog was military, a fellow soldier. I've met a few like him, and they're more than companions to their handlers. But all that aside, I can't imagine leaving a beloved animal with anyone but the person I trust most."

"Please." I look at her dead-on. "Don't leave me Heart-throb in your will."

She rolls her eyes. "I'm serious, Caprice. There has to be a reason Kyle chose you and not his brother."

"Whatever. Maybe there is." I toss up my hands. "But what if I don't *want* him?"

She makes a show of covering Rufus's ears like I might offend him. "I think you should give him a chance."

I gesture around the room, incredulous. "What exactly would you call this?"

"A mistake. *Your* mistake," she says firmly, looking at me. "Rufus clearly has some trauma. He needs someone who can help him work through it."

I stare at her. "But you don't think the 'dog guru' trainer would be a better fit?"

"Kyle didn't." She shrugs, patting the seat next to her, and Rufus immediately jumps up and starts licking her face. I look away so she won't see my horror. "Oh, you're a kisser, are you?" She laughs, reaching out to stroke the top of his head. He quickly flops onto his side, letting her rub his belly. "Oh my God. Caprice, he's such a lover."

"He's free," I say. "You want him?"

She shakes her head, resting one arm across her belly. "I wish I could. Heartthrob plays well with other dogs, and Rufus seems sweet. But we might find he has other issues. I can't test new canine dynamics with an infant on the way."

"It was worth a shot," I say. She pulls more treats out of her apparently bottomless pockets, and Rufus stands at attention. I close my eyes, let out a long breath. "Give me one."

She dumps the pile into my hand. "He likes those—they're cheese. I'll get you a whole bag."

I hold one out tentatively, and he nearly takes off my fingers again. "*Ouch*, you asshole."

"Try placing one flat on your palm and giving it to him that way," Lydia says.

I follow her instruction, and to my surprise, he eats it more gently from the center of my hand. The dog wags his tail, then politely sits and looks up at me. We study each other for a moment, his golden eyes trained on mine. And I can't help wondering what Kyle thought about when he looked at him. How he must've stared into these eyes . . . and still made the decision to end his life.

I give Rufus one treat at a time until I run out, and then he nudges my hand with his nose and looks at me. But it doesn't seem like he's just looking for more to eat. It almost feels like he's offering some sort of agreement.

"You can do this," Lydia murmurs.

Ugh. Something deep inside me deflates. I stand up to wash my hands, then tie up another full trash bag and place it by the door with the others. "Well, what do people do about . . . *separation anxiety*?" I ask.

Lydia scrunches up her nose. "Work with a trainer?"

CHAPTER
SEVEN

In her quest for sainthood, Lydia stays with me most of Saturday to alleviate the damage to my apartment and, in her words, help the dog and me get to know one another. It isn't quite like the team-building experiences I've had at *Mile High Observer*. I have never in my life picked up another living thing's poop. But it also doesn't involve participating in a game of paintball, or Randall's favorite, all-day personality quizzes and trust activities.

By the time Lydia takes off to join Henry at PetExpo in the late afternoon, we've established that my mattress is salvageable, if not the rest of my bedding. But my sofa is a goner.

"I'll see if Seth's free in the next few days," Lydia says, pulling her coat snug around her baby bump. "He and Anton should be able to carry the couch out for you."

"Great. Thanks." I frown at having to accept anything from the Richie brothers, but I have to admit I could use the help. "I'm sort of scared to invest in a new one. But even if I find another secondhand gem, it'll have to wait till my next paycheck." I glare at the dog.

"I've left you written instructions on basic dog care," Lydia says, handing me a piece of paper. "Feed him two times per day. Walk him at least three. *Play* with him. And refresh his water daily."

"I've got it, Dr. Dolittle." She winces, moving her hand to her side like something hurts. "Are you sure you shouldn't go home and lie down or something? This was a lot of work."

"I'm *fine*—she's just jabbing me in the ribs," Lydia snaps, then gives me an apologetic grimace. "Don't forget to make him an appointment with my vet. I wrote their website and phone number here at the bottom. Oh, and I included the name of a female trainer I've heard good things about too."

"Thanks for all your help." I try to inject my voice with confidence, though I'm admittedly terrified as she turns to leave.

"I ordered you two bags of the cheese treats," she prattles on as she opens the door. "And some toys. They should be here this afternoon."

"You didn't have to do that." I hold up the Ziploc containing the rest of what she had in her pockets. "You're a better friend than I deserve."

"Oh—" She turns back. "This probably doesn't need to be said, but put him in the *crate* if you have to go anywhere."

I put on my best *I'm not completely inept* face, hoping to convince us both.

She purses her lips, surveying my apartment one last time. I made the bed with a backup set of bedding until I can get a new duvet. But my sofa still resembles a half-eaten carcass. That, my pillows, and my Louboutins turned out to be the worst of the damage, though.

If I don't look at my living room or breathe through my nose—because one of us *smells*—I can almost convince myself I'm not living with man's best nightmare.

Lydia hesitates in the doorway, then leans in. I think she's offering me a hug, but as I smile and step toward her, she reaches out to stroke Rufus's head next to me. "You can do this," she repeats. I can't tell which of us she's speaking to.

Once she closes the door, the dog looks at me, almost expectant, and my pulse picks up. From what Lydia explained about separation anxiety, I don't think he'll resume his path of destruction with me here, but it takes real effort not to chase my dog-loving friend down the hall and beg her not to leave me. After a minute, I force myself to swallow, then glance at the list she placed in my hand.

"Okay, you've eaten. You just had a walk. You already *played* with my couch." I glance at the water bowl, which is still full. "What else could you possibly want?"

He lets out a low whine and my throat tightens.

I look at the clock and close my eyes. How is it almost three? "Look, I need to catch up on some work. If you can like . . . *not* do anything bad, I'll take you out again in a couple of hours. Sound good?"

He licks his lips and stares at me, and my confidence wavers. Then I remember and grab the cheese treats from the counter. "Here! I have more of these. Only for *good* dogs."

I roll my eyes at how stupid I sound. It's not like he can understand me. But he takes the cue and sits at least.

"Good boy," I say, creeping toward one of my barstools. He tilts his head, but once I'm in the chair, he seems to lose interest. He wanders around, sniffing, and I open my laptop. But I'm watching him like a hawk, ready to freak out and call Lydia if he does anything destructive.

Finally, after making a circuit of my entire studio, he hops up on the ruined couch.

"Hey—" I start to yell, but he circles twice, then curls up facing me. I frown. "Fine. Since you already murdered it," I say with a curled lip. "But don't think you'll be getting anywhere near a new one."

When he doesn't get up or do anything other than watch me for a whole minute, I open my laptop. I've lost way too much of my weekend to this whole situation.

• • •

I spend the rest of the afternoon catching up on nearly a day's worth of emails. I'm used to keeping one ear to the ground on weekends, but since I'm stuck on the assignment desk, I'm not just monitoring my email, but the general *Observer* inbox and all of our social media. About ninety percent of it is ignorable—complaints about our coverage of the primary elections, opinions from readers on a piece Adrienne did on women in education, a request that we expose Mafia influence over businesses in Commerce City, and a hot tip that aliens have infiltrated the student body at Littleton High School.

I follow up on a couple of messages about a shooting near Five Points and layoffs at a warehouse in Aurora. Then I spot a new email from "Mrs. R."

Saturday, March 13, 20__, 4:02 PM

To: Caprice_Phipps@MHObserver.com

From: Mrs.R@mail.com

Subject: Re: A Proposal

Ms. Phipps,

I originally reached out because of your discerning coverage of the Unmatched app last year. You have a talent for calling out malfeasance without unnecessary sensationalism, which I appreciate.

I would still like to offer you an exclusive opportunity to extend your coverage and further expose those behind the app. I promise this story will be worth your while. But if I don't hear from you by Monday, I will have to take it elsewhere. Please let me know your decision. This is a secure number where I can be reached: 303-555-4462.

Cheers,
Mrs. R.

I look over at the dog asleep on what's left of my couch, like a hyena sated after eating its fill. Next to me on the counter are the remains of my Louboutins—a college graduation gift from my mom and the literal only pair of shoes I own that didn't come from Poshmark or DSW. My savings account was already dwindling before I acquired my new "pet," but when I add up the replacement costs, in addition to my rent and other living expenses, my palms start to sweat.

At that moment, my credit card statement slides into my inbox like a sucker punch, reminding me of the two hundred and fifty dollars I spent last month that I didn't have. Baby gifts for Lydia. A care package for my brother. A bridesmaid dress for my cousin's wedding. I was planning to pay it all off over a couple of months, but add new bedding and furniture, and I'll be lucky to do it in six.

I get up and walk to the windows, soaking up my luxurious view. Moving in here was a stretch a year ago. Until then, I'd been living in a garden-level two-bedroom with a roommate on Capitol Hill. It smelled musty and we had mice, but the rent allowed me to pay down my student loans and even save a little. Then my roommate took a job in Minnesota, and it was either find someone else to share the lease or splurge to get my own studio.

At that time, my career still felt like it was building momentum. I'd received recognition for a piece about artists forming a collective downtown. Shortly after that, I'd earned a nod from the Colorado Press Club for a series I did on cyclist safety in the wake of several high-profile accidents. When I started writing about the locally based cheating app Unmatched, the public response was so overwhelming, it seemed like the story that was going to level up my career.

Until I received my first threat.

The article about the dating app shows what a bitch you are. I know where you live, pretty girl.

I swallow hard, pulling myself away from the mountain

view and wandering back to my computer. When I was little, I'd carry around my mom's legal pad, "interviewing" my dolls, aspiring to become some mashup of Oprah and maybe Katie Couric. Except, I soon realized, I didn't enjoy being on camera. So when I got to high school and discovered a talent writing for the school paper, I leaned into that. I channeled Ida B. Wells, doing internships at our local newspaper, honing my ability to find stories that mattered, intent on my dreams making a difference.

At no point did I dream of being called an ignorant whore. That I deserve to be raped. Or hope to receive messages that I should be hanging in a tree.

My mom always encouraged me to pursue journalism, even while warning me it was a tough career for women. Her intentions were good, but I doubt she had any idea.

Still, news is what I *do*. And much as I like to idealize life as a barista, I doubt I'll ever stop looking for the next story to write. The next issue to shed light on. I just wish I could figure out how to reveal the truth without fearing for my safety . . . or worrying about next month's rent.

My stomach does a nervous flip as I click from my credit card statement back to the email from the Unmatched tipster lady. I lower my head to the counter briefly, hoping my brother forgives me.

Hoping I can forgive myself.

Then I reach over and pick up my phone. A woman answers after the second ring.

"Hello, Ms. Phipps?"

My hands are now shaking, but I pick up my pen. "Um, yes. I'm looking for Mrs. R?"

By the time I hang up, the dog has started whining again behind me. God forbid I be allowed to pretend he isn't there. He started up around five o'clock, but I was still on the phone, frantically filling my notepad, so I dumped food in his dish, hoping that would shut him up until I finished. He licked the bowl clean, then climbed back up on the used-to-be-a couch and settled down, thank goodness. But at some point, he got back up and started pacing. And then the squeaking started. It hasn't even been twenty-four hours, and that sound is already like nails on a chalkboard.

"Can you just be patient?" I mutter. "I need to finish typing up these notes."

I'm almost done transcribing my harried scrawl about cheaters and socialites and pseudonyms into something legible and organized when I register a peculiar squirting sound—and seconds later, a *horrific* odor. I whip my head toward the dog in time to see him squatting by my front door with a stream of liquid shit pouring out from under his tail.

I leap off my barstool, screeching. "What are you doing? *Why?*"

I scramble around, trying to remember where I put the leash while gagging on diarrhea fumes. If the dog is sick, Lydia's going to kill me. But by the time I sprint out the door toward the stairs, Rufus is running alongside me, wagging his tail like we're playing some kind of game.

There must be a front moving in because the moment we step outside, my ponytail whips into my face from an icy March wind. I huddle against the side of my building, still wearing the T-shirt and leggings I changed into at the gym this morning. There's a thin strip of grass against the sidewalk, and I pace back and forth in front of it, watching my breath freeze in the air. The dog takes his time sniffing around in his thick fur coat, but I refuse to step back through the front door until he at least pees on a tree.

Once we make it back to my apartment, we're hit with a stench like a neglected porta-potty on a hot day. Rufus has the gall to leap over the puddle in front of the door and stare back at it like he finds it offensive. I cross the apartment, gagging, and crank open my few operable windows, then swing the bathroom door wide and turn on the exhaust fan.

My phone rings just as I've dropped to my knees with a roll of paper towels. When I see Lydia on the ID, I can't swipe to answer fast enough.

"Hey, just checking in on you and Rufus. How are things going?" Her sweet smile beams at me from the screen.

"Shit—*literal* shit, Lydia." I set the phone down on the coffee table so I can resume cleanup, pausing to gag as I approach the Lake of the Runs.

"What? Caprice, are you okay?"

"*No.* This is the worst fucking day of my life. Please come and get the dog. I don't want him."

I open my trash can, dumping in at least half a roll of paper towels saturated in thick wet shit, before scraping the last of it off the floor and attacking the area with bathroom cleaner. The aforementioned animal just looks on from atop my couch carcass like *I* am somehow responsible.

When I have finished scrubbing every trace of fecal material off my floor, I dump the last of the paper towels, cinch up the trash bag, and carry it toward the door. "Be right back, Lyd. Just taking out a bag of diarrhea."

As soon as I step into the hall, Rufus starts crying and shrieking. I hesitate, then *run* for the waste and recycle room, terrified of the damage he might be able to do in less than a minute. But as I race back toward my door, I almost smack into a guy stepping out of the elevator.

He's sort of hunched, with nondescript baggy clothes, and he's carrying what looks like someone's dinner order. "Sorry," I mutter, hurrying past him for my apartment, which sounds like it is literally screaming.

"Uh, s'cuse me," the guy says, holding up a phone screen. I recognize the name of some meal delivery app. "Do you know where this number is?"

I peer at the address without actually moving closer. "Downstairs. You're one floor too high."

"Ohh, got it." He snickers to himself like it's funny, and something about this, and the fact that I'm alone out here with this guy sends goose flesh rising on my skin. I take a step back.

There's a crash against my door, followed by a wail, and I don't waste any more time getting inside. When I close it behind me and turn the deadbolt, I realize my heart is pounding.

Rufus rushes over, panting and whining as I slump against the door, inserting his cold, wet nose into my hand. The next second, however, his ears prick up—no, his whole body goes alert. He positions himself in front of the doorknob, a low growl deep in his throat.

I stare at the dog, staring at the door.

"Caprice?" Lydia's voice sounds tinny and small from across the room. I walk over to retrieve the phone still lying on my coffee table. Rufus maintains his stance in front of my apartment door, and for the first time all day, I don't mind that he's here. At all.

I hold the camera up to my face as I walk into the kitchen, wincing at my disheveled appearance. I set the phone by the sink where Lydia can see me, and pump soap all over my hands. Rufus is no longer growling, but he doesn't move from his position by the door.

Silently, reluctantly, I allow that my brother might have had a point about Kyle's dog.

When I shut off the faucet, Lydia clears her throat and raises her brows. "So . . . you forgot to walk him?"

CHAPTER
EIGHT

When I wake Sunday, there's a strong, solid body against mine and warm breath on my neck. I leap out of bed so fast, I almost pull a hamstring. Rufus raises his head off my pillow like I've disturbed his beauty rest.

"Dog. This is *my* bed."

His head tilts at my words and he stretches, black-tipped tail slapping the bedding.

"Get *off*," I order, pointing to the floor.

Immediately, he does exactly what I say, leaping lightly from the bed and coming to stand in front of me.

I straighten in surprise. "Um . . . good boy?"

This is where Lydia would probably tell me to give him a reward. I applaud myself for thinking of it and grab the last couple cheese treats from the counter. Guess I should walk him and see if her delivery arrived downstairs.

But first, I stumble over to my coffeemaker. It was a long night. I must've fallen asleep eventually, but I laid awake until at least one a.m. brainstorming questions for my interview today, and listening to every sound the dog made, terrified he was going to sully my floor again. I got up and walked him sometime around midnight, but all he did was lift his leg on a tree. So while the coffee machine fills my mug, I feed him and pull on clothes.

Lydia gave me a tongue-lashing about taking him out—not that I needed it after that cleanup—and made me set alarms on my phone so it wouldn't happen again. The first one is set for seven a.m., and we're outside before it goes off. After Rufus has done what he needs to do (picking up solid poop, while still disgusting, beats wiping its liquid form off my floor), I head back inside to assemble an outfit and work on my hair.

"Mrs. R." wants to meet at ten o'clock a.m. at the Fillmore Hotel in Cherry Creek. Not exactly a casual venue, and I'm getting a clear sense the woman herself isn't either. Which shouldn't make me uncomfortable. Except the Fillmore is exactly the sort of place Kyle and I used to land with his parents back in high school, sitting through hours-long dinners as they highlighted his flaws and demanded he shape himself to their expectations. He'd started inviting me along hoping to get his parents to tone it down. Unfortunately, that was not the effect. While the Doctors Forbes didn't overtly object to my presence, they made very clear that I did not, nor would I ever, belong.

I select a wool cowl-neck dress because it's still chilly out and decide to stick with the sleek ponytail I've been wearing most of the time since I relaxed my hair. Once I've contoured and perfected a daytime cat eye, I shoot Rufus a glare and slip into a pair of Jessica Simpson pumps in lieu of my destroyed Louboutins. He watches me without a sound until I grab my purse and notebook off the counter. Then, heeding Lydia's instructions, I use a couple of treats to lure him into the ugly crate next to my bed. He issues one low groan and starts panting as I close him inside, but that's all. At least what's left of my apartment will be safe while I'm gone.

On my way down to meet my Uber, my phone pings with a text.

THEO

I'll be out of service at least a week starting tomorrow. You still have the number for my friend in Colorado Springs?

I'm not calling the dude with the skull tattoos.

THEO

Dwayne's a good guy. He would help, no questions, if you needed anything.

How was Mom?

THEO

Annoyed she hasn't seen you for a month.

On my to-do list. Right below fifty other things.

THEO

Think I'd rather track down terrorists than ask about that.

How's it going with our furry friend?

I pause a moment, briefly considering inundating him with poop emojis and pictures of my desecrated couch. But I don't want to stress him out or give him more to worry about if he's getting ready for a mission.

Lydia has been super helpful.

I'm down a pair of shoes, but he seems to be settling in.

The lobby of the Fillmore Hotel in Denver's Cherry Creek North neighborhood is one of those spaces that clearly had considerable styling put into it, and the result feels effortlessly elegant. There's no flashy branding or over-the-top decadence. The colors are muted, the woods and fabrics of the furniture are high quality, and the spaces are illuminated without the lighting itself being a feature. The overall effect is understated luxury. As soon as you walk in, you can tell you're in a place for people who have money, who don't need to wave it around just to let everyone know.

"Hi," I say to a prim middle-aged woman behind the front desk. "I'm Caprice Phipps. I'm here for a meeting with um . . . someone in room 211."

She does a five-second assessment of me as she glances up. I know she can't possibly read the labels of anything I'm wearing or guess the balance of my bank account, but that doesn't stop my palms from sweating like she's a bouncer who might deny me access to an exclusive club. My skin prickles when I look around and find I'm the brownest person in this lobby.

"Ah, yes," she says. If there's any layer of judgment, she hides it well. "We were told to expect you, Ms. Phipps. If you'll follow me . . ."

She glides from behind the desk, clicking across the hardwood in a gorgeous pair of Manolos without looking back. So I click along after her in my Jessicas. It's a quick elevator ride to the second floor, and before I know it, she knocks once on a door halfway down a wide hall.

We are greeted almost immediately by a middle-aged blonde woman with a wide smile. She passes a cash tip to the concierge with such subtlety I almost miss it. "Nice to meet you, Ms. Phipps. Please, come in."

The woman doesn't extend her hand, so I don't either, waiting to speak until the door clicks shut behind me. "Mrs. R., I—"

"I'm in here," a voice says from an adjacent room. I follow the blonde through a doorway into a brightly lit sitting area decorated in the same tasteful aesthetic as downstairs. A different woman rises as we walk in—slightly older, with brunette hair styled in such perfect loose waves around her shoulders I wonder briefly if it's a wig. She wears a blouse and stylish white pants, her head topped with a striking cowgirl hat that could only be pulled off by a wealthy white woman of a certain age. Whom she clearly is.

"Uh, Mrs. R?" I ask just to be sure, taking her extended hand.

"Yes, that'd be me," she says with a sharkish smile—one that strikes me as vaguely familiar. She gestures to the well-dressed blonde. "This is my assistant, Beth."

"Nice to meet you." I nod.

Mrs. R. offers me a seat, and Beth pours tea for both of us.

"You're younger than I expected. But I've read every one of your Unmatched articles, and I'm thrilled we get to sit down and chat."

"It's my pleasure. And thank you." I take my phone and a small notebook out of my purse, trying to think where to start. "Unmatched was sort of a passion project for me."

"Oh? Do you have firsthand experience?" Mrs. R. asks point-blank, jingling a set of gold bangles on one wrist. I don't even blink. I've been asked this before.

"Ah, no . . . I'm not in a relationship. But I found a good friend's husband on the app."

She tuts in a way that makes me think she's been there and done that.

"So," I go on, opening my notebook. "I'm curious. When we spoke, you said your husband was on Unmatched too. I'm sorry to hear that. But what made you reach out to me?"

Revenge, most likely. But I want to hear it in her own words.

"My husband is a philanderer and always has been." She waves her hand dismissively, but I don't miss the pain in her eyes. "I figured that out within our first year of marriage, which was . . . not recent."

Her eyes hold mine. Perhaps waiting for me to balk or question her choices. But I've done this enough and have met plenty of women in her situation who made the same decision. I nod for her to continue.

"It's one thing to make that choice within a marriage. To be *that* sort of husband." She rolls her eyes. "I guess I took issue when I realized he was advertising it to others—enticing, giving permission, *capitalizing* on it."

I pause, trying to make sure I'm getting her subtext.

"Are you saying your husband is—"

"He founded Unmatched." Her lip curls. "It's his baby."

I straighten in my chair, letting this information sink in. I'd been prepared for this woman to be a wronged socialite at the very least. She and her husband are clearly wealthy and probably influential. I don't even know who they are yet, but ever since I walked through the doors of the Fillmore, I've been sure *whatever* she wanted me to know would at least make local waves.

Over months of research, I found plenty of users and victims, but I'd gotten nowhere trying to figure out who had cultivated the Unmatched app. On record, it's owned by some alphabet soup shell company. But I knew there had to be someone, or even several someones, at the heart of its existence. Some man who sat down one day and said, *You know what would make a great business idea? An app that helps married guys get more tail.*

"Do you mind if I record our conversation?" I ask, reaching for my phone.

She places her hand over mine. A variety of jewels glitter across her fingers. "Before we go any further, I want to ensure you know what you're getting yourself into."

I meet her gaze, pretty sure I know what she means. An assortment of hard-to-forget emails and social media messages floats through my mind. Racial slurs. Dick pics. Threats. The ones that say I'm an ugly bitch and they hope I die. And a few that are even worse.

"Thank you for asking," I say, swallowing hard. This is my opportunity to back out. Run for the hills—or at least down to Starbucks to ask about benefits. But then I imagine moving back to that garden apartment with the mice. Losing my beautiful, expensive view. And I think of the lady journalists who came before me who didn't back down just because they were scared.

And then, of all things, I remember something Kyle said after I published one of my very first features—a piece about abuse claims at a juvenile detention facility.

Some people can't tell their own stories—they need you to write them.

I take a shaky breath. "There are certain risks that come with this job. But I take them because it's important."

She appraises me for an interminable minute, then gives me a sober nod. "And I'm sure you're aware of the risks in exposing . . . well, certain members of society."

My focus lasers in on her. I don't really follow local gossip, but she has seemed familiar since I walked in. And suddenly I care less about a handful of cowardly online threats than I do about the truth.

"Let's do this, 'Mrs. R.'"

"Very well." She gestures at my phone. "Record anything you like."

I pull up the voice-activated software I use for this type of interview, then ask her to state the date and her full name.

"It's Sunday, March fourteenth. My first name is Margaret, but I go by Mimi. My husband is Colin Vanderpool."

CHAPTER
NINE

I step onto the street outside the Fillmore an hour and a half later, phone gripped tight in my hand. As soon as I've ordered my Uber, I dial Randall.

"Is a zombie horde descending on downtown Denver?" he asks.

"Biggest story all year—if my brain doesn't get eaten before I can write it."

"Figured you must have a good reason to call me at my kid's soccer game on a Sunday."

I grimace. Then my ride, a red Subaru, pulls up to the curb, so I don't waste any more words. "Can we meet first thing tomorrow before the staff meeting?"

"I . . . yes?" Randall pauses as I greet my driver and check her photo. "But I was planning to—"

"You're going to want to make the time."

Suspicion creeps into his voice. "Look, Caprice, if this is about covering PetExpo, I know it's not your typical thing—"

"It isn't about pets," I say, buckling my seatbelt. "I need a little guidance."

He doesn't reply right away, and I can guess the look on

his face. He makes this sound when he purses his lips, like a fish drowning in oxygen.

I glance at the driver and lower my voice. "I followed up on that lead you sent—the one you must've known I wouldn't want?"

"Did you now?" he says, voice pitching with interest.

"Yeah. Don't get proud."

He chuckles. "All right. And something came of it?"

"You could say that." My heart starts racing again, the way it did the whole last hour in that Fillmore hotel room. "Did you know who she really was when you sent her to me, Randall?"

"No. Why?" His tone is curious. "Anybody I should have recognized?"

I let out a long, low breath. "I want to talk about that raise you're giving me. Your office, nine a.m."

By the time my Uber drops me in front of my building, I've collected myself some. Still jittery, but maybe less freaked out and a little more excited. Unmatched was initially a hot story due to its scandalous nature alone. But now that I know who founded it, there's no way I can *not* write more about this. Colin Vanderpool is the longtime CEO of Denver-based Green Industries, one of the biggest energy companies west of the Mississippi. He's also a major local philanthropist. He and his wife give enough money to arts and charitable organizations to have their names on half the museums and hospitals in the state. They're basically Colorado royalty.

It makes sense now that I felt so targeted after the initial articles. Mimi suggested her husband probably hired someone to scare me off. And of course, it worked. I backed off the topic—hell, I considered leaving journalism. But now I know who he is. I'm not foolish enough to think that guarantees my safety, especially against a person with so much influence. In some ways, it's scarier. But this whole experience has helped me remember that exposing abuses of power is one of the reasons journalism is so important.

If I don't break this story, someone else will. And after all I've been through, after looking over my shoulder and losing sleep the last six months, I'll be damned if I don't at least get my rent money out of it.

My phone rings as I enter my building, but I bite my lip and send it to voicemail when I see my mom's name pop up. I'll call her back later. I just need to get home, change out of these stupid heels, and go for a run to try and figure out my next move.

But as the elevator door opens on my floor, I am greeted by a too-familiar shrieking sound, and my pulse immediately spikes. I forgot about the goddamn dog.

"*Fuck*," I mutter when I see my neighbor Darius, a broad six-foot-four half-Samoan man, pounding on my door in his pajamas amid the howling.

"Dar—hey, I'm home," I say, rushing down the hall.

He gives me a tolerant, bloodshot nod as I approach. Darius is an ER nurse over at Denver Health, and judging by the look on his face, he just got off a very long night shift.

Another shrieking, banshee-yell issues from my apartment as I fumble to get my key in the lock.

"You got a dog?" he asks, folding his arms.

"Um . . . it's complicated," I say, finally shoving the door open.

I'm terrified to look inside, and unnerved when I find my apartment whole. Unmarred. Well, except for the already half-eaten couch. And the giant dog crate, which is now halfway across the room from where it had been sitting beside my bed. Inside, I see flashes of tan and black as the dog spins, barks, and cries to be let out. I set my purse on the counter and dash over to open the door so he'll shut the hell up.

Which is a mistake.

The dog shoots out past me, snarling and charging straight for Darius, who is still standing in my open door.

"Rufus, *no!* Sit! Oh fu—"

But before he can spring from the floor to rip out my neighbor's jugular, Darius kneels and holds out his palm. "Hey, boy." Rufus stops in his tracks, posture stiff. He gives him a cautious sniff, still emitting a low growl. "Oh my, you're vicious, aren't you?" Darius says in a playful tone.

Rufus eyes him a moment longer, then sneezes and licks his hand, wagging his tail.

Very gently, Darius reaches under Rufus's chin and strokes his neck.

"H-how did you . . . ?" I rasp.

My neighbor sits back on his heels and gives me a relieved look, like he hadn't been sure how that would pan out either. "Todd's sister is a K-9 officer up in Longmont. First time her shepherd ran at me like that, I nearly peed my pants." He gives a tired laugh. "She told me it's my size they don't like."

He rises back up to his full height, but apparently has passed the Rufus test, because the dog comes to stand by my side, nudging me with his cold nose.

I pull my hand away.

"Um, wow. I'm glad you knew that," I say, reaching for Rufus's leash. Darius does look intimidating at first glance, but he and his boyfriend, Todd, are literally the sweetest couple in my building.

Darius glances around my apartment and whistles. "*Ouch.* He do that to your couch?"

"Yeah," I say, dragging my hand over my face.

"What's his name? Where'd you get him from?"

"His name is Rufus." I wince when I think of Kyle's will, trying to come up with a condensed story for my neighbor. "Um, I sort of inherited him. He's an ex-military dog."

His eyes widen. "Well, I hate to be a bitch, but I just

finished a twelve-hour shift and I couldn't sleep with all that noise."

"I'm *so* sorry." My shoulders tighten. "I didn't know he was going to do that. I'll make sure he's quiet the rest of the day."

"Thanks, Caprice." He stoops to pet Rufus again, who hops up to lick his face. Darius laughs. "Oh man, you're some scary bomb dog."

I follow him into the hall with Rufus on his leash since I'm not taking chances with poop anymore. "My friend says he probably has some issues since he was military."

"Ya think?" Darius chuckles, returning to his own door. "Apparently he doesn't like that crate. Hey, you want me to ask Todd's sister for advice? Police dogs might be similar."

"Would you?" I raise my brows, hitting the button for the elevator. "That's a great idea, thank you."

"Sure." He rubs the dog's head one last time. "Nice to meet you, Rufus. Hope not to hear you in my dreams."

I dial Lydia as soon as we're on the street. "Hey, what do I need to do if I want to bring Rufus to The Pooch Park tomorrow?"

"Um . . ." She hesitates. "You could time travel and get on our waitlist two months ago?"

I start to laugh, but quickly sober when she doesn't join in. "That's not some woo-woo manifesting talk, is it? You're really booked?"

"Achievement unlocked," she says, sounding a little guilty. "We had to start turning people away after the holidays."

"Wow, that's . . ." I inhale deeply through my nose, glancing at the dog calmly sniffing the sidewalk beside me. Who apparently only loses his mind when I leave. "That's *amazing*, Lydia. Congratulations."

"Thanks," she says, excitement palpable through the receiver. "But even if I could squeeze him in, I doubt Rufus would be ready for daycare tomorrow."

"Oh . . . um, why?"

"He needs some established normalcy first," she says, like this should have occurred to me. "The poor dog lost Kyle, then lived with a foster for who knows how long. Then your brother swept in and flew him across the country, and now he's living with a woman he doesn't know or trust."

"Why wouldn't he trust me?" I frown, thinking about the creepy dude in the hall yesterday, and the way Rufus stood by the door and growled. "I thought dogs had instincts about people."

She snorts. "Sure. What do you suppose Heartthrob's instincts tell him about you?"

I scowl. I tolerate Lydia's dog slightly better than I tolerate her husband.

"I'm just saying," she says more gently, "Starting daycare will be too much for him right now. First, you need to get to know each other better."

"Okay, fine. We'll start having date nights. But in the meantime, I need to be able to go to work, and this crate thing is not happening."

"What do you mean?"

I grit my teeth. "I mean, I fed and walked him this morning just like you told me, and then I put him in there and left to do an interview. But according to my neighbor, he acted out scenes from *The Exorcist* the whole time I was gone."

"Oh . . . that's a problem."

"Exactly." The dog rounds the corner and I follow with a sigh, waiting while he lifts his leg on a lamppost. "Lydia, I have to be able to leave him. I'm working on this story, and I just—I have a meeting tomorrow at nine. I *have* to go to work."

"Right, okay. I just need to think . . ." Her tone doesn't exactly inspire confidence. "Any chance you can work remotely for a while?"

I'm about to tell her exactly why that isn't an option when my phone vibrates and I glance at the screen. A glimmer of hope blooms in my chest. "Hang on. Darius just sent some kind of possibility. I'll call you later."

CHAPTER
TEN

It starts sleeting as soon as I pull up the address my neighbor sent. I'm huddled under a tree, about to turn tail and head back into my building, when I realize the place Todd's sister recommended is only a few blocks over, off Logan Street. I look down at the heels I never changed out of, then glance at the dog. Lydia assured me he wouldn't be able to destroy anything from inside the crate, and my apartment didn't directly suffer this time, but I think she underestimated his ability to destroy my life. I don't know how I'll be able to get to work this week without getting evicted, and I'm not about to sacrifice my career—or my apartment—because of an animal I don't even want.

Rufus looks up from the end of the lead with his tongue hanging out, like he's just a normal dog and not a demon sent from beyond the grave by my ex to cause further pain. I curse Kyle under my breath, wondering for the billionth time *why* he did this to me. Then, as the sleet eases up, I tug on the leash and head for a place called K9 Academy.

It doesn't look like much from the outside when I find it. Just a door on a storefront in the middle of the block. There's a sign, but it isn't decorated with bones and paw prints or anything. Just black-and-white lettering and the profile of a German shepherd. I'm actually relieved it isn't overly cutesy. Lydia's businesses are one thing. But if this place had been called Pawfect Poochie and decorated with pink poodles or something, I'm not sure I could have convinced myself to go in.

Rufus seems eager to check it out as we approach, nose to the ground, sniffing carefully all the way up to the door. I don't know if they even take walk-ins, but I need someone to teach this dog not to flip out whenever I leave, so in we go.

Inside the door, we find a retail section full of toys and treats and a small reception desk. Beyond that, on the other side of a low wall, is a vast space that feels like a warehouse. The place must span several storefronts. It's bigger than I expected.

Rufus's interest skyrockets as soon as we step inside. I adjust my grip on the leash, wrapping it around my wrist a few times as he does his sniff-every-corner thing, tail wagging fast like it's some kind of game. I can hear voices coming from the warehouse area, but can't see around the racks of toys and treats at the front of the space. As we make our way toward the empty desk, however, I spot a group of people on the other side of the wall, standing in a wide circle with dogs on leashes around a man giving some kind of instruction.

I brighten. They must be holding a training class right now.

Everyone is quietly focused on the guy speaking, and since no one's here in reception, I open the little gate next to the desk and slip through with Rufus to join them. As soon as it latches behind us, the tiny white dog closest to us breaks away from the circle and starts lunging at the end of its leash, barking hysterically.

The instant this happens, Rufus transforms from curious companion into a hound straight out of hell, flying to the end of the lead, snapping, snarling, and barking. A number of the other dogs react similarly while their owners struggle for control. And it's a damn good thing I have a firm hold on the leash because it takes *all* my strength to keep him from swooping into the group and devouring every living creature in the room.

"Rufus, no!" I yell, trying to yank him back toward the reception area.

The woman with the little white dog is screeching. Several other people are struggling with their pets. And the trainer from the center of the group, who does *not* have a dog, comes storming toward me.

"What are you doing?" he snarls. "You can't walk in here with him like that."

I look up at the voice. The familiar face. The scowl burned into my brain.

No. I don't deserve this.

Rufus chooses this moment to fling himself to the end of the leash. And because I'm still wearing the dumb heels I'd put on for my interview and not my practical Hokas, I lose my balance when he yanks me forward—face-planting straight into Drew Forbes's rock-solid chest. I get a whiff of something like sandalwood as he catches me. Before he wrenches all three of us through the low gate and back into the waiting area.

"I've got him. You can leave now," he snaps, letting go of my arms.

It takes a second to collect myself once the noise dies down, and when I do, I realize he's holding Rufus's leash like he owns him. "Wait, what?"

He glances at his watch. "You lasted about thirty-six hours. Longer than I expected."

I look around the space, still completely disoriented. "This is where you *work*?"

"This is my business," he says sharply.

"Uh, Drew?" A woman with blue hair in her twenties,

wearing a shirt that says *K9 Academy*—just like the one Drew is wearing—breaks away from the group of dogs and owners. "Should I take over the class?"

His expression darkens, and he shakes his head. "I'm done here."

The next thing I know, he's turning his back, leading Rufus away from me.

"Hold up. Where are you going?"

He stops at the low gate and just looks at me like he can't figure out why I'm still here. "Are you waiting for a thank you? For disrupting my class?"

My hands curl into fists. "No. I want to know what you're doing with him."

Rufus looks back at me and emits a low whine.

Drew rolls his eyes, then points over my shoulder, speaking to me like I'm a preschooler. "The exit is that way."

My mouth drops open. "You think I came here to *give* him to you?"

"Why else would you be here?" he sneers.

I glance at Rufus, still at the end of the leash in Drew's hands, and admittedly much calmer now. He's watching me closely, but I can't argue—he already seems like a different animal than he was a second ago. What did Lydia call Drew? A dog guru?

Clearly he's better with dogs than he is with people.

I think of the scene I came home to yesterday. My ruined apartment. My couch. It's hard to think after spending most of the night worrying about poop. And I still haven't figured out work tomorrow. If I just let Drew have the dog, all of my problems would be solved.

Except something about that bothers me.

Why didn't Kyle want his dog-whispering brother to have Rufus? Wouldn't it have made a thousand times more sense for him to choose Drew over me?

"Were you and Kyle even speaking before he died?"

Drew's perpetual scowl intensifies. "Excuse me?"

"You heard what I said."

He turns his head and barks an order at the woman wearing the K9 Academy shirt. She looks mildly terrified, but scurries off to take over the class.

"My relationship with my brother is none of your business," Drew says, so low I almost can't hear.

I fold my arms. Kyle and Drew had been close when they were kids—that much I knew. But Kyle hardly mentioned his brother when we were in high school. And the fact that Drew declined our wedding invite and then showed up anyway tells me he's as manipulative as their parents.

"There's a notarized document with Kyle's signature stating he didn't want you to have this dog," I say. "Why?"

"That's not what it—"

"I asked you a question."

I would not be even a little shocked if lasers came shooting out of Drew Forbes's eyes in a moment. Which is an unfortunate thought because his resemblance to my longtime crush, Clark Kent, is intense. But that fades away as he steps toward me, speaking in a rumble that sounds nothing like Kyle or Superman.

"That's also none of your business." A muscle tics in his jaw. "But I can tell you Kyle would be here with me now, taking care of his own dog, if it wasn't for you."

The first time this guy launched that particular assault, I was so unprepared I couldn't respond. Now, I bristle. "Nice try. I hadn't even seen Kyle for an entire year before he died." I narrow my eyes. "When was the last time *you* saw him?"

Drew's mouth is a thin line drawn in concrete.

I hold out my hand for the leash. "Seems he liked you slightly less than he even liked me. Now, if you'll please let me have *my dog*, I suggest we let the dead rest in peace."

When he makes no move to hand Rufus over, I snatch the leather out of his hand.

He glowers, but doesn't stop me.

"You never said why you came in," he mutters as I head for the door.

"I was looking for a dog trainer," I say, trying not to lose my balance again as Rufus tugs me.

"From what I can see, you still need one."

"I doubt we'd be a good fit." I reach for the door, letting the leash slide down my wrist.

"*Stop*," Drew says abruptly. When I turn, he's coming toward me, stiff and robotic. He grabs the loose leash, and just as I'm about to protest, takes me by the hand.

"What—?"

"You can't go onto the street like that. If you hold it like this, without too much slack . . ." He loops the leather over my left thumb, then presses both sides of the leash down into my palm, closing my fingers around it. "You'll have more control."

He lets go as fast as he stepped in, and I look up into his face, open-mouthed, as the scent of sandalwood reaches me again.

"I . . ." I can't bring myself to say thanks, so I just nod. "Good to know."

He seems to realize how close we're standing because he stiffens and steps back, folding his arms so his biceps strain against his sleeves. "You'll give up eventually. I'm just ensuring you don't lose him in the meantime."

CHAPTER
ELEVEN

MONDAY MORNING, I AM SUDDENLY AND UNFORTUNATELY stricken with a stomach flu so bad I have to call out of work from my bathroom floor. Or, this is the situation I describe in my email to Randall, taking care to include a couple of well-placed typos and the suggestion I might be contagious. This should give me at least forty-eight hours to figure out what to do with Rufus—maybe three days if I push. In the meantime, I research dog sitters. Make an appointment with a vet. And at Lydia's suggestion, leave messages for a few other trainers. One never returns my call. The second suggests I find a psychic to help Rufus. The third says she can come over at two o'clock.

In between phone calls and dog walks, I sift through the file folder Mimi Vanderpool sent home with me, which is chock full of photographs, emails, and other documentation connecting her husband to the Unmatched app beyond any shadow of a doubt. But listening back through our interview is what lights a fire under me. I'm not someone who's easily moved, but I get a lump in my throat all over again hearing her describe years of standing by her husband's side while he lavished affection on other women and encouraged the men around him to follow his lead. The quaver of betrayal in her voice convinces me I have to make this story *hers*. Give her back some of the power he took away. I have plenty of material to do it in a riveting, lengthy feature, but I'm desperate to consult with my editor before I begin. And pissed at my ex's dog for getting in the way of that.

By afternoon, I decide to just get it out of my system and start writing, drawing a new portrait of a man most people in Denver think they already know: Colin Vanderpool—energy executive, arts benefactor, and founder of a notorious married cheaters app.

Theo would lose his shit if he knew I was pursuing this. He raged about the base-level hate mail and messages I received *before* the Unmatched articles. After I pissed off all those cheating men last year and he saw how much it intensified, I thought he was going to drop in from a helicopter and extract me to a safe house.

Which is why I'm glad I didn't mention this lead when he asked how things were going. As much time as he spends worrying about my safety, I'm not the one in the top-secret, high-danger, people-shoot-at-you profession. He doesn't need extra distractions.

Rufus starts what I've come to think of as his low-level bathroom whining a little before noon.

"Let me guess. Time to pee on trees?" I ask.

He tilts his head.

"Fantastic," I say, grabbing my earbuds and his leash. "Now I'm having conversations with you like all the other nutjob dog people."

Despite the sleet and cold yesterday, it's almost seventy degrees by the time we walk outside. Typical bipolar spring in Colorado. Blue skies stretch for miles up and down the Front Range, making the snow-capped mountains to the west stand out in high relief. Reminding every single resident why they live in the Mile High City.

Since we still have a couple of hours before the trainer shows up, and I'm never going to see the inside of a gym again, I head for the park this time instead of rounding the block. The trail around the edge of Washington Park is crowded in the mild weather, and after seeing Rufus lose his mind at those other dogs yesterday, I keep the leash looped over my thumb the way the *dog guru* showed me. I have to admit it does seem to give me more control. But I hate that Drew Forbes had any useful advice to offer.

My phone rings as we walk around the lake on the south end of the park, and I'm not surprised so much as resigned when I see my mother's name on the screen. The Zen half of me wants to ignore the call, keep this time to myself to enjoy the weather and collect my thoughts. But my guilty half has teeth, gnashing at my own needs. I am her only reachable child. It's my duty to answer, to fill some ill-defined void while my brother's gone.

"Hey, Mom. I was just about to—"

"How *are* you, Caprice?"

Her tone gives me pause. The last time I spoke to my mother, she was trying to convince me to attend some sort of luncheon benefit for her art gallery. A passion she returned to after retiring from school administration.

"I'm . . . fine. Did you and Theo have a good visit?"

She sighs. "Too brief, but yes. And I suppose I have you to thank for seeing him at all before he shipped out." Her voice sobers. "I heard about Kyle's dog. How is it going?"

Ohh. This.

"Um, I'm going to need a new couch. But otherwise, I'm handling it." I glance at the dog as if he might have some opinion to add.

My mom pauses, waiting for more. And I know exactly what she wants, but it will hurt too much to give it to her. Unfortunately, that doesn't stop her from pushing.

"This must be so difficult to deal with after only a year . . ."

Her words disappear under the buzzing in my ears. My grip tightens around the leash. I take a hard left off the path into the trees, but not before the inside of my chest starts disintegrating.

I have grieved Kyle Forbes on so many levels—before and after he died. When he left to enlist in the military. When he came back a shadow of the man I'd kissed goodbye. When he returned to the service rather than marry me.

And finally, when he left us all for the last time.

I stumble toward a tree, sinking down against its trunk before my knees completely fail me. The dog watches, clearly confused, but when he attempts to lick my face, I push him away. I can't bring myself to look into his eyes, knowing they must have been the last eyes Kyle stared into.

My mom waits. I rest my head on my knees. And when I speak, I change the subject. "How was the new opening this month?"

There's a pause. Mom definitely likes to push. But if there's one thing I appreciate about her, it's that she can also tell when to back off.

"Oh, it was phenomenal," she says. "I wish you'd been able to see it."

By the time she's finished raving about the new photographer she discovered, I've dragged myself back to my feet. I'm taking a first hesitant step toward the jogging path when a flicker of movement catches my eye. It seems the dog noticed it too because he turns his head in the same direction. And for just a moment, I think I see a figure through the trees. Someone tall, with dark hair and glasses. But when I stop and really look, no one is there at all. My neck prickles.

"You *have* to come to First Friday in April," Mom continues. "It's been ages since you made it, and there are so many fun people I can introduce you to."

Translation: there are men she wants me to meet.

I straighten, putting my shields back into place. As someone who has generally fared better with fewer men in her life, it still shocks me when my mom takes up this cause. But maybe that's one of the reasons I've been avoiding First Friday. "I'll think about it for sure, Mom. Just need Rufus to settle in a bit first."

The dog looks up at his name, perhaps detecting some minute gratitude in my voice. I can give him that—he's a convenient excuse. I want to support the new life my mother is carving out for herself in retirement. But of all people, does she really think I can fill the hole in my heart with the right man?

"Oh, Caprice." She chuckles. "I can't believe Theo got you to agree to this."

I curl my lip, tossing a bag of poop into a trash can as I exit the park. "Me neither."

At two o'clock sharp, I buzz in Sara Radcliffe, the third dog trainer on Lydia's list. She's a short, curvy strawberry blonde who focuses entirely on Rufus from the moment she walks in. My apartment soon reeks of hot dogs from the endless supply of tiny pieces she feeds him, but he takes no time to decide she's an acceptable visitor, so I guess I can't knock her strategy.

"This is mostly a meet-and-greet so we can get a sense of each other and decide if we'll be a good fit." She looks around my apartment. "I understand you just got him, but are you planning to move to a bigger place?"

"Uh, no. I hadn't considered it."

A look I can't quite process passes over her face. "This is a really small space for a dog like this."

"Well, I inherited him," I say too sharply. "And I renewed my lease right before that, so moving's not really an option."

Her mouth presses into a line, but she turns back to Rufus, running through a few basic commands—*sit, down, stay*—all of which he seems eager to follow.

"You said he's a retired military working dog? Do you know why they retired him so young?"

My mood darkens, and Kyle drifts through my mind. "No."

She doles out more hot dogs from her fanny pack, eyeballing the couch carcass. "I'm guessing he did that?"

I clear my throat. "Um, yeah. He kind of flips out if I leave him alone."

She nods at the crate. "How about if you put him in there?"

"He goes inside it fine." I shrug. "But my neighbors have a problem with the nonstop screaming when I'm gone."

"That sounds about right . . ."

"For what?" I ask, trying to hide the desperation in my voice. "Please. I—I just need to know where to start. I *do* want to try and make this work."

These words surprise me. But even as they come tumbling out of my mouth, I glance at Rufus and realize I mean it. I don't love him. I've never been a dog person, and I'm sure I never will be. But I couldn't leave the one creature Kyle Forbes actually loved at a shelter. And what are my other options? Give him to someone else? I picture Drew Forbes at his training business, rubbing his hands together like an eager villain.

God. *Why*, Kyle?

"I've just never had a dog before . . ."

Sara raises her eyebrows like that was the obvious statement of the year. But to my relief, she offers a sympathetic smile. "I can tell you're trying."

"You can?"

She laughs. "You're here, talking to a dog trainer, after he terrorized your neighbors and did that to your sofa." Her smile fades. "Some people abandon animals in the mountains for less."

I press my lips together. I might have spent the last seventy-two hours cleaning shit off my floor and cursing my dead ex, but I can't imagine doing something like that.

Sara sinks to the edge of the dead couch, right in a large patch of dog hair. "Look, I'll be honest," she says. "Most of what I do is pretty basic. Obedience training new puppies, teaching them to heel." Rufus plants himself in front of her, and she reaches out to rub his velvety ears. "But this guy already knows all that. He's had rigorous training—he knows his commands. I just think he's also had some trauma."

Somewhere in the back of my mind, I know Theo must've mentioned that.

"But when Drew warned me not to take you as a client, I have to admit I was curious."

Suddenly the air feels thicker. Heavier. "I'm sorry . . . Drew? Forbes?"

"He can be a dick, right?" She shakes her head. "We dated a couple of times—small industry. But honestly, I've had more engaging conversations with a block of wood."

I blink, trying to comprehend the scope of what she's saying. Did he somehow know who I would reach out to?

"But why would—he actually called you up and warned you not to work with me?"

"It wasn't quite like that," she admits. "He said he was trying to save me some trouble because the dog didn't need a trainer . . . and he was right."

"Really," I say, balling my fists up to conceal my rage as I imagine Drew Forbes casually calling every dog trainer in Denver, telling them to stay away from me.

She just laughs while Rufus licks hot dog off her fingers.

"So, what did the *dog guru* think he needs?" I say in a flat voice.

Sara shrugs, drops her hands to her lap, and gives me a

reluctant smile. "I'll just tell you what I think. When you have a dog who's experienced trauma, especially if you're not quite sure what kind, it's usually best to consult a behaviorist."

My stomach sinks. I have a feeling I already know what she's going to say, but I have to ask anyway.

"Who would you suggest?"

CHAPTER
TWELVE

I SPEND DAYS TWO AND THREE OF MY CANINE CONFINEMENT much the same as I did day one. Well, minus time spent with a dog trainer, because that was enough of that. I continue writing my Unmatched piece, carefully reviewing notes from my interview with Mimi Vanderpool. I don't go to the gym. I walk the dog at seven a.m. At ten a.m. At one o'clock, five o'clock, and nine o'clock. Consider becoming a professional dog walker. I reply to emails and order groceries because I can't go to the store. Try not to lose my mind.

I resort to doing crunches and lifting a few hand weights in my living room in a desperate effort to keep up my muscle tone, but between the lack of cardio and my boss asking when I might return to the office, I don't know how I'll keep up this existence.

Wednesday morning, after pulling dog hair out of my coffee and finding it plastered to my leggings, I attempt to vacuum. But as soon as I turn on my little apartment-sized stick vac, Rufus freaks out, leaping back and forth, whining and growling at the appliance like it's some kind of malicious robot. I ignore him, heading straight for the hair-covered dead couch. But when he escalates, snarling and barking like he might actually attack, I turn the thing off.

We both back away, a little surprised, before he settles back into an urgent whine. He doesn't take his eyes off the vacuum until I've put it back in my front closet. Then he starts pacing and whimpering.

I stare at him.

He stares at me.

I let out a long breath.

Then I crumple to my knees. I thought this would settle into some sort of routine. I'd take care of him, meet his needs, live my life around him—coexist. He eats enthusiastically. He clearly likes his walks. But for the past day or so, when we come home, he won't lie down. I can't clean. I can't even close the door of the bathroom to pee. I can't *leave*. He just paces around and cries, even if I'm here, no matter what I do. This seems like the opposite of settling in.

When I raise my head, the dog is two inches from my face. His tongue curls toward my cheek. I push him away.

Wednesday, March 17, 20__, 11:24 AM

To: <u>Kyle.Forbes@mail.com</u>

From: <u>Caprice_Phipps@mail.com</u>

Subject: Re: Re: no subject

Dear Kyle,

Your stupid, smelly dog is ruining my life, and he wants you to know the mission was successful—I hate both of you now. Also, he would've been happier with your idiot brother. I don't care about your reasons. Clearly you were shit at good decisions.

C

Lydia stops by on her way home from a prenatal appointment Wednesday evening, and I meet her at the door with a new level of desperation. "Can you *please* just walk him up and down the hall for ten minutes while I clean?" I plead. "He thinks the vacuum is the enemy. But I'm starting to feel like I live in a barn."

She takes pity on me. Even brings him outside to do his business. By the time she returns, I have sucked up literal tumbleweeds of dog hair from all over my apartment, and finally achieved a level of mental peace I didn't even realize I'd been missing.

It evaporates as soon as they walk back through the door.

"I think Anton and Seth can get this out of here Sunday," Lydia says, gesturing to the former couch. She unclips Rufus's leash and watches him circle my apartment, panting. "Did you feed him tonight?"

"Yeah. Two *hours* ago," I snarl. "I can't go on like this, Lydia. I'm doing everything you said, but even when I'm home now, this is all he does. When he's not stealing my stuff."

She raises her eyebrows. "What does he steal?"

"The other day I caught him with my phone in his mouth —why would that even taste good? He's taken a bagel off my plate. He steals my underwear if I don't put it right in the laundry . . ."

She watches him circle the coffee table, another nails-on-chalkboard whine starting up in his throat. "It seems to me like he's bored."

"Are you sure he can't come to The Pooch Park?" I beg. "Just for a few hours?"

She gives me a sympathetic smile. "Maybe eventually. But I wouldn't even let him take our entrance test if he can't settle down at home first."

"They have to take a *test*?" I study her face for some sign she's joking, but she just nods.

"I had to turn down a standard poodle from the waitlist

last week when he snapped at Henry's Frenchie." She points to the top of my bookshelf. "Why is his Kong toy up there?"

I follow her gaze to the ugly cone-shaped rubber thing she ordered. "He just kept flinging it around. It broke my favorite coffee mug."

"It should settle him down if you're filling it with stuff he likes."

I blink. "I'm supposed to put something in it?"

Lydia releases a slow breath, the way she's been doing since she and Anton started childbirth class. Then she reaches on her tiptoes to retrieve the dog toy and carries it to the kitchen.

"You can fill it with food, treats, peanut butter . . . if you stick it in the freezer overnight, it will keep him busy even longer." She rummages through my pantry, pulling out ingredients, then systematically loads them inside the red toy. When she's done, she offers it to Rufus, who immediately stops pacing. He circles the apartment once with it in his mouth, but does not whine. Then he jumps on the couch with it and starts working to get the food out.

I squeeze my eyes shut. "I had no idea peanut butter was the answer to all my problems."

"It's good to entertain him, but I doubt it will help if he's left alone," she says, hoisting herself awkwardly onto a barstool. "How're you holding up with work?"

I plop onto the seat next to her, relishing the momentary lack of noise. I didn't even realize how pervasive the whining was until it stopped.

"Uh, pretty sure Randall knows I'm not sick. But he also knows I have a lead on a big potential story, so I think that's keeping him off my back."

"The one about Unmatched?" she asks.

I flinch when she says the name, even though she doesn't. No memory stays with you quite like telling your best friend you found her husband on a cheating app.

"Yeah, that one." I swallow. "Actually, the founder's wife got in touch with me."

Her eyes widen. She folds her hands protectively over her belly. "That sounds significant."

I nod. She knows I don't like to share tons of details when I'm working on a story, but right now it's a relief talking it over with someone I don't need to explain it to. Sadly, Lydia has more intimate knowledge of Unmatched than most people.

"I'm still trying to figure out the best approach."

"And the safest one?" she adds.

I nod without meeting her eyes. "I have to admit, I'm a little freaked out. I mean, it seems like there's a level of safety in exposing the guy. But I don't think I should count on that." I grit my teeth. "I just don't want to blow the opportunity. Randall promised me a raise, but also . . ."

"Also?" she prompts when I trail off.

"I don't know." I exhale. "He keeps whispering in my ear about my potential. He even suggested I'm good enough for *Denver Editorial*."

"You are," she says without hesitation. "Even I can see how a story like this would do big things for your career. But you're right to be careful."

One of the best things about Lydia is that she never purports to know what's best for me. She's been as freaked out as Theo about some of the harassment and email messages, but she never suggests I write about something else. She knows where my passions lie. And while it's clear she worries about me, I appreciate her faith in my choices.

At least when it comes to anything besides dogs.

"But I can't do any of this if I can't leave my apartment." I cut a glance at Rufus, who's still licking at the peanut butter.

She crosses her arms over her belly, clearly weighing several options before meeting me with a reluctant gaze. "I hate to say it, but the trainer you met with was probably right. You need a behaviorist."

I bristle. When I look at her, she bites her lip, and that's all I need to understand exactly what she's thinking.

"No."

"He's the best in town, Caprice . . ."

"I don't care. I am *not* asking that guy for help."

"Maybe you could just do a consultation?"

"I basically did when I was at his facility the other day. He tried to take Rufus. And when I wouldn't let him, he told me to give up. I can't give him the satisfaction of watching me crawl back begging for help."

"But you wouldn't—"

Behind us, the rubber Kong hits the floor with a heavy bounce. Rufus jumps down from his throne and nudges the now-empty toy with his nose, glances at us, and starts whining and pacing again.

Lydia's voice softens. "He needs help, Caprice."

"What does he need?" I snap. "He has a home. I feed him. I walk him. I don't use my vacuum for him!"

She raises her shoulders. "If I could tell you, I'd be opening a new branch of my business. But this is what Drew Forbes does, and by all accounts he does it well. There's this dalmatian that comes to The Pooch Park. The owners couldn't leave him home either—they couldn't even walk him. But after working with Drew, the dog transformed. They swear he changed their lives."

"Sounds nice." I slide off my stool. "But I have a policy against working with douchebags."

"I just don't know what else to suggest."

I shake my head, grabbing Rufus's leash for the fiftieth time today. "There's got to be another way. I'm taking him to the vet tomorrow. It could be his diet . . . or something. Maybe they'll prescribe him CBD oil."

Lydia looks doubtful as she gathers her things and follows

us to the elevator, but she doesn't argue. "It wouldn't hurt to ask."

"Dietary issues can affect lots of things," I say, running with this solution. "You think you're having a crisis—but it could totally be indigestion."

"Dogs aren't much different from people," Lydia concedes, giving Rufus a pat goodbye on the sidewalk before folding me into a hug. "Just try to remember . . . *he's* having a hard time too."

CHAPTER
THIRTEEN

I am bleary-eyed when I stumble through the door for Rufus's vet appointment the next morning. He literally whined until two a.m., when I finally put him in the crate and turned up the white noise app on my phone. I wasn't sorry to skip a Zoom meeting about an *Observer* potluck to take the vet's one and only opening. I was half joking when I mentioned CBD oil to Lydia, but I'm ready to try pretty much anything a doctor suggests.

And we get off to a good start. The vet asks at least a hundred questions starting the moment we walk in. How long have I had him? What's his background? What are his habits? She performs a physical exam, weighs him, listens to his heart, looks in his ears. They even draw blood to rule out any kind of imbalance.

But by the end of the appointment, we run into the same wall.

"Overall, he's really healthy," she says, draping her stethoscope around her neck. "But since he was a military dog and you don't really know what he was exposed to, it's hard to pin down what's causing him to be so anxious now. I'm kind of limited to what he's experiencing physically," she admits.

"Unless something weird comes back in his bloodwork, this sounds like it's more behavioral."

"Okay, sure . . ." I say, grasping at straws. "But what can I *do*? Can you give him Prozac or something? Are there like, CBD edibles for dogs?"

She looks at Rufus, who sits against my calf, panting and covering my leggings with dog hair. Gross.

"There isn't much actual data on CBD for canine anxiety. But yeah, we could try fluoxetine," she says thoughtfully. "It's been shown to improve separation anxiety, among other things, though it's a gradual process. It's usually four to six weeks before you see a result."

My stomach drops at the timeframe, but I need something. "Let's try it."

"I'll put in the prescription." She makes a note on her computer. "In the meantime, you could also consult a behaviorist. There's a guy locally who—"

"Please—if you're going to recommend Drew Forbes?" I frown. "I know him, and I'm not a fan."

She pauses, chuckling. "Okay . . . he *can* be a bit prickly. But he's amazing with dogs."

"So I keep hearing," I mutter. "You mentioned some kind of drops earlier that I could put on the dog food?"

"Rescue Remedy, yeah," she says mildly. "It's homeopathic, but we have clients who swear by it. I can email you an estimate for acupuncture too."

"Sure," I say. Because woo-woo alternative medicine for dogs is exactly how desperate I am.

"Okay. You can order the Rescue Remedy online or pick it up at a Pets 'N Co. I'll let you know how his bloodwork looks in a day or two." She pauses, giving Rufus a scratch before she heads out the door. "He does seem like a really nice boy. He might just need time. But give me a call next month and let me know how the fluoxetine is working."

I look at Rufus, who wags his tail and tries to lick my hand before I pull it back.

The receptionist smiles when we head out to the front desk. "Can he have a treat?"

I nod, fumbling with the leash because there's some guy over in the corner with a German shepherd, and the last thing I need after this frustrating visit is for Rufus to freak out again.

"Great. And here is your total for today," the woman says. "Do you want to put that on a card?"

My heart skips a beat as I look at her screen. "I'm sorry . . . this was *how* much?"

She details the charges for the exam, the bloodwork, and the Prozac, minus the portion of my soul I must have handed over. I look down at my whiny, high-maintenance, inherited dog, and scowl. "I should sell you."

"I'll buy," a deep voice says from across the room.

This time, I can't even feign surprise. It has started to feel like I'm living a *why choose* where everything in the universe wants to screw me at once. And here I am, being ordered to bend over again. Only it isn't even fun.

"You couldn't afford him," I mutter.

My already-erratic pulse spikes as Drew Forbes rises from his chair and approaches. "Name your price."

The German shepherd at his feet stays where he left it, chill on the floor. I pull out my credit card as fast as I can. "I was joking. He's not for sale."

But the man keeps coming. I brace myself, tightening my grip on the leash. Just when I think he's going to get in my face and snatch the leash, though, the misanthropic trainer drops to one knee. And starts petting my dog.

"How you holding up, Ruf?"

Of course the beast responds by putting his feet on Drew's shoulders and licking his face like it's covered in Salisbury steak. And the man just lets him, tipping his head back and closing his eyes until an ache starts up in my chest because he *is* Kyle. His angular, handsome face is calm, free of shadows and turmoil, relaxed and at peace—because of a canine. He doesn't even correct the dog when it knocks his glasses askew. But when he catches me watching, his mouth dips into a frown and the spell breaks. I look away.

The receptionist hands me the receipt for a bill that almost matches my rent payment, and I just stand there hoping Rufus decides Drew tastes so good he bites his face off.

"Is he sick?" he asks, running his hands over the dog like he's checking for illness. And from the bitter tone of his voice, any blame is clearly directed at me.

"He's fine," I say, tugging the leash. "Just anxious."

Rufus finally backs off, and when he does, Drew rises to his feet until he's towering over me. And all at once, everything shifts. My breath stutters. Kyle wasn't a small guy, but Drew is taller, maybe even broader. It's not so much his size, though, as his presence. Something about the way he takes up space, maybe his scent. I feel completely off-balance.

He looks me up and down in my athletic wear, and the way my skin heats in response is freaking embarrassing. "You should be running him," he says.

His cranky tone reminds me I'm angry. "Excuse me?"

"He needs activity—he needs to run. It would help," he says, going for condescending and landing it like the professional he is.

I school my face and straighten my spine. "Maybe I do take him running."

He snorts. "You don't."

"How would you—" But then I stop. Because he sounds so certain, and then one tiny bit of data connects with another inside my brain, and I step back. "Oh my God. I knew I saw you at the park."

A look flashes over his face. It's fast, but it's enough. I think back over the last few times I've walked there with

Rufus. I'll admit, I'm generally paranoid about being watched, but I've been looking over my shoulder more this week, and now I know why.

I lower my voice. "Have you been following me?"

"Of course not," he says, but he avoids my eyes.

My skin prickles. "*Why?*"

He glances at the desk, but the receptionist has disappeared into the back to get my prescription. "No need to inflate your ego. I live by the same park."

I step toward him, shaking my head. I've been honing my interview skills for years—I can tell when I'm being lied to. And while Drew Forbes following me in the park is surface-level upsetting, after the threats I've received this year, my tolerance for creepy men is shot.

"I don't know what your obsession is with this dog," I hiss. "But if you don't back off, I will report you for harassment. I've got no time for any more psychos in my life."

His brow furrows.

Just then, a door swings open, and a tech with two braids and a nose ring comes bouncing toward the German shepherd. "Is that my Diesel?"

The dog looks over at Drew, who mutters, "Release."

The shepherd immediately rises, albeit stiffly, from the floor and wags its tail as she offers him treats. "Who's ready for acupuncture?" She rubs his neck. "Are *you*?"

Drew glares back in my direction. But just when I think he's finally going to leave, he leans close, voice low in my ear. "I meant what I said." He strokes Rufus's chin one last time. "I'll pay cash if you'll let me have him. And cover his vet bill too."

I press my lips together, needing no reminder of my financial straits. But when his cold green eyes meet mine, my vision darkens around the edges. I learned a long time ago never to trust the Forbes family. Starting the day Kyle enlisted, when they turned their backs on him. And reinforced when they declined the invitation to our ill-fated wedding. But worst of all, not *one* of them bothered to call me when Kyle died. I only found out by chance, on social media, of all places. And when I showed up at the memorial service, they actually seemed surprised. Just another reason I can't bring myself to hand one of them his dog.

I rise on tiptoe, bringing my lips close to Drew's ear. "I'd sell him to a sausage factory before I'd sell him to you."

"Here's Rufus's prescription," the receptionist says, blustering toward me with an orange pill bottle. "Sorry about the wait."

Drew watches with an icy stare as she goes over the instructions, his expression so tight I'm tempted to punch him and see if he breaks.

"Puppy Prozac." I wave the bottle at him as I head for the door. "Maybe you should try some—though I hear nothing helps bad breeding."

I don't sleep much again that night. I have this weird dream where I keep running into Kyle, except every time he turns around, it's actually Drew. My brain finally ceases this torture around one a.m., when I get out of bed to make herbal tea. And wind up taking the dog out because he thinks it's morning.

Once we're back inside, I head for my closet, to the shoebox shoved in the back with the garment bag still holding my wedding dress. The dog watches as I take it out and set it on the bed, but has the decency to stay over on the couch.

Lifting the lid feels like exhuming a grave.

There's an assortment of history inside. Documents. Trinkets. A ring box.

I remove the one I'm interested in—a framed photo stored face-down—and quickly replace the lid. But it takes a few minutes before I'm ready to turn it over and look at the picture.

When I do, it feels like I'm staring at a pair of strangers from long ago. A carefree girl lifted off her feet in the arms of her handsome, rugged hero. They're both grinning, like neither of them has a worry in the world. Because they have no idea what's to come.

I let out a long-held breath. Then I rise from the bed, ready to bury the frame back in the box.

Except I can't.

My chest aches at the thought. Or maybe, after a night of bad dreams, I just need comfort. So I wander around my tiny apartment until I find a place for the photo on a little table by my door. Where I can look at it and remember that once, a long time ago, Kyle and I were enough for each other.

DREW

"Drew, dear, would you pass the butter?"

He raised his eyes from his plate for the first time that evening, dutifully passing the crystal dish to his mother. For the last twenty minutes, they'd been listening to his father complain about patients whose lives he'd saved. People who didn't speak English or didn't have insurance. People he deemed "indigents" while making sure to highlight his generosity in helping them.

"It's lucky you knew how to treat them," Drew recited from his bank of acceptable responses.

His mother smiled warmly, tucking her smooth gray hair behind her ear.

Dr. W. Andrew Forbes straightened in his chair. "When you have a gift, it's important to share it with the world."

Drew stuffed his mouth full of coq au vin.

"Speaking of sharing talent, I'm *very* enthusiastic about our first scholarship recipient," said his mother. "Such a deserving, disadvantaged young man. A great pick to begin your brother's legacy."

He twisted his napkin in his lap, forcing himself to chew and swallow. Drew couldn't help morbidly wondering if Kyle might have reconsidered killing himself if he'd had any idea how their parents would distort his memory. But he supposed that wasn't fair.

"Anyway, I'm glad you could make it to dinner this week so we can discuss the ceremony," Dr. Patricia Forbes said pointedly.

His father raised a brow. "Yes, what kept you last week?"

Drew brought his linen napkin to his mouth, debating what to share while he finished chewing. Family dinner had felt like a dismal farce for the last eleven months. Kyle had stopped coming years ago, but it was a new level of dysfunction that they could still sit here with his empty chair, going through the motions, when he would never join them again.

"Well, I was . . ." He couldn't bring himself to mention Rufus, and certainly not Caprice Phipps. But when he thought about his business, the one he ran because of Kyle, exciting things *were* happening. "Actually, I was invited to speak and do a few demos at a convention last weekend," he said, clearing his throat.

Both of his parents perked up, focusing immediately on him. Which he honestly hadn't expected. But maybe they'd finally had a change of heart a year after losing Kyle. He held his breath, offering up a little more.

"It was a major industry event and turned out to be great exposure for the training center. Our phone has been ringing pretty steadily ever since."

The Forbeses shared a look—surprise, understanding, followed by tolerant bemusement. And in that moment, Drew realized he'd read them wrong.

Dr. Patricia Forbes brought her napkin to her mouth, covering an indulgent smile. "Oh, Drew, we thought you meant a *medical* convention, of course."

His back hit his chair as he went over his own words. Finally, he managed a strangled chuckle. "Of course."

He fixed his eyes back on his dinner plate, one his mother

had always deemed "for the children" because of a tiny chip in the porcelain rim.

"It's nice that you can fit in some recreation before your return to medicine," his father said, neatly cutting him down while somehow also sounding generous.

"Yes," Drew said. "It's nice."

He gripped his own knee under the table since there was nothing else to reach for. His brother was dead. And dogs were not allowed at family dinner.

"You know, I read an interesting orthopedics study out of Johns Hopkins this week . . ." Dr. W. Andrew Forbes said, changing the subject.

Drew remained in his chair, dutifully cutting his food and nodding, making himself appear riveted by his father's monologue. A skill he'd been honing since he was ten.

His PetExpo talk on behavior analysis in training had been attended with standing room only. He and Blitz had brought home several agility and obedience awards. And just last week, K9 Academy had received a coveted *Best Of Denver* distinction.

But he might as well have told his parents he'd spent the weekend scrubbing toilets.

He closed his eyes, hoping to channel his brother, who had somehow managed not to care whether they approved of his choices or not.

Or maybe he had.

By the time the senior Forbeses concluded a highly intellectual debate regarding possibilities in joint replacement that would have bored the Colorado Medical Board, Drew looked down to find his chipped plate empty. He excused himself to clear the dishes, passing up an after-dinner cocktail so he could sink his arms into soapy, scalding water and feel his skin burn.

But as he stood alone in the kitchen, studiously washing and drying the silver and china, his mind wandered back to

Rufus. It killed him, not even knowing what the dog was struggling with. He could guess PTSD of some kind, but how did it affect him? What were his triggers? Loud sounds were a safe bet, but there could be sights, smells, or situations that bothered him. And what would his new "owner" do about it? Other than try to drug him so he wouldn't cramp her lifestyle.

He *had* been watching her at the park. He hadn't meant to scare her and felt awful about it now. He just needed to know how Rufus was doing. It was obvious she had no idea what to do with him. He just couldn't understand why she was so determined to keep him.

For the thousandth time that year, he wondered what the hell Kyle had been thinking. Why do this to Rufus *or* Caprice?

A soapy crystal goblet slipped out of his hands, shattering into somewhere near a million shards all over the travertine floors.

He exhaled. It felt like he'd been holding his breath a year.

"Well, that's why you didn't become a surgeon," his mother tsked, surveying the broken glass from the doorway.

Drew frowned as she crunched across the floor to retrieve the broom and dustpan.

"Mom, let me—"

"I've got it." She brushed him off. "You think I'm afraid of a little mess after raising two boys?"

His throat felt thick.

She looked at his face and hummed, sweeping the glass into a neat pile and dumping the shards in the trash. "There. Some things are easy to fix."

He didn't point out that the glass wasn't fixed. Now it was just missing.

"Oh, Drew." She leaned on the broom handle, considering him. "I see you, you know."

He swallowed and looked straight at her for the first time in a month.

"Do this work right now if it's what you need." She

sighed. "You're already a brilliant physician. You'll get another fellowship."

He frowned. "Mom, I don't—"

"We all grieve in our own ways. I'm focusing on this scholarship. Your father drank boxed wine for a month after Kyle's death." She curled her lip. "He got through it, and you will too."

He had no idea what to say, so he just nodded.

"Your brother left a hole we will never fill." Her face fell briefly, but then she plastered on a smile. "We know you'll make us proud. And we'll be cheering when you do."

CHAPTER
FOURTEEN

I take Rufus for a run after lunch, resenting Drew Forbes with every breath in and out, even though my body *thrills* from the cardio. The dog seems just as into it, matching my pace easily, panting in a more athletic and less frantic way. We don't see any surly dog trainers lurking behind trees, and that's just as well. I didn't get much sleep. If I spotted him today, I'm not sure I could land a roundhouse kick to the chest the way I'd like.

As we make our way from the elevator to my apartment door, both of us exhausted to the point we may have actually reached calm, my phone pings with a remote meeting invite from Randall. It starts in five minutes.

I curse out loud, trying to figure out what to do. Ask for vacation time starting immediately? I doubt I could get family leave approved to take care of an animal, even if I asked a month ahead of time. Instead, I rush into my bathroom to check my sweaty hair and face, and pull a CU sweatshirt over my grubby tank top. The *Mile High Observer* office tends to be more casual, but after four days at home and the first real sprints I've done in a week, my look is definitely more sweaty than glowy.

I splash water on my face, smooth my ponytail, and then brush my teeth—if only for mental preparation. When I log into the meeting, I flip on the studio filter and smile when Randall appears on the screen.

"Caprice! You're looking healthier than I expected."

Crap. I tried too hard.

"Yeah, I'm . . . feeling much better finally, thank you. Been a rough week."

Randall's sitting in his office at our building on South Broadway. He's wearing a white shirt that matches his goatee and accentuates the glare of lights off his pale forehead. He eyeballs the screen, speaking in his slow drawl. "Just wanted to make sure you're okay. You get a stomach bug, or what?"

I turn to the side, conjuring up a cough, trying to buy myself a moment. It was dumb to say I was sick. I've stayed on top of every one of the assignment desk emails as long as they didn't require I go anywhere or talk to anyone in person. I probably should've passed off more stuff to Jana, but my work ethic is too strong.

"Uh, no, not sure what it was. But I'm feeling better now, thanks."

"Good. I'm bringing the team together tomorrow to discuss some of the spring features, and I'm hoping you'll join us. Last we talked, you sounded pretty excited about that lead you were pursuing. Is that still in the works?"

I open my mouth, trying to figure out how to answer. I'm almost finished writing the Vanderpool feature. It would be ready in time for our next print issue. But I'm still not sure if publishing it will be an excellent career move or the biggest mistake of my life.

"Look, Randall, I've been . . ." Behind me, Rufus starts up a mid-level whine, and I glare at him. He can't do this to me right now. We literally *just* came back from a run.

"What's that?" My editor peers more closely at the screen.

I have my background blurred, but I'm sure the noise is coming through crystal clear.

"Um, well, it's—" Suddenly, Rufus thrusts his nose into my lap and looks right at the camera. I rear back in my chair. "*What* are you doing?"

Randall's brow furrows at the black and gold monster suddenly occupying my lap. Rufus just stares up at me like his head is too heavy to move. I shove his nose off my thighs.

"Caprice?"

"Okay!" I cross my arms, letting out a deep sigh, positive my job is now on the line. What have I got to lose? "Randall, if you want the truth, I have a situation I'm trying to deal with."

He tents his fingers over his desk as if he's been waiting for us to get here. Dammit.

"It's a long story, and I won't bore you with the details." Rufus is back to pacing and whining. I close my eyes. "I inherited . . . a dog. A *really* high-maintenance one. I know this is stupid, but I haven't been coming in because I've been trying to figure out what to do with him."

Randall's bushy white eyebrows shoot up like this is the last thing he expected me to say. Which makes two of us.

"A dog?"

"Yeah . . ." I sink in my chair. Generally, our office is a pretty low-key place to work. People come and go during the day depending on what they're working on, but there's still a level of professionalism I know I'm *not* achieving right now. I watch my boss and start mentally updating my resumé.

But then the edge of Randall's mouth quirks. "What kind?"

"Beg your pardon?"

"What breed is he?"

"Oh." Rufus has climbed back up on top of his carcass throne, but he jumps back down and approaches like he knows he's the topic of conversation. "Uh, a Belgian Malinois?"

"Cool! Like the police use? Can I see him?"

"Um . . . sure?" I reach to unblur my screen and glare at Rufus. "My *boss* wants to see you."

And now I'm clearly losing it because I'm speaking to him the way Lydia does. Except the dog comes over and sits in front of the computer like he understands. He waits patiently as I angle the camera down, staring at the screen like Randall might reach through and offer him a treat.

God, who even cares at this point? At least he stopped whining.

"Oh, you are a handsome fella, aren't you?" Randall says in the same voice I've heard every single one of Lydia's clients use to speak to their pets. "What's his name?"

"Rufus," I mutter, wondering if I should just let the two of them finish this meeting.

"Hello, Rufus! Are you a good boy?" Randall chuckles.

I angle the screen back up at my face. "*Anyway.* I'm sorry I've been out this week," I say with complete sincerity. "I just haven't been able to . . ." I exhale. "He kind of freaks out if I leave him home alone."

"Ah. Separation anxiety?" Randall asks. Because I guess this is a thing dog people know about. "We went through that with our whoodle."

"Your what?" I deadpan.

"You've met Alfonse. He's a wheaten-poodle mix?"

Somewhere in the foggy recesses of my brain, I remember Randall bringing a black medium-sized dog with him to the office a year or so back. I only remember because our receptionist Tracy cooed over him all day, forgot to make the coffee, and managed to lose track of an important delivery I'd been waiting for.

"Right. Yeah, Alfonse."

"He goes to doggie daycare now. Actually, I think you mentioned the place in your PetExpo feature—The Pooch Park? It's fantastic. They've really saved us."

I rub my palms into my eyes, wishing I could just hang up now. "Yeah . . . I talked to them. Apparently Rufus has some issues he needs to work through before they'll take him."

Randall nods, like this makes so much sense. And now I'm convinced everyone else must share some gene I'm missing. "I mean, when we were going through it with Alphonse, I brought him to work with me for a while . . ."

His voice echoes through the speakers. I couldn't have heard that correctly.

"Sorry. Did you just suggest I bring the dog with me to the office?"

Randall shrugs. "Is he friendly?"

"Er, he seems to be . . . ?" Briefly, an image of Rufus tearing across my apartment, aiming for my neighbor's jugular, flashes through my mind. But in the days since that happened, Darius has stopped to get *Rufus kisses* every time he's seen us in the hall. The dog has barely even growled, except at the training place when that fluffy white terror lunged for him. Well, and any time he hears people in the hall.

I glance at the door, my stomach twisting uncomfortably.

"I tell you what," Randall says, leaning forward at his desk. "Let's make a deal."

My skin prickles. I do *not* like the sound of this, though I've already guessed where it's going.

"You can bring Rufus into the office tomorrow, and we'll see how it goes . . . if you'll bring me up to speed right now on what you're doing with that Unmatched lead."

I swallow, clicking over to the document I've been working on the last few days. The one that's been shaping all week into a first-rate exposé. "I can do you one better,

Randall," I say in a husky voice. "Hang up with me right now, and I'll come in tomorrow morning with both the dog and a finished story you're going to want to put on the cover next week."

CHAPTER
FIFTEEN

THE SHORT WALK THROUGH THE FRONT DOORS OF THE *MILE HIGH Observer*, past the front desk, and down the hall to Randall's office usually takes less than thirty seconds and would never be worth a mention. But Friday morning with Rufus in tow, this journey takes a full ten minutes, and the whole experience is like something out of *Alice's Adventures in Wonderland*, with dog-obsessed eccentrics coming at me from all directions.

"Oh my goodness!" Tracy almost falls out of her seat at reception, somehow procuring dog treats out of thin air. "Who's our new office pup?"

A guy I vaguely recognize from IT peeks his head around the corner and grins. "I didn't know we had a new staff member. Can I say hi?"

"Of course," I say through my teeth.

"This breed is so intelligent," he says, letting the dog sniff him.

At that moment, Jana appears out of nowhere and immediately drops to her knees. "Caprice! He's adorable—I'm so jealous!"

I inch down the hall amid a chorus of *awwwws*, getting

peppered with questions about where Rufus came from and why he's here. I've distilled the information to a sentence or two, but I didn't factor in how much his orphan story would pull everyone's dog-loving heartstrings.

"God, I'm sorry about your ex. But wow—you're so lucky!" Jana says. "My sister had to take in our grandma's cocker spaniel, and all he does is pee on the rug."

I turn to look at her, kneeling on the floor with my sixty-pound beast. I consider pulling up pictures of my late couch while she makes heart eyes and strokes Rufus's ears. But we're only a few feet from Randall's door.

"Um, Rufus has a meeting to get to, but if anyone wants to walk him at lunch, I'd be happy to let you draw straws." I pull the dog into the office and shut the door like I'm hiding some tween heartthrob from his adoring fans.

"There's the big fella!" Randall hops out of his chair and approaches Rufus with his palm extended. I have to hand it to the dog. He hasn't whined once since we got here and has been surprisingly chill amid all this attention. Maybe he was used to meeting lots of people in new environments on deployments with Kyle.

My heart nose-dives at that thought, and I let go of the leash to sink into one of Randall's chairs. Rufus starts up his sniff-every-corner-of-the-room thing, and once he's satisfied with his inspection, Randall offers him a dog bed and something to chew.

"I emailed you the feature when I left home," I say when my boss finally shifts out of dog mode and returns to his desk.

His eyes sparkle. "I finished it just before you walked in. Caprice, this is some of your finest work. The way you approached it from his wife's perspective . . ." He shakes his head, but his grin shines with approval. "Though even I still can't believe we're talking about Colin freaking *Vanderpool*."

I bite my lip, leaning forward in my chair. "So . . . you want to publish it?"

His eyes flash to mine. "Is there any reason not to?"

"Only a couple dozen." A nervous laugh escapes my lips.

My boss rests his elbows on his desk, taking me in. I styled my hair and dressed in something other than athleisure for the first time all week, but between writing this article and dealing with my new roommate the last few days, I feel like my edges are frayed.

"What are you most worried about?" he asks. "By the way, I've already submitted your raise to HR. The Vanderpools are well known, even outside of Denver. I wouldn't be surprised if this went a little viral."

The tightness in my chest eases a fraction at the thought of the boost in income. But when I look at him, it's hard to swallow. "What am I always worried about, Randall?"

He has the humility to look chastened.

My boss and I have had numerous conversations about safety over the last few years. He knows about almost every threat and slur I received after the first Unmatched article, and he's been nothing but supportive and sympathetic. He understands why I'm having reservations as much as a compassionate middle-aged white guy ever could.

"Vanderpool's stature as a philanthropist and his political aspirations will make this hit on a whole different level than your other articles," he says.

"Exactly," I say in a shaky voice. "And if angering your average married cheaters earned me rape and death threats, what will happen when I piss off a powerful, influential one?"

Neither of us speaks for a minute. But then Randall folds his hands and looks right at me. "So you're going to let that stop you?"

"I beg your pardon?"

He leans back in his chair. "Look, I'm not trying to minimize anything that's been said or done to you. The comment sections, even on our own platform, are their own circle of hell. But maybe this is a good time to revisit why you got into journalism in the first place."

I stare at him. He knows my answer. We've talked about it annually at my employee review for the last five years, but I decide to play along. "I want to tell people's stories."

"Okay. So you're telling Colin Vanderpool's story?"

"What? *No.*" Rufus stops chewing and looks up when I raise my voice. "Did you even read my article? I've never spoken to Colin Vanderpool. This piece is about his wife. And the thousands of other women affected by the Unmatched app."

Randall looks back at me with a slow smile.

"*Her* story is important. We both know that," he goes on. "But if you don't tell it, someone else will. And they'll most certainly make it about him."

I hold his gaze for another moment, then let out a low breath. Because he's right.

"And it isn't just this story." His voice grows gentler. "I'm thinking about your career, Caprice. I know what happened last year was scary. But this is your chance to prove you're not going to let anyone bully you out of a profession where you're destined for stardom."

My chest fills at his words. But my gaze drops to my lap. "What if I'm scared?"

He doesn't reply right away. Instead, he calls the dog. Rufus jumps right up and eagerly follows directions as Randall runs him through random commands. He tells him to sit, stay, and roll over, getting on the floor with him to play and rub his belly while I pull dog hairs off my slacks.

"God, this guy is smart," my boss says.

"He likes you," I mutter. "Maybe your dog needs a brother."

He chuckles. "My daughter's allergic, or I'd take him in a

heartbeat." He glances up at me. "You're not really a dog person, are you?"

Before I can answer, someone knocks on the door, then opens it without waiting for an answer. Rufus goes from upside down on the floor wagging his tail to charging across the room, snarling and gnashing his teeth, in a split second.

"Jesus!" Brian sees him and retreats so fast he forgets to look superior, slamming the door between him and the dog just as Rufus launches for his neck. "Goddamn, Caprice," he shouts through the wood. "I'm reporting this to HR!"

Rufus stands growling and barking at the door until Brian apparently goes away. Then he comes over to where I've drawn my body into a tight, tense ball in my chair, and licks my hand.

Randall busts out laughing.

"Well done, Rufus." He claps his hands, then looks at me. "Maybe your new companion can help keep the bad guys at bay."

I stare at the dog, who stares back with those golden eyes, and a surprisingly loyal expression. "You sound like my brother," I mumble.

Only Theo would definitely *not* approve of me publishing this article. He's team barista all the way.

The thing is, I made my decision before I even walked in here. And the damn dog had zero to do with it. I uncurl myself from the chair, inserting my feet back into my heels. "I think we both know safety is never a guarantee." I sigh. "But I guess I don't mind some added protection."

"So I can print it?" Randall clarifies.

"You know I'm not going to just sit back and watch someone else break my story."

My boss's whole demeanor shifts. He doesn't fist-pump, but his bushy eyebrows basically do. "All right. It'll go out online and in the print edition next week," he says, opening his laptop. "I can't lie, I'm happy the *Observer* will get to drop this. But I want you to tell me immediately if *any* issues arise."

"Will do," I mutter. "And . . . thanks for the raise."

"You deserve it." He straightens in his chair, the glimmer returning to his eye. "And it'll put you in a better position to negotiate your salary elsewhere."

I roll my eyes, feeling certain of nothing except the need to see this through. For Mimi Vanderpool, for Lydia . . . and maybe for myself.

"Whatever. See if HR will accommodate my 'support animal.'" I sigh. "And tell Brian he might want to keep some Milk-Bones in his pockets from now on."

"You've got it," Randall says, smirking.

"And can someone else take the assignment desk now?"

He narrows his eyes. "Tell you what—let's wait till this drops on Wednesday. Then I'll hand it to Jana."

"Deal."

I rise from my chair and pick up Rufus's leash, bracing myself to face the throngs of his new fan club. If I can just make it to my desk and start sifting through complaints in the inbox, I'll have less space to wonder if I've just made a huge mistake.

"Oh, I have one other assignment for you," Randall says as I reach the door. "We were asked to cover an event in Castle Rock this weekend. Might be a good palate cleanser after the Vanderpool thing."

I look back at him with a raised brow. "That sounds more enticing than it probably is."

He shrugs. "There are a couple of doctors handing out a new scholarship in memory of their son. Seemed like a decent feel-good story."

Something about this pings in my gut. Probably because I know a couple of doctors from Castle Rock who lost a son. "What, ah . . . what's the name of the family?"

Randall checks his computer and looks up at me. "Forbes?"

My stomach knots. And now I'm right back to believing the planets have aligned to ensure my demise. I wouldn't be surprised if I walked outside and got hit by a meteorite. But even as these thoughts swirl through my mind, I hear myself say, "Sure, a scholarship. I'll cover it. That's definitely not sex or dating."

When I return to my desk after a detour outside for Rufus to pee, I open my browser in an effort to collect myself. Or at least figure out what I'm doing. But when I find the event I committed to covering this weekend, the world seems to shrink.

Saturday, March 21st - Castle Rock High School:
First Annual Kyle Forbes Scholarship Award Ceremony

Suddenly, I'm sitting here at my desk a year ago, combing the internet for topics to write about when I stumbled on a social media post from a high school friend that rocked my foundation in three words: *RIP, Kyle Forbes.*

On some level, I'd probably seen it coming. Only it felt like a sneak attack. Was this really how I would learn the man I'd been in love with since I was sixteen was dead? But when I clicked with numb fingers, the internet confirmed the news. Kyle had already been gone a week. I'd lived seven entire days on this earth without him, and I hadn't even known.

Because no one had bothered to tell me.

Something lands on my thighs, jarring me into the present. I look down to find the Kong toy in my lap and a pair of gold-colored eyes looking at me that seem to echo the emptiness in my heart. He was there. He was with Kyle when he did it—he must have been. And I'm furious he didn't stop him. If this animal is as smart as everyone says, couldn't he tell how bad it was? He could've alerted someone. Done *something*.

Rufus rests his muzzle on my leg, and I'm about to shove him away when our eyes meet again, and I pause. Because there's something else I recognize that's hard to describe. We stare at each other for another moment. And then, slowly, I place my hand on his head. Run my fingers over the velvety fur on his ears.

Because maybe he's also hurt. Maybe he misses Kyle as much as I do.

CHAPTER
SIXTEEN

I borrow Lydia's car for the second time in a week, exchanging it for a quart of peanut butter cup ice cream and a dozen promises to fill it with gas, until she reminds me it's electric. While there was no way to strap Rufus to my Vespa for the thirty-minute drive to Castle Rock, I'm trying to ignore how the dog has increased my need to own a vehicle.

Wind tosses the naked tree branches when I pull into the driveway of my childhood home. The sky is darkening, and the faint odor of petrichor hangs in the afternoon air. But it's March in Colorado, which means the forecast could go any number of ways. It might rain, but we might also have three feet of snow by tomorrow. Or it might be sunny and clear in an hour. The weather forecasters were so vague on the drive down, I gave up and listened to music instead.

"Hi, thanks again for doing this," I say, avoiding Mom's eyes when she opens her front door. She's dressed as casual as she ever gets, with wide-leg pants and a loose sweater draped over her slim frame. Her dark hair is swept back in a way that makes her gray streak even more dramatic against her pale, rose-dusted cheeks. "I don't have much time, but here's his Kong toy and some extra treats."

She ushers us inside and takes the leash, immediately offering one of the cheese squares to Rufus. "Oh, he's a sweetheart. But he looks just like one of those police dogs, doesn't he?"

"Uh, sure." I hesitate, glancing to where he's straining at the end of the leash, scanning her modest living room with his sharp, golden eyes. "Here, he likes to do this thing . . ."

I unclip the leash, and Rufus immediately darts around the house, sniffing the furniture and sticking his nose in every corner the way I've gotten used to him doing each time we enter my apartment.

He's already panting heavily, and for a second, I bite my lip, wondering if it's a mistake to leave him here. What if he loses his mind and destroys *her* couch after I go? I have to cover this scholarship ceremony—want to, if I'm honest with myself. But Rufus is technically not a service dog, and I don't want to risk bringing him anywhere near the Forbes family.

"I'm just going to get a few quotes and come right back," I say.

"I'll be fine, Caprice. Remember, I had a springer spaniel before you and your brother were born." She hesitates, then adds, "I wish I could go with you."

I glance up, and her hazel eyes are so full of feeling, I have to look away. We've hardly talked about Kyle since he died, but I know Mom loved him. He spent more time at our house growing up, either with me or Theo, than he probably ever did at his own. He would offer to help her with chores and always called her "ma'am." She took pictures of us here when he picked me up for prom.

"Sweetheart?" Mom says as I reach for the door. "You look really nice."

I look down at my black button-up pencil dress and basic pumps. I wore my hair down, styled in loose waves for a change, but I appear more like I'm going to a funeral than a celebration. And I wonder if she would be so chill if she knew what the dog did to my Louboutins.

"Thanks," I say, trying to ignore the way Rufus whines, following me with his eyes as I let myself out. "Call me if he becomes a problem. And remember, he can't be left alone if you value anything in your house."

I drive Lydia's car along the same route I took every day as a teenager. Out of our cramped little neighborhood with the sagging RVs in the driveways and the Christmas lights still up in March, across the highway to Castle High School, where the ceremony is being held. The building had been state-of-the-art fifteen years ago and surprises me now by looking almost exactly the same.

I haven't walked through the blue front doors since the day we graduated, and I'm unprepared, because the second I do, I'm surrounded by ghosts.

Of Kyle. Of myself. Of the past.

I can almost feel his strong arm slipping around my waist as I enter the main hallway. His voice a deep and raspy greeting in my ear, his lips grazing my hair. We both played every sport we could fit into our schedules, and on the way to the auditorium, I pass the gym doors where we used to meet up after practice. The little hallway outside the locker rooms where we would steal an extra kiss. Gooseflesh rises over my body with each step.

There's a bigger crowd in the auditorium than I expected. And so many familiar faces. I almost turn around and run back out to the car when they start to register. It's funny, Denver sits barely thirty miles to the north, but it's an easy place to disappear just a stone's throw from my past. I notice friends of Kyle's. Friends of ours. Some of them already hardly recognizable eleven years after graduation; some still exactly the way they appeared last I saw them. I lower my head. I don't want to look into these faces and see their sympathy—or judgment, I guess, depending on what stories they heard after we departed these halls.

Hell, maybe that already happened. They were all probably at the memorial service a year ago. But that whole experience was like moving through a black cloud. I'm not sure I would remember if someone had come up and slapped me in the middle of it.

"Caprice? Oh, my gosh." I should probably be grateful Tania Riley is the first person to talk to me. She falls into the camp of people who look mostly unchanged. Her natural hair is pulled back in braids, highlighting the gorgeous tone of her dark brown skin. Her eye makeup is more sophisticated than I remember, her frame a little curvier, but I don't see any other notable difference. We weren't super close growing up, but we offered each other comfort by mere existence, as two of only a few non-white faces in our very suburban school. Tania wasn't a member of any particular clique—she's one of those people who gets along with everyone, and wants everyone to get along. It was always a relief to be paired with her for a group project. She's good people.

"Hey, Tania," I say, accepting an awkward hug.

"I'm . . . I'm sorry we're here for this," she offers, and while her sentiment is clearly sincere, it's also obligatory. She might have heard what happened with the wedding, but she also knows Kyle and I were inseparable during eleventh and twelfth grades.

"Me too."

We file down the aisle of the auditorium together and she clears her throat, gesturing toward the stage. "My, um, cousin is receiving the scholarship."

I follow the direction she points to the small group clustered at the front of the room. The instant knot that tightens in my stomach makes me glad I skipped breakfast. Because there are the Doctors Forbes. Her, a slim white woman in a dark skirt suit, her short, practical hair a little grayer than I remember. A white lily dominates her lapel. Her husband stands next to her, tall and distinguished, but less broad than their sons. His light eyes and silver mustache project authority, though he's somehow slightly warmer than his wife.

They stand with a well-dressed young Black man whose face definitely contains some echo of Tania's. They share the same broad cheekbones and handsome arched brow. His stance is a little stiff, but his easy smile tells me this is not his first award and certainly won't be his last.

"Congratulations," I say, then decide to feign ignorance. "And it's a scholarship for . . . ?"

"Kenyon's going to Northwestern, pre-med," she says, her whole face lighting up. "Smartest kid in our family. None of us were sure how he'd ever pay for school, so this award is pretty game-changing." She hesitates, casting her eyes down. "Obviously, though, we all wish Kyle hadn't . . ."

My throat burns, but I lay a gentle hand on her arm. "Kyle had a lot of demons."

The back of my neck prickles just then, and as Tania says goodbye to join the rest of her family, I turn and scan the room. It only takes two seconds to find Drew Forbes leaning against a wall, staring right at me. He stands out in this crowd, even with his shoulders hunched. The few times I've seen him, he's been casual, in jeans and T-shirts with a few days' stubble. This afternoon, he's clean-shaven and dressed up in a slim-cut gray suit. Perhaps the only nod to his more casual lifestyle is the dark, slightly too-long hair curling against any attempts to be styled.

I raise my chin and meet the stormy eyes boring through his glasses. His gaze drifts down to my side, mouth pressing into a hard line, and I wonder if he's looking for the dog. Like I could have brought him here.

Someone taps the mic, and I glance back at the stage, to his mother and father now gazing out at the room next to

Principal Beck, waiting for everyone to finish taking their seats. For a second, I wish I *had* brought Rufus. My mouth quirks. Kyle would have enjoyed that.

When I look back, Drew has slunk out of view. So I find a seat on the aisle and shift into journalist mode, taking out a notebook and pen as our former principal welcomes the attendees.

The auditorium isn't full, but it's a decent crowd. Upon closer inspection, mostly friends and family of the Forbeses and Kenyon Riley. But I spot a photographer and a few journalists I recognize. That doesn't surprise me. I'm sure the whole point is to publicize the Forbeses' generosity. After a few brief words, mostly about Kyle's athletic stats in high school, Beck turns the mic over to the waiting doctors. Watching them approach the lectern hand in hand, with their stiff upper lips, you might easily pity them. Look at these good people who lost a good son in such a terrible personal tragedy.

If I weren't one hundred percent certain their utter rejection of who Kyle was—who he wanted to be—played a major part in the spiral he eventually got lost in, I might feel sorry for them too.

But I set all that aside as best I can because it won't bring Kyle back, and there's a pit in my stomach reminding me I still need to do my job. Actually, if this didn't hit so close to home, I might enjoy writing about something other than Unmatched.

I jot down a few pleasant details as they weave a brief tale about Kyle Forbes, the hero, before quickly shifting focus to Kenyon Riley's achievements and potential. There is a round of applause, after which Kenyon says a few words about his dreams and ambitions for medicine, which are inspiring, and I decide that's really all my article needs to be about.

The next thing I know, people are applauding, and Drew is up on stage with his parents, posing for photos and shaking

Kenyon's hand. The Forbeses' smiles are all so practiced and plastic, my stomach is starting to feel sick. Kyle hated that his parents could make themselves look so open, loving, and supportive when they were rarely that way at home. Someone announces that the ceremony will be followed by light refreshments in the cafeteria, and this seems like a great time for me to jet back to my mom.

Rather than walking up the center aisle to the back of the auditorium with everyone else, I duck out a side door. One I know snakes around by the drama department before emptying back into the main hall.

I'm almost to the front doors, desperate for a clean breath of air, when I hear the soft slap of footsteps coming up behind me. I wince and turn back, ready to apologize to Tania for leaving without saying goodbye. But when I turn, I find myself facing down a storm in Drew Forbes's eyes.

We both open our mouths, but I shut mine again, deciding it's best just to leave.

"Where is he?" he says.

I roll my eyes. This guy is like one of those dolls with a string you pull to make them say pre-recorded phrases: *You don't deserve the dog. I hate you. Where is the dog?*

"I dropped him at an animal shelter on my way over." I turn for the exit, but a large hand encircles my arm. Like, my entire bicep.

I freeze, heart pounding like a caught animal, before my brain kicks in and I yank out of his grip. "What do you think you're doing?"

His eyes go wide, tracking from my arm to his empty hand. Then he pales and steps back. "Nothing."

I take the opportunity to make for the exit, propelling myself toward the doors.

Until quietly, behind me, I hear, "I just wanted to know— is he okay?"

Somehow, I'm disarmed by the soft concern in his tone. I

look back before I can stop myself, and find his eyes warring with emotion. It makes me think of Rufus's face when I left him today. I swallow hard.

"He's with my mother, okay?" I'm just trying to say words to appease him, so I can safely leave. But when I note the relief on his face, I add, "I—I took him for a run this morning. It does seem to help."

He lets out a slow breath, and I frown.

A pair of heels clicks down the hall behind me, but I'm so focused on the enemy in front of me I don't think to prepare myself for someone worse.

"Drew, I've been looking everywhere for—" His mother cuts off her sentence as soon as I turn and we register one another. "Ms. Phipps."

Somehow, she utters my name as though she's been bitten.

"Dr. Forbes," I say.

Drew steps away, closing ranks with his mother.

"I must say I'm shocked to see you here," she says. "I didn't think you had any interest in Kyle's legacy."

I flinch at her choice of words, fighting to keep my voice steady. "Is that what you're calling it? I bet Kyle would be shocked too."

And now it's clear where Drew Forbes gets his laser glares.

I hold up my notebook, pen, and press pass like I'm Perseus facing Medusa. "Actually, I'm here in a professional capacity."

She eyeballs my ID with a curling lip. "The *Mile High Observer?*"

My chest tightens. Just the way it did every time I stood by Kyle's side, watching her knock him down a peg.

You don't want to go into medicine? Fine. But if that's your choice, we'll give you nothing, and you will be *nothing.*

"That's correct. You might remember I'm a journalist." I clear my throat. "Would you care to make a statement regarding the scholarship you've set up in the name of your late son? It's such an interesting choice, honoring a soldier's memory by setting up civilian students to go to med school."

Drew grunts beside her, his expression dark. And in that moment, looking at them standing together, I do pity them. They might be shitty people, but when all is said and done, they lost a son, a brother. That pain has clearly done nothing to soften them, but they're still grieving, just like me.

"Andrew," Dr. Forbes says in a tone I haven't heard since high school. "I need to return to the reception. Please see that Ms. Phipps finds her way out."

I don't respond. Just watch her turn on her heel, more relieved with each step she takes away from me. "And to think I never got to call you Mom," I mutter, finally shoving through the doors into the open air.

I'm hit with a powerful gust of wind when I exit the school. To the west, black clouds are gathering above the mountains, and now I'm sure we're in for a storm of some kind.

I'm halfway to Lydia's car before I register Drew behind me, but as soon as I do, my skin prickles and I slide my keychain pepper spray into my hand. We're out in the open, but the parking lot is deserted, and I can think of no good reason he'd be following me out here. I round to the other side of the car, putting the vehicle between us before I whirl to face him.

"What? What else do you and your fucked-up family want?"

He startles, like he wasn't expecting me to notice a man closing in on me like a predator through the rows of cars. But when our eyes meet, his expression shifts. His mouth presses into a line, then parts again.

"I—" He stops, looking from me back to the school, then down at his hands. "I'm sorry about . . . in there."

I frown, fingering my keys. That's literally the last thing I expected from him, and now I have no idea what to say.

"What do you *want*?" I repeat.

He exhales and digs in his pocket, then holds out a slightly creased business card. "You can call. If you need help. I . . . I just want to protect him."

I stare at the rectangle with his business name and number, wondering if this is a peace offering or just a new battle maneuver. But when I finally take it and look up into those achingly familiar green eyes, my face heats. Suddenly, my heart is pounding in my chest. It doesn't seem fair that this feels like something I *miss*. I lick my lips and refocus, looking for something to anchor my brain because my body is clearly confused. Then I find it—his glasses. Thank God Drew wears glasses and Kyle sure as hell didn't.

"Thanks." I shove the card in my pocket, slide into the SUV, and lock the doors. But by the time I pull out of the parking lot, I'm blinking through tears, remembering the one and only time I spoke to Kyle after he broke my heart.

I'm sorry, Caprice. I just want to protect you.

CHAPTER
SEVENTEEN

BY THE TIME I MAKE IT BACK TO MY MOM'S, THE CLOUDS HAVE started to descend over the edge of the mountains. The air has actually warmed since I dropped Rufus off, but it hasn't begun raining. I'm sure the highway will be a mess before I get home. I just want to get back to Denver and into a pair of leggings so I can do some squats or *something* to control my heart rate.

When I walk up her front steps, everything seems surprisingly calm. I'm not sure what I expected to find. The house in flames? Half-eaten? First responders gathered on the street, trying to save her from the dog?

I let myself in with a light knock to announce my arrival, which inadvertently summons the beast. Rufus comes barreling out of the kitchen, barking like a hellhound— vicious and snarling, ready to tear out my jugular. But as he registers me, his booming bark shifts into that godforsaken low-level whine. He runs two circles around me, then leans against my legs, tongue hanging out and tail wagging, plastering golden hair all over my dress.

"He seems pretty attached to you." My mom chuckles.

"Well, I'm not attached to him." I sink into a chair and

touch the top of his head lightly, grimacing when he shoves his nose into my hand. "What's the damage?"

"He pooped in my flower bed. But when he wasn't checking out the window to see if you'd come back, he mostly worked on this," she says, handing me the empty Kong. "He did seem to get more agitated in the last half hour, though."

I roll my eyes. "The vet said it'll take a while for the Prozac to start working."

"I'm not sure if it's just anxiety." She pats his head, and he leans in like he enjoys it, but his eyes stay trained on me. "See what I mean? He just adores you."

"More proof there's something wrong with him." I fold my arms and look away.

Mom stays quiet. When she doesn't say anything else, I glance back, and her face is thoughtful. "We couldn't afford to have pets after your dad left. I always regretted that—learning to love animals is so good for children."

I bristle at the mention of my father. As a successful attorney, Anthony Phipps could have easily provided for us, but he chose not to. She almost never mentions him, which suits everyone. But right now her gaze is far away.

I want to tell her I regret every *other* sacrifice she made raising us on her own, setting her dreams aside because she was too proud to pursue child support. But my mom isn't the one who deserves that ire.

"Kyle was always convinced he could change my mind about dogs," I grumble.

Her face softens as she strokes Rufus's ears. "How did it go at the school?"

I glance out the window at the incoming wall of clouds, thinking again of Drew's stormy eyes. "Fine. They awarded the scholarship to Tania Riley's cousin."

"Oh, nice." She nods, then asks more quietly, "Did you talk to the Forbeses?"

"Unfortunately." I curl my lip. "In case you had any

doubt, they're still assholes. I'll just write my article about Kenyon."

She shakes her head mutely, and I don't want to talk about it anymore, so I rise from my chair, collecting my purse and Rufus's things.

"Thanks again for dog sitting, Mom. I promise I'll come by the gallery soon."

Her eyes light up. "I have a new photographer I'd love you to meet." She laughs at my expression and slips Rufus an extra treat. "But if it means I'll see you more often, I'll watch my 'granddog' anytime you want."

I stop and look at her. "Please don't ever call him that again."

She winks, but I can tell she has more to say as I clip the leash to Rufus's collar.

"You know, I did a little searching while you were gone. It's unusual for a military dog this young to be retired."

"Oh yeah?" I say, eyeing the sky as we step outside.

She nods. "Normally, if something happens to the handler . . ." She glances at me, her pale cheeks flushing pink. "Well, anyway, there must have been a good reason they discharged him."

I frown, looking at the dog, who glues himself to my leg. "Maybe he ate some five-star general's couch."

We make it home just as large drops of rain begin splashing down on the sidewalk. The sky is almost completely black, and there's no break in the clouds on the horizon. But even after I've changed into workout clothes and completed thirty minutes of squats and lunges in my living room, my mood hasn't improved. I am sick thinking about Kyle's parents and their decision to "honor" his memory—forcing him to fit their mold, even now. It's almost enough for me to understand the choice he made.

Except I could never understand that choice.

Saturday, March 20, 20__, 7:09 PM

To: Kyle.Forbes@mail.com

From: Caprice_Phipps@mail.com

Subject: Re: Re: Re: no subject

Dear Kyle,

I had to see your family today. If you thought your parents would change with you gone, you were wrong. They're actually worse. Please come back from the grave and haunt the shit out of them. I'm doing the best I can with Rufus, but I have no idea what I'm doing.

Why did you do this to me?

C

I make myself a mug of tea and settle in front of my laptop at the counter. I've felt like some kind of void opened inside me since I turned in my Unmatched piece. Maybe the sooner I write about this stupid scholarship instead, the faster it'll go away.

But like everything today, it's so much harder than it should be. I spend way too long typing, then deleting. Writing out words I want to say, then replacing them with the words I need. In the end, I wind up drafting two entirely different pieces. One that feels like my life's most mediocre piece of journalism, and another that feels like the beginning of something so real, I have to close it and bury it in a hidden folder just so I can breathe.

By the time I send off the boring, official version to my editor, my apartment is almost fully dark, and the silence is only broken by a low rumble of thunder.

The silence.

I turn on my stool, scanning my small living space. Rufus

isn't on the couch carcass where he's taken to sleeping. He also isn't pacing the room whining or crying, sleeping in his crate, or in the kitchen getting a drink. I don't see him anywhere.

A flash of lightning suddenly illuminates my whole apartment, and I spot a shape on the floor between the remnants of the couch and my coffee table. In the dark, it almost looked like part of the rug, but now I recognize the furry legs and black-tipped tail.

I slide off my stool, approaching cautiously. His head and shoulders are fully under the couch frame, which I've never seen him do except briefly to retrieve his Kong. But he's just lying there, not moving. I reach out an unsteady hand to touch him, and when I do, his whole body is trembling.

"Rufus?" I say, glancing at my kitchen clock. "It's um . . . it's time for your walk."

Last week, "walk" had been this animal's favorite word. Anytime I said it, he'd drop everything and run to the door where I keep his leash. Now he doesn't even shift.

"Rufus? Are you hungry?"

I go to the kitchen and fill his dish with food. Another thing that normally has him sitting at eager attention in front of me. I bring the food dish close to his head and give it a little shake, but he remains still. Something tightens in my belly.

I find this half-stuffed llama thing he has been systematically destroying. The squeaker still works, and normally when I pick it up, he spins in circles wanting to play. But now, when I squeeze it right next to him, he makes no response.

I pull out my phone and dial Lydia. Get her voicemail immediately.

I dial again, and it's the same. Somewhere in the back of my mind, I remember her saying Anton was planning a date for them this weekend. Was it tonight? That would figure.

Her husband would totally get in the way right when I could really use her advice.

Another flash of lightning brightens the room, then we're plunged back into darkness. I flip on the lights just as the requisite rumble of thunder rolls through. The dog still doesn't move, but I can *see* him shaking.

I sink to my knees and turn on my phone's flashlight, trying to see his face jammed under my couch. He's turned at an angle, facing away, but my eyes widen when I notice a clear liquid puddle of drool under his muzzle.

I sit up. Touch his body again. He shudders and tenses.

I dial the vet, aware of my pulse picking up. But it's after five on a Saturday, and I get a message saying they're closed. It directs me to call an emergency number, so I do.

"Hi, this is Veterinary Emergency. How can I help you?"

"Um, hello." I clear my throat, my voice weirdly choked. "Uh, there's something the matter with my dog. I . . . I'm kind of worried?"

The voice is calm. "Sure. Can you describe what's going on?"

"Well, he's under the couch and he won't respond to anything."

"What kind of dog is this? How old is he? Has he eaten anything recently? Is there a chance he swallowed something he shouldn't have?" The questions come so fast I can hardly follow. "What's his respiration? Have you taken his temperature?"

"His temperature?" I touch his limp tail on the floor. How do you even do that? "Look, I don't have a lot of equipment. He isn't that old—can you just tell me what's wrong?"

"Not without getting a picture of what might have happened, unfortunately. If you're not sure, you might want to bring him in so we can examine him."

I jot down the address before darting into the hall and

knocking on Darius and Todd's door. When nobody answers, I knock harder. The elevator pings behind me, and my neighbor Arlene gets out wearing one of those plastic rain bonnet things over her gray-blue hair.

"Boy, I tell you, it's cats and dogs out there. I nearly got soaked just getting from my Uber into the building." She pauses, looking at me banging like an idiot on Darius's door. "You know those boys went down to Mount Princeton for their anniversary."

"I . . . they did?"

She nods with a warm smile. "My husband used to take me down there. Hot springs are so romantic."

For a moment I consider begging her to help me get the dog out from under my couch. Until I remember she's eighty-four and gets winded carrying her grocery bags in from the elevator.

I slip back into my apartment, half hoping Rufus will be running around freaking out because I left. Or even just bark or run to greet me. But he's in the same spot. If anything, the amount of drool pooling under my sofa has grown. Never in a million years did I think I'd wish to hear his whimpering whine again, but now, as I lay a hand on his trembling leg, I think I'd give anything to see him wandering around, pacing and making that sound.

A loud clap of thunder breaks the silence, and we both jerk in response. I need to get him to the vet, but when I pull out my phone, I don't know who else to dial. I wish I could call Kyle, ask him what I should do. Tell him I'm trying to take care of his dog like he wanted, but I don't know how.

I pull my knees to my chest and start to rock because it's happening again—I'm *failing* him. I don't know what to do.

And then I feel a crumpled piece of paper in my leggings pocket. I pull it out and stare at the creased business card for K9 Academy. What else have I got to lose?

The phone rings and rings. I doubt anyone will answer

after hours, and I'm right. It goes straight to voicemail. But I dial again, trying to decide whether it's worth leaving a message, because I don't have any other options. But then the ringing stops, and a deep, too-familiar voice comes on the line.

"Hello? This is Drew."

CHAPTER
EIGHTEEN

D REW F ORBES FILLS MY ENTIRE DOORFRAME WHEN I ANSWER HIS knock. His hair is wet. As is his jacket. Raindrop dot his glasses, and behind them, his green eyes flash with something unreadable. Contempt, if I had to guess. For a moment, I consider blocking his way. After he grabbed me back at the high school, I don't want him anywhere near me *or* the dog, let alone in my apartment. When I racked my brain trying to figure out how to help Rufus, this man was my literal last resort. The only reason I called him was because he's asked about the dog every time I've seen him. I figured if he truly cares on any level, he might at least help me get him to the vet. But now that he's here, glaring at me from the hall, I'm afraid this was a mistake. Do I offer him a towel or shut the door in his face?

"Are you going to let me in so I can help him?" he asks.

I frown at his tone and point to my doorbell camera. "There's time-stamped video of you arriving, already uploaded to the cloud. My brother can access it any time. I also texted my best friend. She knows you're here too."

His brows rise. "What . . . ?" But then his mouth presses into a line, and he just nods. I take a breath and step aside.

"He's under the couch."

Drew crosses the threshold, spotting Rufus on the floor as he moves into my living room. "How long has he been like this?"

I glance at the clock and wince. "I'm not sure. Maybe a couple hours?"

"You're not sure?" He makes a sound that resembles a growl, but he's already kneeling on the floor next to Rufus, setting a backpack down next to him.

"Look, if you can just help me get him to the vet, I'm sure I can—"

"He doesn't need a vet," Drew snarls.

My throat dries up. The dog is obviously sick, but as I open my mouth to tell him so, he starts rummaging through his bag, moving into action. He takes out a Bluetooth speaker first, which he turns on and places next to Rufus, tapping his phone until the air fills with loud, but soothing classical music. Next, he plugs something into the wall that resembles a diffuser and takes out these gray sock-looking things, slipping them onto each of the dog's legs. Rufus hardly moves in response, and my stomach churns as I watch.

Drew produces what looks like a larger matching gray coat. He considers the dog and couch a moment, then removes his jacket and flattens on his back against the floor, squeezing his big body under my couch frame next to Rufus like a mechanic slipping under a car. I kneel on the rug beside my dog, trying to follow what he's doing without getting in the way, but I'm left staring at the man's massive legs and torso. His blue Henley rides up as he reaches farther under the couch, revealing a set of *very* toned abs and a trail of dark hair disappearing into his cargo pants. I force myself to look away.

The whole time he works, he's stroking Rufus gently, muttering to him in a deep, reassuring voice. And then suddenly he slides back out from under my sofa and we nearly collide as he sits up, straightening his glasses.

"Sorry—I—is he okay?"

"Have you been giving him the Prozac?"

I frown. "Yes, but the vet said—"

"It won't be effective yet. I know. Just make sure you're giving it to him. He's probably going to need it this summer."

"This summer?" I look to where the dog lies. "What's the matter with him?"

"It's the storm," Drew says, like that's something every preschooler would know. "Lots of dogs are afraid of thunder, but for Rufus it's a thousand times worse because it's triggering his PTSD."

I swallow before trying to speak. This is a term I've only really ever considered in my attempts to understand Kyle and what he did. "The *dog* has post-traumatic stress disorder?"

Drew just looks at me like he's hoping I'll challenge him, but I won't give him the satisfaction. I look down at my limp dog half-buried beneath the couch. He's now wearing the gray coat thing, which Drew somehow slipped over his head and wrapped tightly around his body. It has a hood that extends up his neck, covering his ears and leaving only his face exposed. The whole thing would look silly if he weren't so unresponsive.

"Should we at least get him out from under there?"

"Absolutely not," Drew snaps. "We're not going to take him out of a safe place *he* chose because it's what we want."

"Okay . . ." I say slowly, shoring up my patience because he knows more about this than me. "Then what should we *do*?"

He gives me this look like he wants to tell me to go away and let him handle it, but has to concede he can't tell me to leave my own home. "We sit with him. We keep him safe. And we wait it out."

I shoot a doubtful glance out the windows. Rain still

comes down in sheets, and if anything, the sky is blacker than it was when we got home. This kind of storm doesn't happen often in Denver, but when it does, the intensity is always semi-biblical. If I didn't have a clock to tell me it's close to ten p.m., I'd have no way of guessing the time at all.

Drew has gone back to stroking his big hands down Rufus's body and murmuring to him over the music. If I don't fully focus my eyes and simply listen to the rumble of his voice, my brain could almost believe he's Kyle.

Something hot sears through my chest at this thought, and I cough to conceal what was starting to feel like a sob. I look away, trying to block out the big, muscular man on my floor who clearly loathes me, trying to separate him from the man in my head who I *know* loved me—just not enough.

I rise from where I kneel, moving to Rufus's other side, determined to do something to help the dog left in my charge.

I hesitate a moment, trying to figure out how to approach. Rufus's back is to me, and Drew is on his other side, massaging his paws. I run my hand down his back a few times, trailing my fingers along the soft, feathery golden fur that isn't covered by the coat. I've just registered that his whole body isn't trembling quite the same way it was before Drew got here when another loud clap of thunder breaks through the music and he goes rigid under my touch.

I can just make out Drew's words over the violins and flute as the thunder subsides. "Hey buddy, it's okay, you're safe, you're going to be okay . . ."

Rufus's body is still tense under my hands. I look around for a tool that might help, but I only find the squeaky llama he didn't respond to before. I'm willing to bet he still doesn't want food. So, I act on impulse and lie down next to him. I dip my head under the edge of my couch so I'm closer to his ears, and then I press my body up against his, spooning him the way I might if he were Kyle.

"Rufus, I'm right here," I say in the most soothing voice I can muster. "I know it's scary, but it's going to be okay."

There's a lull in the music, and though I can still hear the rain coming down, thankfully, there's no thunder. But in that quiet moment, I catch the faintest whine. It's such a small sound—more like a whimper—and it breaks something loose in my chest. I would never claim to speak dog, but this clearly sounds like a cry for help. I press my face into the back of Rufus's neck and stroke my fingers gently over the soft fur of his nose, repeating my words, or versions of them. Meanwhile, my brain *floods* with thoughts of Kyle feeling lost and helpless, the exact way his dog feels right now.

I shut my eyes, imagining myself pressed against his body. Saying words I never got to say.

I'm right here; it's going to be okay.

Thunder crashes again around us, but I just stay there, tears streaming down my face as I whisper and pet the dog. My dog. The lights in the room are still on, diminishing the flashes from the windows. And even though I know Drew Forbes is also here because I can hear his low voice still talking, on some level, I register the feeling Rufus must have sought under my couch. Some semblance of safety—like nothing can get us if we just stay here together.

I don't know how much time passes under that half-dead couch. Too much. Eventually, I open my eyes and notice the light has completely shifted. It's brighter. Quieter somehow.

I raise my head, and my neck is stiff, like it's been weirdly positioned for hours. And when I peer at where my arm is slung over the blond fur next to me, there's a large, warm hand resting over mine.

I blink. The hand is connected to a muscular arm and body, awkwardly sprawled unconscious on my floor, glasses askew. My heart thuds once in my chest because, asleep,

Drew Forbes looks both more *and* less like his brother, and noticing this makes weird things happen inside me. Carefully, I slide my fingers out from under his, pulling my hand toward me over the dog's ribcage.

In response, Rufus raises his head and looks back at me, eyes shining with a light I didn't even realize was missing last night, but I'm relieved to see. He comes to life, twisting ungracefully to extract himself from under my couch skeleton, and I follow suit. By the time the dog is standing in front of me, wagging his tail like absolutely nothing unusual has happened, Drew is also sitting up on my floor, looking like he wishes he were anywhere else.

The dog does one of those full-body shakes and starts pawing at his head. Drew refocuses on him, removing the coat and leg warmer things that are clearly annoying him now. I take the opportunity to slip behind the counter into my kitchen, noting the clock—6:04 a.m., *how?*—and picking up the stainless steel food dish to prepare Rufus's breakfast. As soon as he's free of his accessories, he runs over, sitting obediently in front of me and licking his lips like he hasn't eaten in days.

"You seem none the worse for wear," I mutter, watching him inhale the food I just set down. I glance over at Drew, now standing in my living room, taking up more space than any man I can remember coming through my door. And looking entirely rumpled all the way from his hair down to his sneakers. "Um . . . do you . . . want some orange juice?" I ask, admittedly sounding like I don't actually want to give it to him.

He looks up, like he just realized I wasn't offering it to the dog. "No-no, thank you," he says with those impeccable manners that made my mom sweet on Kyle, then looks quickly away to zip his backpack. He watches Rufus licking his dish across the floor. "I . . . need to go."

"Right. Yeah."

We both move for the apartment door—me, remembering my own manners and trying to show him out at the same moment he apparently decides to make a break for it. We reach the handle together, then overcorrect in the small space, repelling each other like polarized magnets. It's an uneasy two seconds before Rufus comes trotting over, spinning in circles between us and nudging his leash hanging on the wall.

"I bet he really needs to go," I mutter, peeking in the mirror through the bathroom door and smoothing my slept-on-the-floor hair.

When I look back, Drew is running a hand through his too. Not making it neater at all, but somehow more appealingly disheveled. And in that moment, even though we literally spent the last eight hours under a couch with a traumatized animal, my cheeks warm like the night was something else.

"Thanks for your help," I say lamely, kneeling to clip the leash to Rufus's collar. I give his head a pat when he looks up with his tongue hanging out. "You can send me a bill . . . or whatever."

"Sure." His tone is clipped, and I immediately feel foolish, remembering who I'm talking to. I *hate* the way his looks, his voice, keep blurring in my head, echoing my heart's permanent ache. "Look, um . . ."

I glance up, bracing myself for his standard scowl paired with whatever he's about to say. Another demand to give him the dog, or some threat about taking proper care of him, no doubt. But he's trailed off, gaze fixed on the framed photo on the little table by my door. He picks up the picture taken a million years ago, in which I'm lifted off my feet, swept up in his brother's arms.

I raise my eyes to Drew's, challenging him to do or say anything—try to touch that memory. Except he already has. *You're the reason my brother killed himself.*

But when he drags his gaze to mine, his expression seems . . . surprised? Confused?

He hesitates, clears his throat. Rufus comes over and licks his hand, which apparently startles him because the frame slips and falls to the floor with a crack.

"*Oh—*" I swat him out of my way, lunging to pick it up. The frame itself isn't damaged, but when I turn the picture over, there's a thin crack through the glass, running right down the center, visually separating Kyle and me.

I run my fingers along the line like I could wipe it away, put us back together—and then all at once, every feeling and memory I'd managed to hold at bay the last twenty-four hours seems to flood through this hairline crack. The visit home, the school, the familiar faces. The scholarship "honoring" Kyle. Having to see his mother and father, who clearly don't get him any more now than when he was alive. Tense hours of rain and thunder, ruminating on how I'd failed him and would also fail his dog.

I open the apartment door wide, glaring at Drew through a sheen of tears.

He makes a sound like he wants to say something, but nothing follows. Instead, he sets the gray coat and leg warmers on the little table where the photograph used to sit, runs a hand over Rufus's ears. And then he's gone.

I close the door, leaning back against the wood as my vision blurs. Then I sink to the floor and put my arms around Kyle's dog.

DREW

He let himself in the door quietly, guiltily, as if he was slinking home after a one-night stand.

Diesel raised his head from where he lay on the couch, too old and stiff to hop up and give him the third degree. He delegated that work to his underlings. Pudding was already at Drew's heels, running circles, and Blitz would have been if Drew hadn't placed him in his crate with music playing before leaving the previous night. The border collie was also not a fan of thunder, though he didn't melt down the way Rufus did. Still, Drew had no intention of being gone all night.

Once the dogs had forgiven him, which took all of sixty seconds, he offered them breakfast topped with half a sardine each as an apology, made a cup of coffee, and took the trio into the yard. His manager ran K9 Academy for him every other Sunday, thank God. Dealing with people was hard enough when Drew was relaxed and well-rested. Today, the entire left side of his neck and shoulders was stiff and sore from falling asleep on Caprice Phipps's floor, and his mood had been completely trampled on top of that. He would do well to stick to dogs and avoid humans the rest of the weekend.

But conflicted as he felt, he didn't regret going over there. He'd worked through storm anxiety with all kinds of animals, and Rufus's case was severe. Caprice obviously didn't know what she was doing. He hadn't been surprised by her call—actually, he'd gone over there thinking it was his big chance. She didn't care about the dog. She was just petty and didn't want Drew to have him. But he was confident she was already so close to the edge that however Rufus reacted during the storm would have her begging Drew to take him off her hands.

Except that's not what happened at all.

She'd spent the entire night on the floor alongside him, soothing the dog. Stroking and comforting him through the worst of the storm. It was clear she had no idea what techniques would work or why. She was only emulating Drew's actions. But by morning, one thing was indisputable—Caprice Phipps *cared* about Rufus.

And Drew no longer knew what to think.

But he couldn't stop thinking about her. His brother's former fiancée. The woman who'd led Kyle astray and then left him when he was most vulnerable. Drew had every reason to hate Caprice, and the feeling was obviously mutual. So why did his mind keep returning to her whispers to Rufus that she wouldn't let anything hurt him? The pretty way her lashes fluttered as she struggled to remain conscious while petting him. Or how those same eyes welled with tears when the photo of her and Kyle hit the floor?

If his brother meant so little to her, why did she have that picture at all?

Drew's vision glossed over. He'd recognized the photo from a shelf in the background of a distinct memory. One that ambushed him regularly, refusing to fade.

"Just come back to Colorado and recuperate for a while. I'm

already building the business. You can step in whenever you're feeling better."

"I feel fine," Kyle said in a voice so flat it was an obvious lie.

"Of course you do." Drew masked his concern. "But, you know, it seems like the perfect time."

The shadows on Kyle's face made it look like his eyes were sinking into his head. "Yeah. Medical retirement. Just what I've been waiting for."

It was a struggle, but Drew managed to keep his expression neutral. "Look, I know this wasn't part of your plan—"

"What are you trying to accomplish, Doctor Forbes?" Kyle asked.

"I told you, I'm done with medicine," Drew whispered. "You and me—we're going to chase our dream."

For a second, it looked like Kyle considered it. Then he shook his head and limped to the window. No specialist had been able to explain the limp, not medically. But it was there, nonetheless, every time he moved. "No, thanks."

"Why?" Drew's voice came out harsher than he intended. His eyes followed Kyle's to a photograph on an otherwise bare shelf. "Because you don't want to be near her?*"*

"No." Kyle's voice was far away. Across the room, his recently retired military working dog, a handsome Belgian Malinois named Rufus, lifted his head, keying in on his tone. Or maybe his respiration. Or some pheromone in the air.

Drew waited for his brother to say more, but when he didn't, he just shrugged. "Maybe she's one thing Mom and Dad were right about."

Kyle's head snapped up, nostrils flaring. "Caprice was the best fucking thing that ever happened to me."

"Then why isn't she here with you?" Drew snapped, losing out to frustration. "Why would she let you live through the worst time of your life alone?"

Kyle pressed his lips together but directed his gaze back out the window. The dog got up and crossed the room, laid his chin in his lap, and looked doubtfully at Drew.

"Look, I even have plenty of room for this guy." Drew took a gentler tone, gripping his brother's shoulder. He leaned down and gave Rufus an affectionate pat. "Just come stay with me. We'll figure out the rest."

"I'm staying here." Kyle's hollow, stubborn voice set Drew's skin prickling.

"Why?" Drew looked around the tiny, barely furnished apartment. "There's no reason to stay here. You don't even have a job."

"Maybe I'll greet people at Walmart."

"There's a Walmart back home."

"Maybe I don't want to go home," Kyle snarled. "Or be anywhere near you, or Mom, or Dad."

Drew flinched, his mouth hardening into a line. But he couldn't help feeling some relief at his brother's ire. At least when Kyle got angry, he seemed alive.

"Look, I'm just thinking about what your doctors said—"

"Believe me," Kyle spat. "I heard it."

Drew watched the shadows creep back over his brother's face. His physical wounds had mostly healed, but PTSD and a traumatic brain injury had left him unable to carry out his duties—or do much of anything aside from sitting around this apartment. The neurologists suggested he could heal with time and support, but they couldn't make him want to. The one thing that gave Drew hope was that Kyle had Rufus, whose own discharge for canine PTSD felt like some unfortunate consolation prize after what they'd been through. But if they could somehow heal together, Drew was confident he could get his brother back on his feet.

"Okay, look. I have to get back to Denver for the training facility opening—I thought you'd be coming with me. But I'll be back in a couple of weeks. Just think about it, Kyle." He put a hand on his brother's shoulder. "You're going to get through this. And when you do, we'll run the business together . . . like we always said we would."

Kyle didn't respond. Didn't even look at him. He just sat there with one hand on the dog.

There was nothing left for Drew to do but give Rufus a last pat and head for the door, holding on to the hope that the dog would be enough. That if Kyle did nothing else, he'd take care of himself for Rufus's sake.

He'd been wrong. So incredibly wrong.

Eight days later, Kyle had left Rufus with someone who ran a rescue for retired military working dogs. Then he'd gone home, dialed a number four times from his cell phone, but never actually called. Instead of leaving a voicemail, he left a legally binding will and instructions on how to find and care for his dog.

And then, he was gone.

CHAPTER
NINETEEN

ANTON AND SETH RICHIE ARE THE LAST TWO PEOPLE I EXPECT TO see outside my apartment door Sunday morning when Rufus and I return from our walk. Lydia's husband stands tall, chiseled, and broad-chested, looking like He's Just Ken, with his matching blond brother waving behind him.

"Hey, Caprice." Seth grins. "Richie brothers furniture moving service here. We have been instructed to remove your couch?"

I blink, my brain running sluggishly through recent conversations and landing on a shadowy memory of this plan. I automatically reach for my leggings pocket, only remembering as I find it empty that I left my phone somewhere under said couch.

"Where's Lydia?" I ask, narrowing my eyes. Anton avoids my scrutiny, running a hand through his disheveled brown hair. In answer, the elevator dings behind me, and out steps my somehow more-pregnant-looking-than-last-week best friend. She smiles and comes down the hall, wielding a bag of what I'm one hundred percent certain must be dog supplies.

"Good morning!" she says, beaming way too brightly for

someone with restricted caffeine. "I came to pick up my car. And as promised, I brought the couch removal crew."

"I . . . remember that now," I mutter, taking the bag out of her hands.

She raises her eyebrows. "Has there been a change of plan?"

I look down at Rufus, who is currently eyeing Anton with what looks like suspicion—this dog just keeps growing on me. But when I think about him crammed under the remnants of my sofa last night like he was hiding from incoming mortars, I frown. There isn't enough money in my bank account to purchase furniture right now, and there isn't going to be before the next thunderstorm.

"I just think it makes more sense to wait until I get a new one," I say, not wanting to rehash my night while we're standing in the hall. "Guess you're off the hook, boys."

The Doublemint twins look at each other and shrug.

"Wanna grab a game of squash?" Seth asks.

Anton hesitates, glancing uneasily at Lydia, who gives an exasperated laugh. "Oh my God, go. I don't need you to stand here and *watch* me be pregnant. I'm going to hang for a bit with Caprice, then I'll drive myself home. I'll be fine. Have fun!"

Her husband reddens a little, but embraces her like she's made of solid gold, kissing her cheek before disappearing with his brother down the stairs.

"You guys are gross," I mutter, unlocking my apartment door.

Lydia just smiles, following me in, waiting until I disconnect Rufus's leash before giving him a proper Lydia Richie greeting. This involves several treats and a game of tug, after which she actually looks winded and perches on one of the less-destroyed portions of my couch.

"Now," she says. "Tell me the real reason you're keeping this monstrosity."

I fill my water bottle at the fridge, closing my eyes in an effort to center myself. "Okay. So, that thunderstorm we had last night . . . ?"

Realization dawns on her face as she brings her hand to her mouth. "Oh no. We were—Anton made me turn off my phone. Did you call me? Did he freak out?"

I shake my head, watching her grip her belly. "It wound up being okay."

Her shoulders relax a little, but worry lingers in her eyes. "Sorry. He did this whole elaborate romantic evening with candles and melted chocolate and whipped cream . . ." She smiles to herself, then glances at me, face instantly reddening. "Um, I knew turning off the phone was a bad idea."

"It's okay, Lydia. I—I called Drew."

Her mouth immediately clamps shut. She studies me. Then, after at least half a minute, she speaks with a measure of caution. "And that went . . . well?"

I sink onto the more-damaged portion of the couch, drawing my knees to my chest. "If you're asking if it was awkward and uncomfortable, but we managed to help Rufus, then yes?"

Lydia knits her brows. But then Rufus pads over from the water dish, rests his chin in her lap, and gazes up with literal puppy dog eyes. She dissolves into adorations, totally disregarding the water dripping all over her leggings.

"He seems to have recovered," she finally says, stroking down his neck.

I nod. "Drew wrapped him in this shirt and leggings getup and played music." I glance toward the door, where the photo of Kyle and me used to sit and the dog clothes still rest in a neatly folded pile. "But before that, Rufus was hiding under the couch, and . . ." I exhale. "Drew said it was important not to take away his safe space."

Lydia hums in approval. "He's probably right." She plucks at some of the stuffing spilling out next to her thigh.

"How's the furniture fund? You still working on that Unmatched article?"

The way she asks is so casual. If I didn't know her well, I might've missed her uneasiness altogether.

"It publishes this week," I say, a knot twisting in my stomach.

She swirls her hands over her belly and releases a low breath. "Okay. Good to know."

I study her with suspicion. "I swear to God, Lydia, Anton better not be back on that fucking app—"

"He's *not*," she says quickly. "We've talked about it in therapy. And actually—I know this won't garner sympathy, but his guilt is overwhelming—he realizes he made the biggest mistake of his life when he went on Unmatched. If anything, a new article is going to intensify his shame." She swallows. "It's really weird feeling sorry for someone who feels guilty for causing you significant pain."

I sneer. "Well, I have zero sympathy. He deserves to simmer in his regret. I hope he never forgets he almost lost the best thing he ever had."

She sighs, arms still wrapped tightly over her rounded midsection. "Well, anyway, thanks for the heads-up. I hope the new article holds the right people accountable *and* earns you a raise." She returns to her comfort zone, refocusing on the dog. "Now, what else did Drew Forbes suggest for Rufus?"

My breath stutters. "Um, he didn't? He left immediately this morning."

"Oh," she says, and I don't miss the way her tone lilts up. "He was here all night?"

There is zero reason I ought to feel anything other than annoyed thinking about that, but my face still heats when she asks. Until I remember his exit. And the picture frame now sitting broken in a drawer.

"It was a really long storm."

She nods, stroking Rufus's nose and staring down into his eyes. "Hmm. Well, Drew Forbes's reputation may precede him. But if he cared enough to stay all night with you and Rufus . . . I might have to revise my opinion of him."

CHAPTER
TWENTY

Tuesday evening, after the longest two workdays of my life, I take Rufus for a run. I ended up tethering his leash to the chair in my cubicle on Monday after he helped himself to some cupcakes left over from a birthday in the break room, as well as a reheated slice of pizza Brian brought for lunch. I had to order a whole pie from down the street just to keep him from filing a complaint with HR. Things seemed pretty under control today until Jana, of all people, popped around the side of my cubicle and asked if I could get the dog to stop whining so she could talk on the phone.

This, on top of him shoving his cold nose in my face repeatedly the last two nights, drooling on my sheets, and squeaking until I finally lost it and locked him in his crate— where he *still* cried.

He needs activity—he needs to run, stupid Drew Forbes repeats in my head like an obnoxious reminder. So that's exactly what I'm doing, hoping to give the dog whatever it is *he* needs so I can meet my own.

The weather has warmed, making like spring instead of winter again for a few days, and I'm far from the only person in Denver rushing out to soak up the sunshine. But surprisingly, the crowded jogging path doesn't faze Rufus. He just seems happy, out from under my desk. By the time we complete our final circuit of the park, the dog and I are both panting, but the way he looks at me as we slow to a walk and head home—I'd almost swear he's grateful.

I grip the leash, and we match pace. I know dogs can't possibly measure time or track significant events. They remember things, obviously, but there's no way Rufus could understand that today marks one year since Kyle's death. Or what that means. He just has one of those expressions that seems like he does.

I take my time returning to our building, stopping along the greenbelt on the way there to do some stretching, loosening up my calves and hamstrings. Now that I don't have work to distract me, I just want to skip over the rest of today.

I try to center my anxiety on the new Unmatched article dropping tomorrow, wondering if I'll have to start looking over my shoulder again after it prints. I'm working so hard to focus on this, and the music drumming in my earbuds, that I don't notice the wall that is Drew Forbes's chest until I nearly walk straight into it.

"Hi, um . . ." He trails off when he sees me. And even though he's literally outside *my* building, he is apparently so unhappy to see me, he drops to his knees and greets the dog instead. Rufus knocks his glasses sideways, licking his face like it's covered in au jus. But I can't help noting the gray pallor of the man's skin. The shadows lingering around his eyes. There's no denying that today sucks for him too.

But why is he *here*?

I stand there, waiting for him to finish communing with Rufus, annoyed that his mere presence precludes my own mental escape. Like I needed a living, breathing, bespectacled reminder of the person I'm trying hardest not to think about today.

Finally, he clears his throat and stands, and I wait for him to explain why he chose to further ruin my already terrible day with his appearance.

Without looking at me, he extends his arm, a small brown paper shopping bag dangling from his fingers. "This is for you."

Wow. I've received literal death threats with more enthusiasm. I give the bag a wary glance before taking it, wondering if it's filled with poison. Or maybe a bomb. I narrow my eyes and reach inside, but what I find is a simple, tasteful wooden picture frame the exact size of the one he dropped. I have to admit, it's nicer than the original.

I hold the frame a moment, trying to figure out how to make speech work, but Mr. Congeniality beats me to it.

"I have a proposal," he says. My eyebrows shoot up. Some part of me actually wants to laugh. He sounds like a goddamn robot.

"Then you should have stayed on your knees," I snark. But when he just looks confused, I roll my eyes. "I took the dog for a run like you suggested. Now I'm in major need of a shower. Hurry up and spit it out."

He straightens, even more stiff and formal, if that's possible. "Today is . . ." He swallows, and for a nauseous moment, I'm sure he's going to drag me with him into a black hole. I step back, consider making a run for it, but then he says, "I think I can help Rufus recover. I'd like to. If you'd be willing to work together."

I was wrong. This *is* a black hole. Just not one I ever saw coming.

"Look," he continues. "I've done some research and have a few ideas about what he's struggling with. We could just try for a week or two. It'll either help, or it won't."

I bite my lip. My knee-jerk reaction is to say no and shove past him. But instead, I force myself to ask a question. "And what would that look like, exactly?"

He shifts his weight uncomfortably. But when he brings

his hand to rest on Rufus's head, something changes. His whole posture is more relaxed, more fluid.

"You could bring him to the training center. Or we could just work in the park at first, if that's more comfortable. I'm sure the running helps. But this dog was trained to follow specific commands, do specific types of jobs . . . My hope is he'll settle down if we let him do them."

I open my mouth, ready to say *yes, please.* Beg for it, for anything that will settle Rufus at all. But I catch myself before I can walk into his web. I almost forgot I'm dealing with a Forbes. And they have a one hundred percent burn rate. I tighten my grip on the leash, moving toward the entrance of my building. "Sorry, I can't afford formal training."

"I won't charge you," he says quickly. "I just want to do it . . . for him."

The gravelly quality of his voice gets my attention. I'm not sure which *him* he means.

Rufus—or Kyle?

I turn to the dog, staring up at me, panting, with his tongue hanging out the side of his mouth. And I swear he has an expression in his eyes like he just wants me to figure things out.

So do I, dog. So do I.

"He needs water," I mutter, opening the lobby door. But the traitorous animal lingers. Drew's long fingers still stroke his ears, his golden eyes relaxed and trusting. I remember something Lydia said once about animals being able to tell things about people's character. I roll my eyes. "I'll think about it, all right?"

Drew nods, giving Rufus a final pat before he steps back. The dog looks from him to me briefly, like he's not sure why we're going separate ways. Then, finally, he follows me through the door.

• • •

Sometime around three a.m., I wake up to an unfamiliar sound. I hadn't been dreaming, or if I was, I don't remember. But I was so deeply asleep, it takes forever to form a coherent thought. I'm not even sure I actually heard something until it starts up again.

Squick, squick, squick . . .

A sort of rubbery, plastic sound. Not close, but definitely coming from inside my apartment. I look around for Rufus, who is usually curled in a ball on a mat next to the bed under the window—when he's not just standing watching me sleep like a creeper. But he isn't there now. Which probably isn't good.

I turn on my bedside light and sit up. The sound seems to come from what's left of the couch, but I can only see the back of it from here. The dog is probably finishing it off or, best-case scenario, chewing on his Kong. But something tells me I should make sure. I swing my legs over the side of the bed, and just as my feet touch the floor, a new sound fills the air. One I recognize immediately.

"Oh no, you didn't, you fucking—"

I rush into my living area and flip on the overhead light. There, perched in the middle of the sofa he single-handedly destroyed, is Rufus. Holding what's left of my favorite, now very chewed up, purple vibrator—currently *vibrating*—in his mouth.

"Give that to me." I lunge for him, but he makes a dramatic escape over the back of the couch like a thief fleeing an art gallery. *"Rufus."*

He looks at me. And then has the nerve to wag his black-tipped tail.

I nearly growl. "You are a very bad dog. Let me have that right now." I come around the couch toward him, trying again to reclaim my sex toy.

Rufus watches my movements, and if I didn't know better, I'd swear something twinkles in his eyes. He makes a playful sound in his throat and launches onto my bed, doing what I can only describe as a bow, stretching his head down toward his front paws with his butt sticking up in the air. The maimed purple cock hangs out the side of his grinning mouth, still vibrating, and I almost scream.

"Goddammit, stop! This isn't funny—just spit it *out* already!"

Immediately, his whole demeanor shifts. He straightens, all sense of play disappearing. The toy falls out of his mouth, landing destroyed on top of the covers where I probably left it last night while trying to escape my grief. When I reach to grab it back from him, he lets out a low, distressed whine.

I hold up the formerly dick-shaped purple silicone, turning it over until I find the power button and shut it off. I rotate it, examining its thoroughly chewed state, and as I do, the very-chewed business end falls off. I let out a long, shaking breath.

"That. Was. My. Favorite!"

Rufus tilts his head, wagging his tail slightly.

I hold it in front of his face, look him in the eye and say, "*Not* a bone."

To his credit, the look the dog gives me is a polite rebuttal.

I cover my face with my hand. "*Fuck!*"

After tossing away the remains of the only reliable dick in my life, and arguably one of my last remaining sources of stress relief, I fire off a text to Drew Forbes, giving exactly zero fucks about what hour of the morning it is.

Meet in the park tomorrow. 5:30p.m.

CHAPTER
TWENTY-ONE

THIS WEEK, THE COVER OF THE *MILE HIGH OBSERVER* IS A HIGHLY recognizable photo of local Green Industries CEO Colin Vanderpool with the Unmatched logo—a white letter *U* encircled by a gold wedding ring—superimposed over his fleshy face. Beneath that, the headline reads:

Unmatched Scandal: The Downfall of a Denver Philanthropist

I have to sit down when I find the print issue waiting for me on my desk. Randall didn't tell me I'd have the front page. A slight thrill runs under my skin, and I force myself to take a slow breath through my nose. I did this—I exposed Colin Vanderpool's wicked deeds. The whole time he was donating hospital wings and attending charity benefits, he was *also* developing an app designed specifically to help himself and other guys fuck around on their spouses.

His wife wanted to nail him for it, and I helped her do it. These are the consequences, fucker. I stare at his smug face, my mind buzzing, waiting for the satisfaction to sink in.

"Nice work," a voice says behind me.

I startle so hard, Rufus comes out from under my desk growling, but quickly wags his tail, looking between Randall and me, confused.

"You currently have the most-clicked article on the *Observer* website." My boss chuckles. "Not that anyone's surprised."

"Thanks," I say, though my voice comes out too small. Apologetic.

I hate it.

My boss kneels to pet Rufus, then says in a low voice, "You nailed the bad guy. But if anyone sends you garbage you're worried about, forward it straight to me."

I let out a low, grateful breath. Maybe I'm obvious, but I'm also glad I don't have to explain. "Thanks, Randall."

I wasn't brave enough to take my phone out of Do Not Disturb when I woke up this morning, and I'm still afraid now. But after my editor heads back to his office and a few coworkers have stopped by to congratulate me on the cover feature, the office falls into its normal, bustling rhythm. This may be as safe as I'm going to get.

I glance down at the animal staring out from under my desk, and I swear his gaze is almost reassuring. So I take a breath and unlock my phone. Immediately, my screen fills with an onslaught of notifications. The headline from my own news organization. Some text messages from colleagues here and at other publications. An encouraging note from Lydia. A slew of social media alerts and emails. No voicemail.

I exhale. Inhale. Continue basic breathing.

Wednesday, March 18, 20__, 7:46 AM

To: Caprice_Phipps@MHObserver.com

From: Mrs.R@mail.com

Subject: Re: Going To Print

Ms. Phipps,

You have exceeded my expectations. As usual, you write beautifully and sensitively, and while I was surprised at the angle you took with the article, I can't help feeling flattered by a feature I was sure I'd have to brace myself to read. Thank you for that, and for exposing my husband as the manipulative philanderer he's always been. I am already out of town, holing up in one of our vacation homes while my lawyer serves up divorce papers.

Thank you for your generous portrayal.
Margaret Vanderpool

My blood starts pumping again with her words. I open my laptop to find other notifications I'm happy to see. Re-posts from my social media. Nods from other journalists and political figures. A few promising-looking nods from larger news organizations.

But Mrs. Vanderpool's email, more than anything else, brings me peace. She's the reason I was willing to do the feature in the first place. After hearing the tearful account of how her husband flaunted his disrespect for their marriage, and for her. How he did whatever he wanted for years while she endured with no voice of her own.

Until today, when I gave her one.

A burst of warmth kindles in my chest when I think about it, keeping me afloat even as I skim through my social media comments. There, inevitably, my confidence is knocked down a couple of pegs by some entitled men defending their rights to women's bodies. But I don't spare them my attention. I can't. Not after the Features editor at *Denver Editorial* sends a personal note complimenting the piece. It's barely two sentences, but I nearly fall off my chair knowing my name is on her radar.

By five o'clock, things have gone better than I imagined they could all day. Even Rufus seemed to whine slightly less while I stayed on top of all the responses, though I did ply him with some of Lydia's chews. We're both ready to leave the desk behind by the end of the day, though, so I tug him with me into the ladies' room to change before we head to the park.

I've hardly had a moment all day to think about meeting Drew, but now the idea of spending time with him after work instead of just going home or for a run puts a hitch in my good mood. I spend an extra moment straightening my desk in a blatant attempt at procrastination and decide to also check my email one last time before packing up my laptop. Unfortunately, this is where what's left of my mood takes a swan dive into the sewer.

Wednesday, March 18, 20__, 5:01 PM

To: Caprice_Phipps@MHObserver.com

From: AnonE@mail.com

Subject: your hair looks nice

You wore your hair down today. I liked it. Better than your fucking article.

My skin freezes over. When I try to swallow, my mouth fills with a sour taste. I had been standing a moment ago, but I realize I'm back in my chair when Rufus's head drops into my lap. The whites of his eyes are visible as he stares up at me and lets out a new, unfamiliar low whine. Unconsciously, my fingers land on a warm place between his ears while my thoughts try to find traction in my brain.

Colin Vanderpool is exposed. This was supposed to be over.

Except somehow, I *know* this is the same person.

How, though? It's been six weeks since I got a message like this. The address is different (it always is), but surely Mr. Vanderpool has more important things to do today than harass a local journalist.

Like meet with his lawyers.

A creepy, unsettling sensation curls through me as the idea that it might *not* be Colin Vanderpool dances at the edge of my mind. But why would anyone else care about the article?

A low moan issues from Rufus's throat, vibrating against my lap. I look down to find his golden eyes less reassuring and more . . . pleading. I glance at the clock, suddenly remembering where we're supposed to be heading.

Quickly, I forward the message to Randall. It wasn't technically a threat, but it sure as hell felt like one. Then I archive it into a folder reserved for exactly this sort of thing, where I can keep it on record without having to look at it. When that's finally done, I stand from my desk and glance over my shoulder, holding tight to the dog's leash.

"Okay, Rufus. One asshole down. Only one more to deal with."

The grass in Washington Park has already turned a gorgeous emerald green thanks to all the moisture we had this week. We enter the green space from Downing Street and head for a clearing on the north end in the trees. I glance over my shoulder *again* as we leave the path, hating how quickly I've fallen back into paranoia. Everyone and their dog is literally here because of the nice weather. The hordes of people ought to be reassuring—safety in numbers, or whatever. But I can't help wishing I were alone in my apartment behind a locked door.

My spirit sinks further when I see the familiar, broad-chested figure waiting in the trees. He's in jeans this time and another stupidly form-fitting Henley. His unruly hair looks like it won a battle with the comb—very *unlike* his brother's high and tight hairstyle. In fact, each time I lay eyes on Drew now, he reminds me less of Kyle. But I guess that only means he's becoming his own obnoxious persona in my life instead of haunting me like a ghost.

He greets me with a nod as we approach, but as soon as Rufus lays eyes on him, I apparently cease to exist. The dog jerks me forward, wagging his tail and bouncing circles around Drew. I roll my eyes and let go of the leash, reminding myself that Rufus only acts like this because the man carries a literal tool belt of dog treats like some Pavlovian superhero. In no time, he moves from licking Drew's face to wriggling upside down in the grass, inviting him to rub the lighter fur on his belly. I glance at my smartwatch, counting the seconds until this "training session" is over.

Drew indulges Rufus for another minute, scratching his ears and stroking him with his enormous hands. But eventually he straightens and utters a low command, and the dynamic between man and dog immediately shifts. Rufus is on his feet at attention, eyes and ears focused intently on Drew, who marches up and down between the trees, giving him different subtle commands. Rufus does all the basics: sits, lies down, and heels so closely at Drew's side it looks like he might trip him.

Once Drew seems to have captured the dog's rapt attention, he starts running him through different drills. He clips a long leash to his collar and makes him stay put from farther and farther away before releasing him. Each time Rufus does whatever it is Drew tells him to do, the man gives him an enthusiastic "*Yes*" and rewards him by letting him tug the end of a blue toy that looks like a ball with a rope handle on the end. After some minutes, I decide I need one of those since Rufus would clearly do anything to chomp his teeth around it.

But eventually, man and dog repeat these commands and rewards so many times, my attention wanders. I sit down against a tree, idly scanning joggers and dog walkers on the path, and farther away along the road. Every one of them looks like they belong here, of course, and also somehow like they might break character and close in on me if I let my guard down.

"Sound good?" Drew grunts directly behind me, and I sit up so fast, my spine cracks against the trunk of the tree.

"What?" I look up, annoyed.

"I *said* this is probably as much as we can do for today. Do you know his basic commands?"

I haul myself to my feet, wiping pine needles off my butt. "Yeah, like, sit, stay, down, whatever."

He frowns. "There are hand signals too. Have you bothered to learn them?"

"Why would I? I thought the training part was your job."

His mouth presses into a line. "If it isn't obvious, Rufus really *wants* to be told what to do."

"Well, that's one of us," I say through my teeth. "Just tell me the command for 'don't chew up my things.'"

Drew's brows draw together and he leans close, voice gravelly. "He wouldn't chew your stuff if he lived with me."

My lip curls as I snatch the leash. "Not a chan—"

The words fall away as sudden movement behind him catches my eye. A twenty-something white man running directly toward me, teeth bared, fists pumping. Without thinking, I shrink against Drew, just trying to put something between me and the approaching man.

Who crashes to the ground ten feet short of us, catching a frisbee just before he hits the grass. Laughing, he gets to his feet and brushes himself off as he walks back toward his friends, and it's a good thing I have a death grip on the leash because Rufus lunges after the guy, suddenly barking and snarling.

"Rufus, settle."

The words rumble against my ear, but only after Rufus immediately obeys do I look up and realize I'm crouched right up against the burly dog trainer. So close I can feel the heat of him. I straighten quickly, ignoring his quizzical stare as I put space between us.

"Are you—?"

"I've got to get going," I say, focusing hard on gathering my things.

When he doesn't answer, I make the mistake of looking up into those sea-green eyes, which swirl with curiosity and something else I can't identify.

"Thanks for um . . . working with him," I say, shifting my attention to Rufus.

The thoughts crossing his features fade, and he nods. "Sure. Tomorrow, you can try running him through the commands too."

My jaw drops. I don't even know where to start with that. "Me? Tomorrow?"

He folds his arms over his muscular chest, the sleeves of his Henley straining against his generous biceps like he's posing for some NSFW dog training calendar. "You're eager for him to stop chewing up your things?"

"Yes." I flatten my mouth into a line, trying hard to picture my couch and not my vibrator while talking with Drew Forbes.

"Then he needs activity. A sense of purpose."

"Okay, fine, but I can't do this *every* day."

His lip curls. "Did you eat today? Breathe air?" His gaze rakes over the bag holding my laptop. "Did you spend time doing meaningful work?"

I rest my hands on my hips. "What's your point?"

He steps closer, eyes darkening. "It's no different for him. You can't just feed and walk him when you feel like it. He needs attention, he needs *love*, just as much as he needs food and water." He takes another step, close enough that I have to tilt my head up to look at him. "You have to *show up* for him. Every day. You can't just leave him behind when things get hard."

This last bit feels like an accusation. The corners of my eyes prick as I curl my hands into fists. Because I have a feeling we're not just talking about the dog.

"I *never*—"

But the words die on my lips, and my chest fissures. Because what if he's right?

I always thought I did everything I could to fight for Kyle, but what if I didn't? What if I could have done something different? He pushed me away—he left *me*. But why didn't I chase after him? Why didn't I try harder?

I close my eyes, tears burning beneath my lids.

But it doesn't matter. Nothing can bring him back now.

I clear my throat, my voice coming out low and steady. "I will give Rufus what he needs."

For a moment we just stand there, too close. Drew, me, and our mutual ghost.

Then the breeze shifts between the trees, and Rufus raises his nose to scent the air. I lay my hand on his head automatically, and I'm surprised by the near-immediate calm that settles over me. I step back, pick up my bag, and loop the leash over my thumb. "We'll be here tomorrow. Same time."

Wednesday, March 24, 20__, 11:59 PM

To: **Kyle.Forbes@mail.com**

From: **Caprice_Phipps@mail.com**

Subject: Re: Re: Re: Re: no subject

Dear Kyle,

Your brother is a bigger dick than I ever imagined. He's a jerk and a bully and I guess I understand now why you didn't want him to have Rufus. But did you really think *I* could do better? What if I don't?

I'm just so scared I'm going to screw up again.

C

CHAPTER
TWENTY-TWO

"Do you want me to come with you this afternoon?" Lydia asks through my earbuds as I exit my building. "It could be like a supervised custody visit. I could just sit and glare at Drew so he stays off your back."

I exhale, simultaneously grateful for her fierce loyalty and determined not to ask her *any* more favors. "Not necessary, but thank you. He can give me all the free training he wants. I'm not giving Rufus to him."

She chuckles. "I'm just . . . still trying to wrap my head around you as a willing dog owner."

I mutter under my breath, and for a second I want to tell her the rest. How Drew didn't just try to take the dog again, but also insinuated that I abandoned Kyle.

"Is it helping at least?" Lydia asks. "Have you seen any progress?"

I glance down at Rufus walking right at my heel. Between taking him for early runs the last two mornings and his structured training every afternoon, he *has* been more mellow. I caught him shredding the laces of one of my Hokas Wednesday night, but now that I think about it, no one even complained about him whining at work yesterday. "I mean, I hate to suggest Drew Forbes was right about anything, but the dog does seem happier."

"Good. And if it means it might be safe to replace your couch, who cares?"

"Yeah." My chest lightens. "I might actually be able to do that soon. The Vanderpool article has gone totally viral again. Last I checked, it was on *BuzzFeed* and *HuffPo*, and *Denver Editorial* even reposted and linked back to my original article. Randall also followed through on the raise he promised."

"Caprice!" Lydia squeals. "I *knew* you'd do it!"

"Eh," I say quickly. "The trick is, I need to *keep* writing stuff like that. But it's been nice, proving I could do it again." Rufus's head perks up, and I follow his gaze to a hooded person shuffling down the sidewalk. With a gentle tug on the leash, I cross the street to avoid them.

"Also, I hate to admit this, but I do feel safer with him."

She hesitates. "With Drew?"

"*What?* No, Rufus."

"Tell me more." Her voice drops and somewhere in the background, I hear a door close. "Something didn't happen, did it?"

I swallow. Both grateful for her best friend intuition and annoyed because I didn't want to worry her with this part. "There were some nasty social media comments and a couple emails after the feature was published, of course. It's creepy, but as the police told Randall, there's no overt threat."

"Are you okay, though?" Lydia says soberly. "You don't sound okay."

"I'm fine," I say, relieved she can't see my face. "I've got Cujo here. I'm totally safe as long as anyone who tries to mess with me doesn't think to bring a Kong toy."

She hums for a second like she's trying to decide whether to believe me.

"Well, I read the feature and it was phenomenal," she finally says. "I'm still in shock that Colin *Vanderpool* is such a slime. He was a major donor to Colorado Humane. But I loved how you presented it from his wife's perspective. I—I'm glad you wrote it."

If anything could reaffirm for me that publishing the article was the right decision, it's this. Because Lydia's one of the people I wrote it for—one of the women who deserved better. And her voice matters to me more than any malicious email.

"Thanks, Lyd," I say, quickly pivoting subjects. "Anyway, how are the birth classes going? Have they found a way to simulate childbirth pain for fathers? I've heard kidney stones are effective."

Her bemused laugh tinkles in my ears, and I quietly treasure it. Because a year ago, I wasn't sure I'd ever hear her laugh that way again.

"They're going well," she says, ignoring my barb. "We met a couple also expecting a little girl and sort of scheduled our first play date."

"Uh . . . do you like, sit with your bellies next to each other, or wait till they're actually born?"

"It won't be until they're like two months old." She snorts, then quickly adds, "But I'm sure it'll be adorable."

My interest in babies is somewhere below my interest in dogs, but this is so bewildering, I have to ask. "What exactly happens at an infant playdate?"

"Um . . . I'm not actually sure." She hesitates. "Maybe I'll ask if they want to bring their dog to play with Heartthrob so it isn't boring."

I smile. It's been hard to imagine Lydia with a baby in tow. I know things will change once her little girl is born, but hearing her focus this major life event around dogs the way she does everything else is somehow reassuring.

"Okay, well, you go get on Pinterest so you can plan your new mom charcuterie," I say, approaching the doors of *Mile High Observer*. "I'm almost to work."

"Sounds good," she says, already distracted by an employee speaking in the background. "Keep me posted on everything—and my offer still stands to chaperone you and Drew!"

Randall meets me at the reception desk as soon as I walk in, and my mood immediately falters. The full cup of coffee he puts in my hand does nothing to distract me from the grim look in his eyes.

"Caprice. Can we chat?"

My stomach drops further when he doesn't even greet Rufus.

I bypass my desk, following him directly to his office, where he closes the door. For a moment, we just look at each other in silence.

"I got an anonymous call early this morning," he says. "A woman who wanted to warn you that Colin Vanderpool isn't the only guy behind Unmatched."

I have the wherewithal to set the coffee on his desk before my butt hits one of the chairs. He takes in my facial expression and continues.

"She said there's at least one more person she knows of." He swallows. "And suggested you be very careful."

My pulse roars through my ears. Randall's mouth is still moving, but I don't hear what he says. The room feels like it's full of water. I can't breathe. I manage a slow blink, but struggle to form words. Finally, I choke out one very stupid question.

"Who was it?"

He just looks at me. And if I could erase the look in his eyes permanently from my memory, I would, because it's pure disappointment. He takes his seat behind the desk and runs a hand over his face. And somehow, this mortifies me enough to kick me back into action.

"Mimi Vanderpool never mentioned anyone else," I say. "Never even hinted."

"She might not have known."

My boss's lips are a thin line. He doesn't even have to say what we're both thinking. *I should have checked.* I took her at her word; I wasn't careful. A rookie mistake when, as a woman of color, I have even less room for error than everyone else. And now I not only look like a fool, but I might have put myself at additional risk.

"Caprice?" Randall says from far away.

My face burns so hot I can't bring myself to look at him. I pick up one of the stuffed toys he now leaves in his office for Rufus. This one's a squeaky coffee cup with an idiotic smiling face.

"Told you I'd be better off as a barista."

Randall lets out an impatient snort. "You know my opinion on latte art."

My vision darkens. "Yeah. You said it would be a waste of my 'talent.' But now we know I never had any in the first place." I hurl the stuffed toy across the room, where it bounces off a picture frame, knocking it askew. The heat instantly drains from my face as my actions catch up with my brain. "Sorry, that was—"

"Understandable?" Randall's eyes follow Rufus as he jumps up and runs after the toy.

I let out a breath, trying to slow my pulse. I've worked with Randall for five years. I consider him a friend, an ally, and a mentor. But I know better than to show aggression like that in the workplace.

"Sorry," I say again as the dog returns, tail wagging.

My boss stares at his desk. "This says nothing about your

talent—only your research." He meets my eyes. "Have there been any more messages?"

My hands start shaking. I fold them in my lap, but it doesn't help. "One. Early this morning."

You'll keep that pretty nose where it belongs if you know what's good for you.

The words land differently now, knowing it likely wasn't from Colin Vanderpool. That there's someone like him still out there . . . someone I need to 'be careful' of.

Randall frowns. "Send it to me. Keep sharing anything that feels remotely off, and I'll keep passing them along to my contact at DPD. We'll need to keep a close eye on all communications as you dig deeper."

"Dig deeper?" I blink at him. "I don't think so, Randall. You can keep me on the assignment desk. I'll write staff articles, maybe some horoscopes if you want to get fancy. But I'm done with investigative features—especially about Unmatched."

My boss folds his hands and looks at me straight-faced. "No, you're not."

"Um, yes, I am? If there was any remaining doubt that I'm not cut out for journalism, this is proof. I thought I could write about things that matter, but I got in way over my head."

He shakes his head. "Caprice, this is the tip of an iceberg."

I bristle. Because that's exactly the problem. "Yeah, I wrote and published an entire story without realizing there was more to it. Not only do I look like a fool, but I might be in even more danger than I even realized. That's a hard stop—I'm not willing to go any further."

"But this is how you get smarter. Safer. The more you practice, the better you'll be."

"No one gets smarter if they're dead." I snort. "Put Brian on it. I'm not interested."

My boss's caterpillar eyebrows confer with each other, and

I can tell my words aren't sinking in. "What was in the email?"

I frown, curling my fists in my lap. "No offense, Randall, but I don't think you understand what this is like. Just *existing* as a woman, let alone a woman journalist whose skin isn't white. I already live in a state of constant hyper-vigilance. Looking over my shoulder. Always taking different routes home. Weighing whether it's safe to go places alone, or just open my apartment door. Even when there are people around, I have to weigh whether they'd help if I needed them or cause me more harm. And that's *without* drawing further attention to myself with my writing.

"Then add in uncomfortable professional situations— inappropriate comments about my hair and skin. Being touched or asked on dates after interviews with men who don't like the word 'no.' Making up boyfriends or commitments because it feels safer than angering a man, but still having to give them my number because they're contacts. Worrying they'll escalate if I block them. I'm exhausted—tired of always being on my guard. I don't need to make things worse for myself when I can't even handle the basics of my job."

His mouth turns down, following the shape of his goatee as he considers my words. "You're right. I don't understand what that's like, and I know I never could," he says. "But you're wrong about the job. You're perfect at it. You've made some mistakes, but your instincts are good and your voice is powerful. You've already shown the world you could expose one asshole, and now you're going to prove that none of them are safe."

"But *I* don't feel safe." I draw my knees to my chest, swallowing around the lump in my throat. "Technically, these guys haven't done anything illegal. They made an app for cheaters; they're douchebags. But it's not like they're going to jail. There's no clear point where it'll end for me."

"What makes you so sure there's nothing illegal?" Randall asks.

I roll my eyes. "Last I checked, cheating was reprehensible, not unlawful."

"Yeah." He nods. "But it kind of makes you wonder . . ."

Our eyes meet, and his question bores into me until I do exactly what I just said I wasn't going to do. "Why are they trying so hard to push me away?" I ask. "Is there something else going on?"

My throat goes dry even as a subtle sparkle returns to my boss's eye.

"Randall, I can't—" My voice breaks.

I close my eyes, my thoughts suddenly on Theo, tracking down bad guys somewhere thousands of miles away. When I open my eyes again, Rufus has planted himself next to my chair, and my hand is buried in his neck fur. He fixes me with his golden eyes, and if he weren't just a dog, I'd think he actually looked concerned.

"You mentioned you've been training Rufus with someone?" Randall asks.

I look at the ceiling. "Yeah, another one of the aforementioned assholes."

His brows draw together. "The trainer? Does he make you uncomfortable too?"

I open my mouth, but stop to consider. For all his crabbiness and bad attitude, I have to admit Drew does not make me feel unsafe. Kind of the opposite. I had every reason to be wary of him at first, but the night he stormed into my apartment, he kept his distance. He wasn't pleasant, but he never acted creepy or tried to touch me. He's texted me since, but only about the dog. I think about waking up on my floor with his hand over mine the morning after the storm, and while that memory ought to be intolerable, oddly, it felt safer than waking up next to any man since Kyle. My face warms.

Drew's never been threatening at all. He just clearly hates my guts.

"No," I finally say, not wanting to explain our shared tragedy to my boss. "I mean, it's uncomfortable, but not in the same way. He's really good with Rufus. I think he's just a jerk to everyone."

"Hmm." Randall nods. "In my experience, people who work with animals tend to prefer their company to other people."

"That's probably for the best." I snort. But when I glance at Rufus all I can think is how relaxed Drew seemed kneeling on the ground while the dog licked his face until his glasses fell off.

"Did you ever find out what kind of training Rufus received with the military?"

"Uh . . . no." I actually don't even know who to ask besides Theo.

"I think most of them are used to sniff out explosives or drugs, but he might've had some protection training." Randall shrugs. "Maybe he could help keep the bad guys away."

I look at Rufus, whose tongue currently hangs out the side of his mouth. If I hadn't personally seen how terrifying he was the times he lunged at Darius and Brian, I might laugh this off. But then I remember the creepy guy in the hall outside my apartment, and the way Rufus stared at the door and growled until the hall was empty. I find myself digging my fingers deeper into his fur. And even when I realize it, I don't let go.

"I guess I could ask his trainer."

"It doesn't solve the safety issue," Randall says. "But it might help."

I let out a low breath, rising and picking up my bag, trying not to think too hard about how Randall managed to turn a conversation about safety concerns into distilled motivation.

Against my better judgment, my mind is already churning through possibilities, wondering who Colin Vanderpool's "partner" might be. I'm itching to send emails. Make phone calls. Start digging.

"Thanks for the coffee," I say, swiping the paper cup off his desk to take with me.

He smiles, managing not to look *too* pleased. "For what it's worth, it was made by a very bored-looking barista."

CHAPTER
TWENTY-THREE

Washington Park is surprisingly empty on Friday evenings.
It's one of the city's larger green spaces, and during the week, you can hardly walk across the grass without dodging a rogue ball or game of one kind or another. Usually, there are volleyball nets everywhere, yoga classes, groups of people playing spikeball, families having picnics. But the whole place is cleared out this evening. A few joggers and dog walkers pass through, but the crowds and parties are absent, the lawn abandoned. I suppose everyone is either out at clubs or on dates—maybe touring art galleries on South Santa Fe Drive.

I cringe, remembering my mom's invitation. I love her, and I'm happy she's finally doing something for herself, but I'm almost grateful to have an excuse not to go. Art galleries really aren't my thing—too much small talk and schmoozing.

Lucky for me, I'm on a double date with anxiety and my dog.

Actually, I will *not* call it that. Not with Drew here.

I adjust the leash in my hand as I make a turn, scanning the path for the umpteenth time before focusing back on Rufus.

"Are you expecting someone?" Drew asks.

I frown. "No, why?"

"You keep looking around like you are."

My face heats. We've been moving Rufus through a single routine for the last twenty minutes. The same one we've been repeating with him all week. Walking him back and forth between the trees, having him sit, lie down, or walk at our heels. Drew hardly speaks except to address the dog, so I've been lost in my head pretty much since we got here. Ruminating on some ideas I want to follow up on about Unmatched. Worrying about what else I might find next time I open my email. And apparently keeping an unconscious eye out for stray bad guys.

I didn't expect him to notice.

"Just practicing situational awareness," I say. "Doubt you'd understand—not really a Y chromosome thing."

His brows draw together. He opens his mouth like he wants to say something, then exhales instead. "Why don't we run him through one more time and call it a night?"

"Thank God," I mutter under my breath. It has been a grind squeezing Rufus's training in on top of everything else each day. Don't get me wrong, my personal life has devolved into a sad rotation of dog walking, work, YouTube strength training videos, ramen noodles, and Netflix. But at least I can do most of that from the security of my locked apartment.

This week was a lot, though, and I've been looking forward to having a couple of days to myself. I'll hunker down tomorrow, touch base with a few contacts I hope will send my research in the right direction, and catch up on a couple of staff articles on local events I promised Randall. Maybe do some living room Pilates. If she's feeling up to it, Lydia might want to dog walk with me. I just really need a couple days where I don't *also* have to see Drew Forbes.

We move through all the training motions again, the same way we have all week—him watching as I march between the trees with Rufus at my heel. Although this time I could swear Drew's gaze follows me as closely as the dog. I stop, use the voice and hand signals he's shown me to have Rufus sit, lie down, and stay. I walk away, ensuring he doesn't move, then give him the command to release. The dog runs to me, wagging his tail when I offer his tug toy like it's the greatest thing since dry kibble.

Drew nods, looking satisfied. Then he pushes his glasses up his nose and looks at me. "Okay, that's good. Although I'd like to try something different with him this weekend."

This weekend.

I blink at him, searching his burly frame for meaning while I try to process his words. He's disrupted his endless rotation of chest-hugging Henleys in favor of a light blue button-down today, and the change would almost be funny if his forearms didn't look so good with the rolled-up sleeves, and if he hadn't just said what I think he just said.

I clear my throat. "I'm sorry, did you mean Saturday or Sunday?"

My annoyance must creep onto my face because the corners of his mouth pull down.

"Both," he says. "Now that we've earned Rufus's trust and he wants to work for us, it's important to maintain consistency. Though I can do more with him if we go to my facility."

My fantasies of not having to look into Drew Forbes's chiseled face for forty-eight hours flit away like a traumatized butterfly.

"Is that really necessary?" I ask.

He has the audacity to look nonplussed. "Rufus is making progress. We don't want to lose this momentum."

"He's not going to notice if we skip one day."

The man bristles, stepping closer. "Because you want to lock him away in that jail cell of an apartment while you do what?"

"Sorry if I have a *life*," I say, even though it feels like a lie. "But I have stuff going on that has nothing to do with pet ownership."

"Then leave him with me," he says.

"No."

"Why?"

I fold my arms, mostly because I don't have an answer other than *I don't like you.* "I don't need you to be my dog sitter."

"I didn't suggest you need me." He glances at Rufus. "But he does."

I roll my eyes. "Look, fine. We can meet *one* day to train him, not both. And I'm not leaving him with you. It's been a busy week and I—I just have a bunch of work to catch up on."

"Oh, yeah." I swear I see his skin prickle. "Saw the article you wrote."

For a moment, I blink. At no point has my writing about Unmatched intersected with our uneasy training relationship, but here he is dragging them together because why not—the only thing that could make our dynamic more unpleasant would be having to endure his criticism of my work. He probably wants to unleash some opinion about how men are allowed to cheat if they want.

"Lovely, thanks for being a reader," I say, trying to shut him down before he starts. "Subscribe to the *Observer* for more exclusive features."

"It was well written." He says this as if it physically pains him to compliment me, and I'm so surprised I almost laugh.

"Yeah, well, have fun debating my content with your girlfriend."

"My . . . what?" His brows draw together behind his glasses like he doesn't follow.

I nearly snort, because of course. Why did I ever think this prickly man would have a woman in his life who willingly spends time with him? I turn away, shaking my head, but as I walk to collect my things from under a tree, a strange warm sensation thuds through my chest.

"Never mind," I snap. "I should go."

I sling my bag over my shoulder, but when I look back, his jaw moves like he's chewing on something. Finally, he says, "My parents will be complaining to the *Observer* . . . I thought you should know."

Now I'm the one not following. I tilt my head, debating whether to ask what he means—until all at once my brain makes the leap. "Oh. The scholarship article?"

He gives me this look like *what else*, and I let my hair fall over my face, fumbling with Rufus's leash. Maybe because it took me a moment, or because his compliment wasn't what I thought it was. Honestly, I had been trying to forget I wrote that piece. I'd done my assignment, included the correct names and information—though I focused most on Kenyon Riley's accomplishments and dreams. I'm not surprised the Doctors Forbes were unhappy.

"Well, they can get in line. Most of our mail is from people griping about our coverage," I say through my teeth. "I think I exercised a great deal of restraint about the award, considering Kyle never wanted to be a doctor."

"No." He nods slowly. "That's what our parents wanted."

Drew's voice is surprisingly soft as he says this. I can't decipher the look on his face, but his words shake loose something I've been ruminating on for a while.

"Didn't *you* go to med school?" I ask. "Why are you a dog trainer and not a physician?"

The look he gives me could freezer burn a glacier. But when he doesn't answer, I ball my fists and step toward him.

"What? Is it some paltry posthumous gesture just like your parents' award? Is opening the business of *Kyle's* dreams supposed to atone for the fact that he's gone?" My lip curls. "That's some self-sacrifice. Maybe if you'd tried it when he was alive, he'd still be here. Probably running it better than you."

I stare right at him, hoping he'll dispute me. I've spent the last year simmering in my feelings about Kyle while biting back replies to unwanted opinions on all my writing. I am ready to unleash.

But it's like watching an iron curtain come down behind his eyes. Drew mutters quietly to Rufus and slips him a treat. Then he collects the few training items scattered around us in the grass.

All I can do is watch, growing more and more annoyed. I want him to grovel, say he's sorry, beg forgiveness—for *both* of us losing Kyle.

So I can stop blaming myself.

Instead, he just turns to go, speaking once over his shoulder in a cracked voice.

"I'll be at K9 Academy tomorrow. Seven p.m."

CHAPTER
TWENTY-FOUR

"Ms. Phipps?" a woman's deep, mature voice greets me over
the phone Saturday morning. "What can I do for you?"

"Yes, hello, Mrs. Vanderpool." I sit up. Her assistant left
me hanging so long, I almost forgot who I was waiting for.
"Thank you for taking my call."

"It's Richards now—Mimi Richards. I'm reverting to my
maiden name."

"Oh, okay . . ." Congratulations doesn't seem like the right
sentiment, but I jot the name amid the notes on my kitchen
counter. "I was just calling to check in now that the article's in
print."

"That's kind of you," she says distractedly. "I believe I
sent an email expressing my gratitude."

"Yes." I clear my throat, hoping my speech doesn't warble
with the pulse pounding in my throat. "I received that, thank
you. I wanted to see how you're doing. Things must be kind
of intense right now."

"That's one way to put it," she says, startling me with a
cackle. "Colin has endured so much fallout the last few days,
I've had to make popcorn."

"Oh—" I try to echo the levity in her voice. "But . . . you've been all right?"

She snorts. "Better than I've been in years."

Keep that pretty nose where it belongs.

"Well, that's great to hear." I clear my throat again, genuinely relieved she hasn't had to deal with the kinds of messages I've received. But something about her tone makes me pause. "If you don't mind, I have one follow-up question I'd like to ask."

"For another feature?"

"Not exactly. I'm just hoping to clear up some confusion."

She hums. "Just so we're clear, I don't consent to another interview. Anything I say now stays completely off record."

"Uh . . . of course." I straighten on my stool, trying to rein in my surprise. "This will be between us."

"Good," she says, voice clipped. "What would you like to know?"

I take a breath, no longer confident I can navigate this conversation. "Well, this week after the feature came out, I learned your husband had a partner working with him on Unmatched."

She doesn't immediately respond, so I continue.

"I have to admit, I was confused," I say carefully. "Did you know Colin had a business partner when we met for our interview?"

She sighs. "Honestly? Yes. I just didn't really care."

My chest flares at her words, but I keep my voice even. "I might have written the feature differently if I'd had that information, ma'am."

"Your article was perfect," she says. "Everyone knows the truth now. I've been offered nothing but sympathy since I filed for divorce."

"Sounds like you got exactly what you wanted," I say, trying to force a smile onto my face.

"Is there something else I can help you with, Ms. Phipps?"

Rufus's muzzle slides into my lap. Usually when he does this, I'm quick to push him away. But I take a moment to stroke his ears as I gather myself. "Yes. I have some real concerns about Mr. Vanderpool's business partners. Do you have any idea who they might be?"

She's quiet for so long, I pull the phone away from my ear to ensure we weren't disconnected.

"Sorry, I can't help you."

"Mrs. Vander—"

"*Richards,*" she corrects. "Sorry, I have no further information, and I have to run. Thank you for your efforts, Ms. Phipps. Please don't contact me again."

After my first phone call gets me absolutely nowhere, I circle the question I wrote down after my meeting with Randall: *Is there something* else *going on with Unmatched?* Then I pour myself another cup of coffee and change my approach.

"Denver County Sheriff's Office, this is Maya."

"Hey Deputy, it's Caprice at *Mile High Observer.*"

"Caprice! I haven't seen you at spin class lately. Did you switch gyms?"

I cut my eyes to Rufus, curled up on the wreck of my couch. "No, I've just been tied up with some stuff. I'm hoping to get back in the rhythm soon."

"I totally get that. What can I help you with today?"

"Actually, I was just thinking about a conversation we had last fall," I say, flipping my notebook to a fresh page. "I think it was right after the Boulder Marathon. You were telling me about some jerk drugging women he met on dating apps?"

Maya snarls. "Oh, I definitely remember that. Pretty sure that dirtbag's case is still pending trial."

"Could I request copies of the police reports on him?"

"It would be my pleasure," she says, tapping at a

keyboard in the background. "But didn't *Denver Editorial* already run a big story about that?"

"Yep. I'm not really interested in him specifically," I say, scanning my notes. "I'm taking a closer look at the dating apps themselves. Has the sheriff's office had to deal with them directly at all?"

"Unfortunately, yes." She scoffs. "Which is one reason I personally won't use any of them."

I straighten in my chair. "Care to tell me more?"

Maya hums into the phone. "They're like a haven for predators. The guys sign up, make a charming profile to lure their victims. And once they get what they want, they delete the whole thing and start over. I followed up with one victim who reported a man she met on Ignite. He'd drugged and assaulted her, then created a new profile two days later. When she contacted the company to flag him, they never even replied to her. They just deleted his original account—*and* hers. So she couldn't even access their chat history, which she needed for evidence."

"*What?* After he assaulted her? Is that even legal?"

"People sign liability agreements when they use these apps." She sniffs. "And the companies make money no matter what happens."

I pick my jaw off the floor and sit on that a minute. "Any chance that victim would be willing to speak with me, Maya?"

"Maybe." She pauses. "But I can't give you her info."

"Right, of course." I rub my hand over my face. "Can I request the report for that case too?"

"It'll be redacted, but sure. I guarantee, though, if you ask around, you'll find plenty of people just like her."

I am so antsy to run by midday, Rufus almost can't keep up on our way to the park. It's the weekend and crowded when we get there, of course. But we fall in with the other joggers along the gravel path, running intermittent sprints around both lakes and the fire station on the north end of the green space. I do jumping lunges the last half mile until my thighs feel like they're going to scream and fall off. After a brief stop at a drinking fountain for both of us, Rufus sacks out in the grass to watch me stretch.

I must've sent twenty emails this morning. I reached out to every contact I had from the original Unmatched feature. Every jilted wife and girlfriend, every person who'd even claimed to have a connection to the dating site. This included Marisol Lopez, a friend of Lydia's whose marriage did not survive after my first article went to print. She was *very* helpful the first time around, but has been frosty ever since.

I'm staring at the sky, debating between walking the dog to Lydia's to drag her out for coffee or heading home to do some upper body lifting, when a strange number rings on my phone. These days, unknown callers tend to put me on guard, but I always have one very good reason to answer rather than let them go to voicemail.

"Bruh."

"Reece! You are not going to believe the weather we're having here."

This is a joke. Since Theo can never even hint at his actual location, he makes shit up every time he calls.

"Let me guess. You're sipping a cocktail on a beautiful white sand beach, it's ninety degrees, the waves are gentle, and a gorgeous girl in a grass skirt is waving a palm frond over your body to keep you cool."

"You ever consider a side hustle as a psychic?"

I snort.

"Good. Cause I'm legit down in a shelter riding out a category four hurricane."

"Oh, hey, Hollywood called," I deadpan. "They said to keep your day job."

He snickers. "Just checking in—I only have a few minutes."

This is also bullshit. Theo never calls without a reason. But I play along.

"Not much to report here. Except next time you want to crash, you'll be sleeping on my floor, courtesy of the patriarchy's best friend."

"So, you and Rufus are warming up to each other?"

I glance at the dog rolling in the grass by my feet. "No comment."

But then the air shifts ever so slightly over the line, or the satellite, or whatever.

"Listen, sis, I just had to call because I read a fascinating article about this rich lady in Denver who outed her husband for being a total cheating douchebag."

And . . . there it is. I sit up in the grass, looping Rufus's leash around my wrist and adjusting my earbuds. "Sounds like quality reporting."

"It was excellent. I only have mild concerns about the author's sanity."

I let out a slow breath and drop the pretense. "I think we've hashed this out before? You literally chase down bad guys with guns for a living, and I . . . write words. Whose mental health do we question?"

"Have you looked at the comments section? What the fuck are you doing?"

I close my eyes. "I don't know, trying to live my life. Have a career."

Failing at both?

"What's the stalker situation?"

I pull myself to my feet and Rufus jumps up, taking his position at my flank. "With all due respect, Theo, you've got to let me handle this. You can't micromanage my safety from wherever the fuck you are on the other side of the world."

The line is quiet for so long, I'm afraid the call might've dropped.

"I already lost my best friend, Caprice," he finally says. "If something happens to you . . ."

It's difficult to breathe with the lump swelling in my throat.

"What Kyle did wasn't your fault, Theo. He wasn't your responsibility. And neither am I."

Something cold touches my palm, and I look down to see Rufus gazing up at me like a soldier reporting for duty.

"Besides. I literally can't go anywhere without this nutso dog. He comes to work with me every day. I can't even leave him alone in my apartment."

Theo makes a sound in his throat. "You take him everywhere?"

"Um, he won't even let me close the door to pee."

"So you're keeping him, then."

He doesn't phrase it as a question, but I stare at Rufus, wondering. Thinking about Kyle.

I'm just trying to protect you.

Problem is, I never figured out what he was protecting me from.

"Maybe." I rub the soft part of Rufus's ear, my voice cracking. "I'm thinking about it."

TWENTY-FIVE

It takes nearly all my physical and emotional strength to drag my feet toward K9 Academy Saturday evening. After chasing leads all day *and* being reminded of the risks to my personal safety, I think I'd rather have laser hair removal on my vulva than spend my free time with Drew. But despite the fact that he got a run today, Rufus started pacing my apartment, looking bored, at five o'clock. And I just couldn't bring myself to put on my headphones and drown him out. Plus, I do feel a *little* bad for ripping into Drew yesterday. Whatever went down between the brothers years ago, he still lost Kyle as much as I did.

When Rufus and I reach the front door of the training school, the door is locked. Dark shades are pulled low over all the windows, and the lights are off. I hesitate, glancing up and down the street before checking the time, even though I just looked at my phone. It's almost seven, right when Drew said to arrive. But maybe after the things I said, he had a change of heart. I hover my thumb over the screen, trying to decide whether to call him, knock on the window, or go home. At least if he's decided to stand me up, that's one more reason never to see him again.

An elderly couple strolls down the sidewalk as I simmer in annoyance. I have emails to catch up on. A staff article to write about chalk art downtown. Also, it's getting dark.

The back of my neck prickles and I shuffle my feet, looking both ways down the street again. I'm not far from home, but these days I like to stick close to my building once the sun goes down.

Rufus whines next to me like he's picking up on my unease, which does nothing to help.

I roll my eyes and raise my knuckles to rap on the glass just as the door swings open. And suddenly I'm staring up into Drew Forbes's scowling face. Except it's not a scowl—not quite. There's no line between his brows or laser eyes. On the contrary, the green of his irises is . . . I wouldn't say warm, but maybe something this side of polar? It's so unlike his usual expression, I forget to speak for a second.

"Good. You're on time," he says, voice heavy with the implication he expected I wouldn't be. All my second-guessing about his expression or what I said yesterday evaporates—he's back to acting like the asshole I expect. I purse my lips, ready to snap that *he* left *us* waiting. But then he steps aside, and the dog immediately rushes through the door and bounces all over him like he's the fun, playful dad and I'm the strict mom who never lets him have any fun.

Drew produces a tug toy seemingly out of thin air, and Rufus grabs on, pulling back and growling, wagging his tail so hard I have to step out of the way. The oversized man is wearing cargo pants and one of those form-fitting Henleys *again*—green waffle weave this time, someone kill me—and I have to snap my eyes back to the dog to refocus on why we're here.

I drop the leash, letting it drag on the floor while I look around. K9 Academy feels different this time. More cavernous and echoey. I guess obviously because it's night, and it's closed, and no one else is here. Drew moves behind me and flips the deadbolt on the door with a click. I tense, my fingers automatically grazing the zipper of my belt bag where my pepper spray is stowed. But he's so focused on the dog, he just moves around me like I'm not even here. He gives Rufus the "out" command to release the toy, then tosses it into the training area and tells him to "get it." The dog complies like it's everything he lives for. I roll my eyes, but make a mental note to try and up my game when we play this at home. Usually I throw his toys across the room just so he'll leave me alone.

The two of them pass through the little gate, and my pulse spikes as I follow, entering the area where everything went sideways last time. Without a class of people and dogs losing their minds at the sight of us, the training area feels bigger. In my memory, it had been mostly empty, but now there's an assortment of equipment arranged like a miniature equestrian arena, with obstacles and jumps set up in a kind of semicircle. It looks a lot like places Kyle would go to work dogs in high school. Only nicer.

I swallow hard. This place would've been a dream to him.

Drew walks Rufus to the center of the room, and I set an alarm on my watch for one hour, determined not to give the man a second more of my time. Then I lean against the half wall, settling in to watch him do whatever he has planned for the dog.

They take their positions and Drew removes the leash, speaking in a low tone. The next thing I know, Rufus is leaping through a suspended colorful tire like it's nothing, following Drew's direction to the next obstacle, which is a jump that resembles a small section of fence. When he clears that with ease, he looks back to Drew, who walks over to a low collapsible tunnel that Rufus shoots into, coming out the other end with his mouth open and eyes bright, like he's enjoying himself. From there, Drew directs him to a tall wooden structure that looks like a ladder. I'm not sure what the dog is supposed to do here, but apparently Rufus knows because he climbs up one side of it and down the other like he's done it hundreds of times.

It occurs to me, watching him go through these motions at Drew's command, that he probably has. I never got to visit where Kyle worked after he enlisted and was accepted into the Military Working Dog Handler training program in San Antonio, but I suppose it might've looked something like this.

The two of them continue, and Rufus easily clears every obstacle and hurdle. Even climbing onto this big seesaw-looking thing, walking up the incline until it tips forward under his weight, then down the other side and back to the floor without hesitation.

They run through the entire course several times, Rufus gaining confidence and speed with each go-round, wagging his tail with his mouth wide like he's grinning. When they finally come to a stop, Drew gets out the tug toy again and Rufus grabs it instantly, pulling back on it with his entire body, eyes bright, growling and jerking his head back and forth, trying to shake the life out of it.

I don't even realize I'm smiling until a laugh escapes my lips.

"Good boy," Drew rumbles in a low tenor. "That's right, who's a good boy?"

My eyes drift from Rufus to the muscular arms wielding the toy. Drew has pushed his sleeves up to his elbows, which has the effect of enhancing both his forearms *and* biceps. And when he slides his glasses up his nose, his eyes are alight— mouth pulled up in a lopsided smile like he's enjoying this as much as the dog.

Just like when we first arrived, his expression, his whole *demeanor*, is suddenly so different he doesn't seem like the same man. Not the cranky dog trainer. Not Kyle's misanthropic brother. Someone I don't know at all.

Finally, he gives the "out" command and stows the toy out

of Rufus's sight. Drew runs a hand through his tousled hair, then turns, smile still on his face. And when his gaze lands on me, something thuds hard and low in my chest.

"If it's okay with you, I'd like to try something with him," he says.

It takes a moment before I register *if it's okay with you*. He isn't barking orders or assuming—he's asking my permission. I shrug and nod at the same time, confused. "Sure. He, uh . . . looks like he's having a good time."

He nods, then reattaches the leash and hands it to me, escorting us both to the reception area. "Okay, just wait here a few minutes," he says, disappearing into a back room.

I pull out my phone to check for replies to any of the emails I sent this afternoon. There aren't any, but I wrinkle my brow when I see a voicemail from an unknown number twenty minutes ago. My phone never rang.

Drew returns and opens the gate just as I finish listening to the message. Or trying to, anyway. It was a two-minute recording of empty air, and what *might* have been someone breathing.

"Everything okay?" he asks, eyes pinging between the phone in my hand and my face.

"Uh . . . yeah. Just a spam call, I think." I lock the screen and shove the device back into my pocket, but my hands are shaking when he reaches out to take the leash. "W-what are you doing with him now?"

"Scent work," he says, looking down at Rufus the way Lydia would, like he understands what this means.

The dog gazes back at him like he's just waiting to be given a command.

"Okay, Rufus. Let's go check," Drew orders in a clipped, authoritative tone.

The dog immediately moves into action, rushing back toward the agility course. Only he approaches it totally differently this time. Rather than making the jumps and navigating the obstacles, he runs around the equipment with his nose to the ground.

It takes me a few moments of watching before I realize he's doing the sniff-every-corner thing he does every time we enter my apartment.

"Check," Drew says, walking alongside him, holding the leash and pointing to a few specific spots around the room. "Check here."

At each place he points, Rufus zeros in to give a more thorough sniff before moving on. Eventually, they make their way to a set of lockers on one of the far walls.

"Check here," Drew repeats, and Rufus does his thing.

But instead of sniffing the metal doors and moving on like everywhere else, his whole body goes alert. He focuses on them, poking his nose all around, clearly ecstatic about something. He looks up at Drew, tail wagging furiously, and this time he sits.

"Good boy, *yes*," Drew says in a subdued tone, immediately producing a Kong toy on a rope, dropping it right between Rufus and the locker door he's obsessed with. Rufus clamps the Kong in his teeth, looking delighted while Drew praises and plays with him.

He hands me the leash and removes an object—presumably the source of the scent—from the locker and returns it to the back room while Rufus is busy with his toy.

When he enters the training room again, he's looking at me. Not with a scowl, but something more like a question.

"What did you put in there?" I ask.

He shrugs. "A scent the military uses for training. To his nose, it mimics explosives."

My mouth drops open, but when I look at Rufus rolling happily on the floor with his reward, something finally clicks.

"I . . . I think I get it now."

Drew's brows rise slightly behind his glasses, and damn if

he doesn't look just the way Clark Kent does when Lois figures out he's Superman. I shift my gaze back to the dog.

"He's been doing this thing since I've had him," I say. "When we go places, or return home, he sniffs all over just the way he did here. Like he's searching for something. I've never understood. I just thought it was some weird quirk. But after watching this . . ." I clear my throat. "Maybe you were right. Maybe he needs this work."

He could completely gloat. Look smug. Say *I told you so*. But Drew Forbes doesn't do any of those things. He just nods and crosses his arms over his chest, which makes my pulse skip involuntarily, since it only enhances his superhero physique. I am almost grateful when Rufus flings the Kong into my legs so hard I have to look away.

"We can skip tomorrow," Drew says in his low, even timbre. He starts disassembling the course and moving the obstacles aside, probably clearing the space for his next training class. "You should still exercise him, though."

I look up, confused. We just agreed this was good for Rufus, and now—I bite my lip, a weight settling in my chest when I remember *I'm* the one who asked for a day off.

"Right . . . yeah, I'll make sure he gets a run."

Rufus lies on his side at my feet, now chewing lazily on his toy. He actually seems kind of tired. Or maybe sated is a better word. My stomach does a guilty little twist for not figuring out what he needed earlier, though I don't know how I could have. Not without the *dog guru*.

"I can come back Monday," I say hastily. "Anything to keep him from eating the other half of my couch."

I add this last part as a joke, but Drew just nods and slides the tire jump thing to one side. Still no sense of humor, but no scowl. And he *seems* less grumpy. Usually, his shoulders are square, back straight, and he walks around with this perma-nent resting assface.

Maybe it's because he proved his point. Or we're on his

turf doing his thing. Probably both. But his eyes suddenly seem softer, his demeanor gentler. The lines across his forehead smoothed out.

Drew folds up the last of the obstacles and sits on the floor beside Rufus. When the dog rolls over to let him rub his belly, I realize they're *both* more relaxed.

A lump rises in my throat, and I wonder if I'm doing the wrong thing, keeping them apart. I still don't know why Kyle left Rufus to me, but it's obvious that he and Drew can meet each other's needs.

My one-hour timer vibrates gently against my wrist. I dismiss it quickly, but can't bring myself to head for the door just yet. "I um . . . I was a little harsh yesterday."

Drew's hand pauses in the golden fur on Rufus's belly, but he doesn't look up. "I was a physician," he says, clearing his throat. "I was going into sports medicine and had just finished my residency the first time Kyle got hurt."

The edges of my vision darken, and I'm hurtling back five years. *The first time.* It should have been the last time. Kyle had been conducting a raid with several other servicemen. They came under enemy fire, and he was badly wounded. But his dog at the time—a German shepherd named Vinca— engaged the enemy long enough that Kyle's unit was able to get him and others to safety. Unfortunately, Vinca did not make it out of that fight.

Kyle never spoke about what happened, not even to me. He came home for a short period during his recovery, but his parents pressed him so hard to leave the service, he returned to duty as soon as he could.

"Even when we were kids, he always carried a . . . darkness inside him."

I close my eyes, letting the tears burn under my lids. Because I know. "It got so much worse after he was hurt," I whisper.

And then he'd been hurt again.

It happened six months before the wedding. Kyle had been back in the field for about a year. It was a struggle, but he'd been assigned a new dog, and we were counting down the days until we tied the knot. We had everything planned out. The church, the honeymoon. After that, I would finally move in with him.

He downplayed the second TBI, more concerned about the dog's injuries than his own. But nothing was ever the same after that.

I sink my fingers into Rufus's fur. I'm not sure when I moved to the floor. It doesn't matter. I just need to feel his warmth. Feel the heartbeat inside him.

"Kyle and I used to dream about training dogs together. Having a place like this." Drew's face is a black cloud as he gestures around the room. "I always wanted to make it happen for him."

I furrow my brow, adding up this information. "But you just said you became a doctor . . ."

"I did." He shrugs.

My gaze flits around K9 Academy before landing back on Drew. "You mean you did this . . . for him?"

He doesn't say anything. He doesn't need to.

I bite my lip, flooded with questions, but the words catch in my throat. When I meet Drew's clear green eyes through his glasses, all I manage to whisper is, "Why?"

"I thought I could save him," he says, voice flat and resigned. "But I guess I wasn't enough."

CHAPTER
TWENTY-SIX

"Let me just make sure I've got all this straight," Lydia says as we take our second slow lap with Rufus around the little park by her house. "Drew Forbes *quit* medicine so he could open a dog training facility to try and help his struggling little brother?"

"That's how I understand it." I keep hoping the knot in my chest will loosen each time I rehash this, but so far it's only pulled tighter. It doesn't help that Lydia's face looks like the holding-back-tears emoji.

"Damn," she says. "That sure makes him less villainous . . ."

"Just hold on to your hormones. He's still a Forbes," I say quickly. "He sided with their parents when it counted. There would've been some catch."

But even as I say this, the malice in my voice falls flat.

I wasn't enough.

Those words could have been pulled from the shards in my chest—but they'd come from Drew. And that's a problem. Because I've spent two years bearing this failure alone, and I am not prepared to share. Especially not with him.

"Kyle and Drew were barely speaking before the

wedding. That relationship was dead. There was no sickening sibling bond like those two have going on." My gaze tracks across the grass to where Lydia's husband and brother-in-law are currently on their tenth set of push-ups, trying to out-fitness each other. Anton's eyes flicker habitually toward us, making clear he thinks I'm overtaxing his pregnant wife. I use my leash hand to flip him a subtle middle finger.

"I guess you can't know what happened between them that last year," Lydia says, maiming me gently. "Either way, this changes things."

"It doesn't change anyth—"

Suddenly, she halts and plops down on a bench. I stop abruptly, studying her for imminent signs of distress, grateful Anton will be here in a hot second if she's not okay. But she just takes a calm sip of water and pats the seat next to her.

"I am not sure who's more high-strung these days—you, or my husband."

I exhale, settling next to her and filling a collapsible water bowl for Rufus. "I object to you putting us in a sentence together."

Lydia rolls her eyes, rubbing Rufus's neck. "Tell me how it's going with *this* guy. If I didn't know better, I'd swear he's turning you into a dog person."

My lip curls at her hostile choice of words. But when I look down, I find my hand already resting on Rufus's head. "Stockholm syndrome," I mutter. "The training is making him more tolerable. He hasn't chewed anything he wasn't supposed to for a week now. He seems calmer when we're home. Drew did this 'scent work' thing with him yesterday, and it was kinda crazy to watch. He seemed to love it."

Lydia watches me carefully while I ignore her obvious satisfaction.

"But Lydia, if I keep him, I'll have to move, and probably buy a car, and . . ." I grimace. "I don't know, that just feels like a lot with things so uncertain at work."

This gets her attention, but only leads to more scrutiny. "I thought you just got a raise?"

I squeeze the leash in my hands. I haven't spoken to anyone other than Randall about my giant *oops* with Unmatched, and it's been killing me. There was no way to tell Theo. I don't want to worry my mom. And while I respect that Lydia doesn't want to be treated like some fragile flower right now, it seems unfair to burden her with undue stress. But after the creepy emails I received last week, and the breathy voicemail Saturday, I feel like I'm going a little crazy.

"I'm just behind on deadlines," I say, dithering. "But since Rufus can come to the office now, I'm catching up."

Lydia's eyes narrow. "I call bullshit. What else is going on?"

"Nothing," I say, dumping out the dog bowl and packing it away.

Rufus sits up and looks back and forth between us, eyes lingering on Lydia as if to say *she's lying*. Then he rests his head in my lap. I stroke his ears and attempt to change the subject.

"How many weeks are you now?" I ask.

She doesn't answer, eyes moving from Rufus back to me. Lydia speaks fluent dog, and Rufus might as well be giving a TED Talk on my anxiety.

"What happened?" she asks, and the compassion in her voice gently crumbles what's left of my walls.

I let out a long breath. "We got an anonymous tip that Colin Vanderpool had a business partner on Unmatched. Or partners—at least one. And I'm pretty sure, whoever they are, they're not happy I've outed him."

She frowns. "So you're investigating?"

"Yes."

There's a long pause, and while I know Lydia won't freak the way my family might, I still regret giving her this to worry about. "I know you'll be smart and as safe as you can." She reaches out to grasp my hand. "Are you scared?"

I swallow, glancing around the little park and nearby playground. I wasn't ready for this question, and I'm afraid the answer is blinking like a neon sign on my face.

"I've been receiving messages like I did after the first article," I say, my voice more level than I expected. "I don't think it was ever Colin Vanderpool sending them."

"Oh." To her credit, Lydia just presses her mouth into a line and nods. "Well, I see you're carrying your Theo arsenal," she says, gesturing to my belt bag. "And you've got Rufus. And the camera on your door."

I'm not sure if she's taking inventory of my armaments to reassure me or herself. I still feel like a soldier going to war with a bag over my head.

"I'll feel better once I know who it is," I say. "I just need to hurry up and figure that out."

Lydia opens her mouth to reply, but is interrupted by a shriek coming from the little playground. I follow her gaze over my shoulder and spot a tiny, pigtailed linebacker screaming toward us across the grass.

"Paloma, *wait*—" A thirty-something Hispanic woman chases after the little girl, coming to an abrupt stop when she throws herself into Lydia's lap.

"Dia!" the little girl cries in a helium voice. "You have donuts?"

Lydia laughs, giving her a hug and waving at the mother —her friend, Marisol. "It's so good to see you! I'm afraid I left my donuts at home today."

Paloma juts out her lower lip like Lydia stepped on her puppy. But then she spots Rufus and nearly lunges off Lydia's lap. "Doggie!" she cries, hands outstretched.

I tighten my grip on the leash and look at Lydia, who is holding back the squirming toddler. "I don't actually know how he is with kids."

Marisol seems to notice me for the first time, and the way her face falls tells me exactly how thrilled she is. We haven't seen each other since Lydia's baby shower nearly a month ago, where we mostly pretended not to know one another.

"Careful, bebé," she says, scooping her daughter out of Lydia's lap. "We don't know this doggie."

I tell Rufus to sit, and he immediately complies with a light tail wag.

"Doggieeeee!" Paloma whines, still reaching for him.

Lydia and Marisol have some sort of nonverbal exchange while I sit there, unsure what to do, but then Marisol steps forward, letting Rufus sniff her outstretched hand and eventually petting his head. When the dog remains calm and engaged, Marisol instructs her daughter to hold her hand out too.

I watch Rufus carefully, not really sure what to look for. I think about the guy with the frisbee the other day and hold tight to the leash. But he just wags his tail a little harder, and when the little girl gets close enough, he starts intently licking her hands.

"Silly doggie!" Paloma gives a delighted squeal, and all of our shoulders relax.

"Doesn't hurt that her fingers are sticky with popsicle juice," Marisol says, offering me a thin smile. "Are you dog sitting or something?"

"No, he's mine . . . long story."

A dog starts barking from across the grass and Paloma immediately zeros in on Lydia's Akita mix, Heartthrob, who's been sitting with the boys watching us circle the park.

"Harbob!" she cries, grabbing Lydia by the hand. "I can pet him!"

Lydia looks at Marisol and shrugs, letting Paloma lead her away across the grass.

Marisol moves to follow them, but I clear my throat and

speak. "Hey, I'm glad to run into you. I actually emailed you a couple days ago."

"Did you?" she asks in a way that tells me she knows I did.

We have zero in common aside from Lydia—and the fact that Marisol was one of my most informative contacts when I wrote the original married cheaters feature about Unmatched.

"Yeah. I'm not trying to beat a dead horse, but I was hoping to ask you some new questions about Unmatched. I wrote a follow-up—"

"Oh, I know." Her tone is chilly, her eyes focused on Lydia, Paloma, and Heartthrob.

I frown. We've never had a warm relationship, but this is frosty even by our standards. "Marisol, what—"

"You need to be careful," she says, low and matter-of-fact. "I don't know how many guys were involved with the app. I didn't even know Vanderpool was one of them until I read your feature." Her lip curls, but I'm surprised to catch a flash of respect in her eyes. "But I will tell you, if my ex was involved, you don't want to look at this any closer."

I frown. Before I wrote the piece that put Unmatched in the public eye, Marisol had been unhappily married to a tech executive named Erik Schneider, who was an obvious ass but seemed about as threatening as a mosquito.

I shift, trying to look her directly in the eye. "Has something changed? Are you okay?"

She pulls her eyes away from her daughter and meets my gaze.

"*I* am fine. Actually, never been better."

"Good. Glad to hear it. All I wanted—" I stop as something slips from the back of my mind. "Did you call the *Observer* and speak to Randall Jones about this?"

Her eyes flicker away, and that's all the answer I need.

"Marisol, what the hell? You know you can just contact me directly."

She shakes her head and glances around. "Look, I don't know if he's really involved, and I'm not even that interested in finding out. I just wanted you to know he's not someone you should provoke."

"But why—"

"Mommy, Mommy, *Mommy!*" We both look up to see Anton cantering toward us with Paloma perched on his shoulders, pulling his hair like she's a tiny jockey. "Dia said she'd give me a puppy!"

Lydia trails behind them at a much slower pace, holding Heartthrob's leash, clearly trying her best not to full-on waddle. "Um, I did not!" she shouts.

Anton raises the little girl over his head and flies her around like an airplane in a clear effort to impress the whole park with his biceps and forearms and daddy vibes before setting her down, giggling. "I don't think that's what she said either, peanut." He presses a thumb to her nose. "But I know she'll let you visit The Pooch Park anytime you want."

"And have donuts?" Paloma says with eyes like an anime character.

Anton glances at his wife and shrugs. "We could get donuts."

Marisol rolls her eyes as Lydia catches up, taking her husband's arm. "You two have about a year and a half to work on setting some boundaries."

"I'll say," I mutter, too low for anyone to hear.

"Paloma, it's time to go," Marisol says, scooping up the toddler. "Say bye to Lydia."

"Buh-*bye*, Dia!" The little girl waves, then turns to Rufus and blows a kiss. "Bye, new doggie!"

Marisol spares me one last fully loaded glance, which makes clear she has nothing left to say to me, and then she's gone. Lydia waves, then hands Heartthrob's leash to Anton and gives me a light hug.

"You want to join us for Sunday dinner?" she asks.

"With you guys and Seth?" I ask, looking over her shoulder at her husband and brother-in-law, whose combined dimples are so sharp they could put an eye out. "Uh, actually, I have plans."

Lydia catches my hand and squeezes. "I know you're never going to forgive Anton. I'm . . . still working on that myself." She frowns, resting her other hand on her belly. "But your walls are high, Caprice."

"What's that supposed to mean?"

Rufus nuzzles against her and she strokes his ear. "I've just been thinking about what you told me about Drew and Kyle."

I step back, but she doesn't let go of my hand. "What about them?"

"You've spent so long beating yourself up about what went wrong. What you could've done differently. But maybe you were never the problem—and maybe Drew wasn't either." She shakes her head. "Maybe it was all Kyle."

Something sears through my chest at her words, burning all the way to the backs of my eyes. But it stops there. Because I *know* in some alternate timeline, where we might've gone through a different series of events, Kyle would still be alive.

I pull my hand out of hers. "You know, I don't really have time to think about that. I've got research to do and articles to write."

Lydia gives me an apologetic smile and nods. "Okay. Well, you're still invited to dinner—any Sunday. If career demands ever let up."

She rejoins her husband across the grass, and as they walk away holding hands, I'm left holding my leash, looking down at Rufus.

"What do you say we order Chinese and go on a research deep dive? I've got a secret bully stick I've been hiding from you."

The dog cocks his head, staring at me with his honey-gold

eyes, and for just a moment, I allow myself to feel guilty. Because I know he'd prefer to run obstacle courses and play hide and seek. And see Drew. Even I sort of wish we were doing that tonight.

Monday, March 28, 20__, 4:17 AM

To: Kyle.Forbes@mail.com

From: Caprice_Phipps@mail.com

Subject: Re: Re: Re: Re: Re: no subject

Dear Kyle,

I'm starting to wonder if you had any idea how much you were loved.

I guess that isn't fair. You'd still be here if you knew. It just kills me that you couldn't see it through the darkness while you were here. I'm sorry we couldn't help you—we just didn't know how.

C

DREW

He'd just completed the Level II class graduation. His manager, Shawna, was handing out treats, certificates, and congratulations, and he was ducking out to take Diesel to acupuncture when the woman approached.

"Drew? Do you have a moment?"

He paused at the door. "Yes, of course. Congrats again to Garbanzo."

He knelt to pet the dog, a strange-looking mix with the body of a basset hound and the spotted coat of a dalmatian. The lady and her daughter had been in his Monday class for several months, but he could only remember the dog's name.

"We just wanted to say thank you," the woman said. He looked up when her voice wavered. "We didn't know what we were doing when we got this dog. We got him because he was cute, but he turned into a little demon. He got into everything, he'd snap at my neighbors. I thought I was going to have to bring him to a shelter, but my kids—"

She glanced at her daughter and swallowed hard.

"Anyway. Coming here was a last resort. I wasn't even sure it would work. But what we learned in your classes *transformed* him. We're so grateful. I-I just wanted you to know."

He blinked. The dog sat patiently, waiting at her heel like he'd been taught, but Drew could remember the demon behavior she described. He *had* been quite a handful.

"I think you're giving me too much credit," he said. "You showed up for the classes. You did most of the work."

But his chest lightened at the thought that the work he loved was keeping *any* dog out of a shelter. Improving people's lives.

He picked a toy from one of the retail displays and presented it to the little girl, who looked about eight. "Here— an extra reward for a job well done. I hope we'll see you in Level III?"

"Absolutely." The woman beamed. "We can't wait."

Her daughter grinned as they headed for the door. "Thanks, Mr. Drew! See you next week!"

He scanned the jogging path at the park as he drove to the vet. It was too early for Caprice and Rufus to be there, but looking for them had become something of a habit. It didn't feel quite as frantic as it used to. He knew exactly where they were right now—she'd told him. Rufus stayed with her during the day, under her desk at the *Observer*. Her boss liked him. He got walks and treats. And in the evening, they came to train with him.

At some point, he realized he looked forward to it. Occasionally, they still had awkward moments, but overall, they'd fallen into an amiable rhythm. The dog came in, had a ball, and went home tired. Caprice mostly sat and watched, but he knew she paid attention. They never talked much, but the times they did were surprisingly easy. Almost pleasant.

Nothing wrong with that—it was better for Rufus if they were getting along.

It only bothered him a little when he caught himself clocking the hours leading up to their meetings. Or when he noticed how quickly their time together seemed to pass. Or that Sunday, the day she'd asked to skip, had felt like the longest day of the whole week.

He'd started to accept the dog was safe, maybe even happy with her. She wasn't the person he thought she was. Sometimes she was even affectionate with Rufus when she didn't realize Drew was watching. She'd rub his ears and look into his eyes with a sad smile, and something would catch in Drew's chest.

He just wasn't sure how he felt about that yet.

CHAPTER
TWENTY-SEVEN

My week starts off with a bang. Monday, I finish two staff articles I pulled from the assignment desk that I researched and wrote around Rufus. By Tuesday, I've scheduled video calls with two potential sources willing to talk more about Unmatched. And on Wednesday, I receive a follow-up from Maya with the sheriff's office, who went above and beyond getting me a list of reports related to dating app safety.

Unfortunately, the week goes downhill from there.

Friday, April 2, 20__, 9:15 AM

To: Caprice_Phipps@MHObserver.com

From: Randall_Jones@MHObserver.com

Subject: FWD: Atrocious Reporting

Caprice,

See below—anything you want to discuss?

Randall

---------- Forwarded message ---------

Friday, April 2, 20__, 7:12 AM

To: Randall_Jones@MHObserver.com

From: WA_Forbes@DenverMedical.org

CC: P_Forbes@DenverMedical.org

Subject: Atrocious Reporting

Dear Mr. Jones,

We notified local news organizations about the Kyle Forbes Memorial Scholarship, created in honor of our late son, in order to raise awareness about the award and increase opportunities for disadvantaged local youth. Every other news outlet in Denver provided adequate coverage of the inaugural award last week except the *Mile High Observer*, whose reporting was lackluster and insufficient. Please note that we will not associate ourselves with your publication again.

Sincerely,

W. Andrew Forbes, MD

Patricia Forbes, MD

Randall finds me on the sidewalk while I'm walking Rufus around the building to pee. I've managed to avoid him most of the morning. I'm pretty sure all I needed to do was reply to his email and acknowledge the feedback, but the longer I sat at my desk and considered what to say about the Forbeses, the harder that simple task seemed.

I guess I owe Drew for the heads-up on some level. Obviously, I knew enough to expect Kyle's parents would be unpleasant. But their style is typically more passive-aggressive. When Kyle and I were together, they would just not invite me to holidays or important family events. If we spoke, they'd pretend not to remember my name. And when they finally had to acknowledge our relationship publicly, they always found a way to make me sound like a charity case.

The *Observer's* coverage of the scholarship was published without a byline. And though the Forbeses didn't call me out personally, they obviously knew who wrote it.

Rufus lights up when he spots my boss, likely because his pockets are permanently stuffed with dog treats. But this works to my advantage while I try to figure out what to say.

"Look, Randall—"

"How's the research going?" he asks while the dog crunches a Milk-Bone. We both know that's not what he came out here for, but this is timely, so I run with it.

"Actually, I've had a bit of a breakthrough," I say, trying to keep my enthusiasm in check. "I think I've identified Colin Vanderpool's business partner on Unmatched."

He crosses his arms with a broad smile. "You don't say? Who have we got? Another society page regular? Someone political?"

"Not this time." I move a little closer, dropping my voice as we stroll. "His name is Erik Schneider. On the surface, he's kind of a nobody. Grew up in Ohio, went to Virginia Tech. Became an IT executive, but not the flashy variety. He was the guy who physically ran the Unmatched app while Vanderpool rubbed all the elbows. But when you look closer, he's one of those men who sits in the background with his hands in everyone else's cookie jar. A total supervillain archetype."

Randall arches a brow, indicating he wants facts. "What villainy was he up to aside from hosting an unsavory, but technically legal dating site?"

"You mean aside from stalking and threatening journalists?"

He stops walking. "You think it's him?"

I lay a hand on Rufus's head, glancing up and down the street. "There's a lot of evidence suggesting it's him. I'm working on this with one of my contacts at the sheriff's office."

"Good."

"But there's more, Randall." I pivot so I can speak directly next to his ear. "I'm pretty sure Schneider and Vanderpool have been turning a blind eye to reported assaults happening via Unmatched."

His face darkens. "Can you prove it?"

"I have copies of police reports and hospital records, and I've conducted interviews with some of the victims. My friend at the sheriff's office says that technically dating apps aren't required to do anything because of the agreements people sign. But it seems like women should at least know which apps are taking measures to protect them and which won't."

"I agree." Randall strokes one hand down his goatee. "I know I don't need to say this, but make sure you verify—"

"*Everything*," I say. "Of course."

He glances at the *Observer* building. "How close are you? When do you think you can have something written up and ready to print?"

"I'm considering breaking it into two parts. Depending on how long it takes me to track everything down, I could have the first one for you by next week?"

"Good." Randall shifts as he considers this. "Have you received any new threats?"

My cheek twitches. "Technically, nothing overtly malicious since last week. I had a strange empty voicemail last weekend, but that was all."

"Okay." He straightens, turning to face me. "Now. Did you get the email I forwarded this morning?"

Crap. I'd almost forgotten why he came out here in the first place. Briefly, I consider faking temporary amnesia. Blanking on how to speak English. Or maybe just pretending my computer died. Instead, I say, "I did," and make a close examination of Rufus's leather leash.

I don't need to see Randall's face to know his eyebrows

are dancing a tarantella. "Was it just me, or did that message seem kinda . . . personal?"

I sigh and finally look at him. "You want the stupid, actual story? Or the embellished, more interesting version with spies and explosions?"

"Just the facts, please," he says, always hot to sound cliché. He reaches into his breast pocket like he wants a cigarette, but Randall doesn't smoke, so I'm not surprised when he holds a Hershey bar out to me.

When I shake my head, he shrugs and bites into the candy himself.

I lean against the red brick side of the building. "So, the scholarship that the Forbeses awarded—it sends a kid to medical school in the name of their son who died."

Randall nods.

"Well, the thing is, Kyle Forbes never wanted to be a doctor. He joined the military just so his parents couldn't force him into it."

Randall breaks off another piece of chocolate, surprising me with a chuckle. "I can't even send you to cover boring local events without you digging up more interesting stuff."

My cheeks warm. I need something to do, so I push off the wall and resume walking toward the *Observer* entrance.

"But you didn't write about that," Randall muses, falling into step beside me. "So how come these doctors are so pissed off?"

I glance over at him, but as soon as I meet his eyes, I can tell he already knows.

"Well, for one, I wrote the piece about the scholarship recipient and not about them." I snort. "But even if I'd written a glowing, complimentary account of their generosity, they would've hated it."

Randall tosses his candy wrapper in a trash can and waits for me to continue.

"Kyle Forbes and I dated all through high school. We got engaged after he enlisted." I stop just short of the *Observer* entrance, having zero desire to share this story with anyone but Randall. "His parents never liked me, and their dislike grew more intense when I encouraged him to follow his own passions instead of theirs. Though I guess if I hadn't—"

My voice breaks, and Rufus shoves his cold nose into my hand.

"I'm sorry for your loss," Randall says quietly, the corners of his mouth turned down.

"Thanks," I say, so low I barely hear myself. "It's complicated. We'd broken up before he passed away . . . Anyway, he left me Rufus."

"Aha . . ." Randall rubs the dog's head gently, obviously piecing things together. "He must've loved you very much."

My eyes snap to his, but I can hardly see his face now through my tears. If Kyle still loved me, there's no way he would've done what he did.

"Perhaps my opinion came through in my article more than I realized," I say unsteadily. "I'm sorry. I should've let someone else do that reporting."

I watch my boss's eyebrows converse before he speaks.

"Actually, I was thinking *that's* quite a story." He glances at me, clearly trying to gauge whether I'm bothered before pressing on. "I know this is personal, but I can't help wondering what you could do with it if you explored more deeply. The scholarship was hardly worth writing about, but the entitlement, the family manipulation . . . the way the son bucked it all to be true to himself? Seems like quite a human interest opportunity."

"Randall . . ." I stare at him, and he has the grace to look apologetic before I look away. He can't know I have a draft of the story he's proposing already started that I've been dithering over for weeks. "I actually wouldn't mind helping

Kyle give his parents one last 'fuck you.' But I already have plenty of powerful, vicious people mad at me. I'm not sure I need more of that."

"You don't," he muses, stroking Rufus's ears. After a minute, he looks up with an inscrutable expression. "Don't take this the wrong way. But I just wonder what their son would want you to do."

And what's strange is, when he says *their son*, Kyle isn't who comes to mind. When I close my eyes, considering, the person I picture is Drew.

Would he care if I wrote about his brother? If I did a deep dive into Kyle's mental health—his passions, motivations? His defeats? Now, suddenly, I'm curious to ask Drew what it was like for *him* growing up. I already know how it was for Kyle. But how did they end up so different? Why was Drew the golden child while Kyle was so firmly the black sheep? Did Drew simply *want* to be a doctor, while Kyle didn't? Or was there more to it than that?

Drew and I have been operating under a sort of peace treaty for the sake of the dog all week, but what would he do if I wrote a feature like this? Would it shift me firmly back to his enemies list? Would he resume trying to take Rufus away from me?

My chest aches. What *would* Kyle want me to do?

I grip the leash tighter in my hand. "I'll have to give that some thought."

Randall pulls open the door as we approach the entrance of the building, and Tracy gives me a warm smile from the front desk. "Hey, Caprice! A card came in the mail for you. Is it your birthday?"

I furrow my brow in confusion. "What? No."

She hands me a plain envelope the size of a greeting card. It's postmarked Denver with no return address. Totally benign by all appearances, but as soon as I touch it, my stomach fists. I slide my finger under the seal and peer inside, trying to decide if concerns about white powders are prudent or paranoid. But all I find is a card with a flower on the front that reads *Thinking Of You . . .*

Inside, there's a handwritten note.

And your little dog too.

CHAPTER
TWENTY-EIGHT

Drew opens the door of K9 Academy, taking the leash from my hands as I step inside. He doesn't speak; he barely makes eye contact. Just focuses on the dog. Which is pretty much how this has gone the last five days. We've fallen into an uneasy rhythm where we meet for the sake of Rufus's needs. We talk about the dog, about when to meet. We do *not* speak any more about Kyle. Honestly, it's been kind of a relief.

"Sit . . . good, *yes*. Now heel," he says, taking Rufus through a series of basic obedience exercises as a warm-up.

Rufus follows in lockstep, eyes glued to the man's chiseled features, ready to do his bidding. I perch on the little half wall, out of the way. The two of them are so relaxed and in sync, it's almost like a dance. And it's actually kind of fun to watch.

Until Drew and I accidentally catch each other's eyes. We both turn away immediately, and I busy myself on my phone. But when I sneak a look at him later, I can't help noticing the tension creeping through his shoulders. Or the way he keeps clenching his hands at his sides.

If the dog has picked up on any of this, he's faking ignorance to have more fun.

"Okay, Rufus, go!" Drew commands.

The dog takes off on the agility course like he's spring-loaded. Drew changes up the order of obstacles each day, presumably to keep it interesting, but the dog doesn't even stop to think about it. He's over the bar jump, up and down the seesaw, and through the tunnel like he's done it a dozen times.

"*Wait,*" Drew prompts as Rufus leaps onto the low table.

I hold my breath. This has been the most challenging part for him, mostly because it requires him to stay still for a full five seconds. It's obviously still cramping his style by the impatient look in his eyes, but he just spins in a circle before lying down flat, eyes still glued to his trainer. When he finally gets the release signal, Rufus takes off, soaring through the remaining obstacles, mouth open, tongue hanging out, wagging his tail and barking like he's the happiest canine on earth.

I clap for him, and when I do, all I can think is how happy this would've made Kyle. Watching his beloved dog having the time of his life in a place that existed in his dreams. The way Drew moves is so like him, I can only imagine what the brothers would have looked like working here side-by-side. Drew cuts a slightly larger figure than Kyle did, but they were both so clearly gifted with animals, it's obvious they could have done something special together. Not to mention these men were blessed with the kind of genetics that go wild on social media. If Drew and Kyle had ever done dog training videos together, it would have been an instant thirst trap.

This makes me snort. Then clap my hand to my mouth. Because both men would have *hated* that.

I must've made too much noise, because when I look up, Drew is staring right at me. And while I *know* he couldn't know what I'm thinking, the look in his eyes sure feels like he does.

Thankfully, Rufus chooses that moment to barrel straight into him, nearly knocking him down to grab the tug toy out of his hands. I cover my mouth, trying not to laugh as my dog runs a victory lap and Drew accounts for all his fingers. Once he's recovered himself, Rufus baits him into a tug-of-war, and it seems truly unclear who will win based on the flex of Drew's shoulders and biceps versus the whole-body pulling and growling Rufus is doing. Eventually, whether it's earned or a forfeit, the dog comes out a winner.

And the next thing I know, Drew is walking to where I'm sitting, holding out the toy.

"You try it now," he says, sage eyes burning into me.

"Me?" I sit forward, glancing at the agility equipment like a kid who wasn't paying attention in class. At the park, Drew had me run Rufus through commands occasionally, which I admit was good practice. But since we've been at K9 Academy, I've been a strict observer. I haven't been watching closely enough to know the right words or gestures to use.

"You're his handler," he says firmly. "He needs his commands to come from you." His voice is brusque, though maybe slightly less barbed than times in the past, which makes it harder for me to bristle a response.

I have no interest in being a dog handler, nor do I even know how. But when the dog looks at me expectantly with those bright golden eyes, I groan. He probably won't care if I screw up as long as he gets a reward.

"Fine." I sigh, slipping off the half wall and taking the toy from Drew's hand. As I do, our fingers touch, and a light shiver passes through me. I look up at him in surprise, and he returns my stare, pulling his hand back slowly like he felt it too. I clear my throat. "Where do I stand?"

"Take your position here," he says, moving to a random spot on the floor. I square my shoulders and follow. When I'm close enough to touch him, but still a comfortable distance, he says, "Good. Now make sure Rufus is where you need him to be."

The dog looks at me like I ought to know what this means, and when it's clear I don't, Drew steps closer, positioning himself parallel to my body. The masculine scent of soap and sandalwood tickles my nose, making my pulse pick up. I straighten my back, focusing *all* my attention on mimicking his posture. We haven't been this close since the night we spent on the floor of my apartment.

"Say, 'Rufus, place,'" he rumbles, breath warm against my ear.

I clear my throat and repeat the magic words while pointing to the floor directly in front of me, since that is also something Drew is doing.

The dog is in the spot before I can blink, sitting and wagging his black-tipped tail, looking back and forth at us like this is some fun new double-trainer game. I keep my eyes on him, afraid to turn my head and find out exactly how close Drew is.

"All right, now he knows what's expected," Drew says. "But he's still going to be looking to you for any changes. Just make sure you maintain your connection."

I nod, though focusing on his words and not his scent is now a significant challenge. I close my eyes briefly, breathing him in. "Okay."

There's a pause, stretching just long enough to be awkward. Then he clears his throat. "Um, you can tell him to start any time."

My eyes fly open almost as fast as the blood rushes to my face. "Rufus, go!"

The dog takes off through the tunnel. Clears the tire jump. Heads up the A-frame and down the other side. He pauses on the table, even though I forget to tell him to wait. Quickly, I position myself between that and the next obstacle.

"Release!"

He leaps down, clears the next hurdle, then picks his way carefully through the weave poles. Once that's completed, he's flying through the tire jump, circling back toward me, and I'm so focused watching him come in for the finish, I gasp when Drew's big hand closes over mine. He extends my wrist out away from my body, and I whip my head to look at him, a question on my lips. Before I can ask, the toy is snatched out of my hand and Rufus is whipping it back and forth, trying to shake it to death.

Drew looks down, and when our eyes meet, I'm aware we've ended up in a strangely *Dirty Dancing* stance—his arm still extended in the air gripping mine, his other hand resting on my waist. Our faces separated by inches.

His breath catches, and my pulse races beneath my skin.

"I—sorry," he says, letting go and stepping back, taking all the air with him. "I didn't want him to knock you over."

I draw my arm down, bringing my hand to my wrist, trapping the lingering warmth of his touch. "Oh. Thanks."

The dog whips the toy into my legs with a painful smack, and I lean down, grateful for the distraction.

"Good boy!" I say, grabbing the end of the rope and pulling, because that's his favorite. I can feel Drew watching, but I'm so confused about what just happened, I can't bring myself to look at his face.

"Yes, that was excellent," he says, and I relax as he resumes his usual clipped tone. "He still followed your direction, even when you mixed up the obstacle order."

"What? I didn't mix it up." Rufus nearly pulls me over while tugging the end of the rope.

"The open tunnel should've come before the seesaw." Drew says this like I got a C on my report card, and I roll my eyes. "But the point is, he didn't hesitate to do what you asked. He's really become attuned to you."

I purse my lips, not sure what to make of that.

"Seems like you've become more attuned to him too," he adds, this time with distinct resignation.

I release the end of the toy and Rufus gives it a vigorous shake, tossing it in the air and chasing it across the floor. He brings it back, and we engage in another brief tug-of-war before I let him win, and he makes a lap around the room wagging his tail. I can't help smiling. Watching him enjoy himself is so different from watching him pace my apartment whining.

"I guess it helps that I understand him better now."

"How's that?"

I shrug. "He was miserable when I didn't know what he needed. We both were. But . . . I don't know, I guess now we have something to offer each other."

I glance at Drew, catching a glimpse of his brother's ghost. A lump forms in my throat. And suddenly, I badly *want* to talk about Kyle.

"You know, he was determined to make me a dog person," I say in a shaky voice. "He and my friend Lydia claimed it was my only major flaw." I look down to where I've been rubbing Rufus's belly unconsciously with my foot. "God, if he could see this, he'd be so smug."

Neither of us speaks for a moment. Then Drew asks, "Why didn't you like dogs?"

I have to stop and think about that. My mom might be right about not growing up with pets, but it feels a little more complicated. I shrug, stroking the soft fur on Rufus's ears, letting my pulse slow down. "I'm still not sure I *do* like dogs in general . . . but maybe this one's growing on me."

A reminder goes off on my phone, and when I see the clock, I rise from my seat.

"Damn. I had no idea it was this late." Our one-hour training session has run closer to two, and when I glance out the windows, the unexpected peace I found here—with the dog, with Drew—evaporates like a mirage.

Thinking of you . . .

I pick up my belt bag, hastily fastening it around my waist, then take inventory of its contents: pepper spray, Taser, personal alarm. An individual arsenal courtesy of my brother. One that felt mildly ridiculous until it didn't—when the mail came this afternoon. "Sorry, I just need to get home."

Drew rises from the floor as I locate my keys. "Is . . . is everything okay?"

I look up, surprised by the soft concern in his voice. For a moment, I even think about telling the truth. No, nothing has felt okay for months. I can't tell if I'm being harassed or truly threatened, but there's a creep out there who wants *something*, and now he's threatening my dog too.

Instead, I let out a slow breath, thinking back to my conversation with Randall. "Do you . . . do you think Rufus was ever trained to attack?"

Drew blinks. He clearly didn't expect this question, and too late, I realize it was the wrong one to ask.

"Sorry. I meant, um . . . is there a way to call him off if he tries to bite someone?"

He stiffens immediately. "*Has* he tried to bite?"

"No, not exactly." Oh God, I'm making this worse. "I mean, he freaked out at my neighbor and a coworker when they surprised him. But he didn't bite. I just wondered . . . is there a command for that? Like, to literally call off the dogs?"

He studies me for an uncomfortable minute, then turns his attention to Rufus, who's gone to sit patiently by his leash. "He probably had bite training. I don't know exactly what that looked like, but I doubt he'd ever attack without being given a specific command." He frowns. "Then again, he was discharged in part because he became unreliable in the field."

"Can you tell me the commands?" I ask. "Just so I know what to say . . . or not say?"

He pauses. "They probably used something like *go get him.* I can find out for sure."

My adrenaline surges with the phrase. *Go get him.* I curl my fists.

"But if he bites someone, it would be serious." His voice is stern. "Military dogs are trained to do damage. Break bones. If he hurts someone, a judge could deem him dangerous, even order to have him put down."

My mouth drops open. I look at Rufus, who gazes back stoically. Loyally. On some level, I like that he might sink his teeth into someone trying to mess with me. But if he hurt an innocent person? I don't think I could handle having to euthanize Kyle's dog.

"To make him stop," Drew continues, "You could say *out,* or *sit.* Just anything that's the opposite of what he's doing. We should probably practice that too."

"*Out* or *sit,* okay . . ." I make a quick note on my phone so I won't forget.

When I look up again, his expression has darkened. "What are you afraid of?"

I look away, forcing a laugh. "Excuse me?"

"Come on, you're on guard all the time. Always looking over your shoulder. For a while I just assumed you didn't trust me, but tonight . . ." he trails off, and when I meet his gaze, his eyes burn into mine. "I don't think it's me."

My heart thuds. He's either been paying real close attention, or I'm a way worse actress than I thought. "Sorry, I don't know what you're talking about."

He arches his eyebrows over his glasses. "I know a scared animal when I see one."

I snort, grabbing Rufus's leash. "You spend too much time with dogs."

"Caprice."

I stop in my tracks. I can't remember if he's ever spoken my first name. Had he been calling me Ms. Phipps? Has he called me anything? And why does he have to sound so much like he cares?

"Look, I don't know what you're trying to do. But just stop." My voice is a low growl. "We're not friends. We're barely acquaintances. I'm never giving you the dog. I'm not even sure why I'm still here." I gesture around the training center. "Maybe Kyle planned all this out just to twist the knife a little harder. But I'm done."

A bitter laugh rumbles from Drew's chest. "Right, because Kyle hurt *you*."

My throat burns. "He sure as hell did."

"You have got some nerve." He steps toward me, malice lacing through his voice.

Tears prick the corners of my eyes. "Pretty sure I have the right. We were together ten years. I was planning to spend the rest of my life with him."

"Until he got hurt. And things got hard."

I snap my head to look at him. "What the hell are you talking about?"

"I was there that day—I watched you *run* out of the church."

A gasp slips from my throat. The air goes still.

"Is that what you think happened?" I close the distance between us, clutching the leash in my trembling fists.

For a second, his eyes flash between mine like he's uncertain. Then he presses his mouth into a thin line. "That *is* what happened."

Something fissures deep inside me. Not my heart, which has been in pieces far too long already, but something else. Something new and fragile that had just started to blossom. Until he wilted it with his words. I step back, away from him.

"So, you're telling me you watched your brother's bride leave him at the altar. And you turned around and left without offering him a word of support."

Drew's eyes narrow, but I don't miss how his face pales.

"You're right, Kyle changed after the second time he was hurt. Things got harder for him. Darker." I shake my head. "I planned the whole wedding thinking we'd be okay if I could just hold him together."

My voice breaks, but I force the rest of the words.

"Kyle never set foot inside the church, which you would have known if you were a *shadow* of the brother you pretend to be. I waited for him in my dress, convinced I could save him if I gave him my heart." I swallow hard, leaning into Rufus for support. "But my love wasn't enough."

CHAPTER
TWENTY-NINE

My follow-up piece about Unmatched drops Wednesday.

And it's a total flop.

Maybe because the man at the center of it wasn't a high-profile philanthropist. Maybe because a couple of *very* famous celebrities renewed the world's faith in love stories by getting engaged the day before. Or maybe a butterfly simply flapped its wings somewhere over the Continental Divide, shifting the winds and the whole world's fates.

Whatever the reason, I start the day fired up, ready to field comments, questions, emails, and re-posts. But by the start of our mid-afternoon meeting, the story only has three likes and two anonymous comments. *"This was well written,"* which I could guess was from Lydia. And another I've decided not to give space in my brain.

"Caprice, can we chat?" Randall asks as my colleagues rise from their chairs.

I look around and nod, hanging back as the conference room empties, offering Brian a somewhat strained high five as he leaves. His piece about teachers needing side hustles to earn a living made the cover of the print edition and turned out to be the star feature. Even I have to admit it was earned.

Randall closes the door as the last person leaves and returns to his seat. "I didn't want to discuss this in front of the entire staff."

"Thank you," I say quietly. He doesn't need to clarify what he means. "I've scrapped the final segment, and I'm back on the assignment desk. I think I'll just focus on that for a while. If you have any events you want me to cover, just let me do it as a staff article."

He frowns. "I don't think I need to tell you every piece can't be a hit."

I close my laptop, sliding it off the table and into my bag. "No. But generally no one expects to follow up a big sensation with a total fail."

"Vanderpool is a prestigious local figure. A lot of people were invested in his downfall. The stakes weren't the same with this Schneider guy."

"I mean, I would expect at least *half* the population would be invested in the safety of online dating, but what do I know?"

Randall sits forward, rubbing his temples. "Maybe the public is just fatigued on Unmatched."

I curl my fists in my lap. I spent hours combing through police reports, speaking to app users, and researching Marisol's ex, who, it turns out, is just as unsavory as she warned. He indisputably covered up for several predators, letting them hide behind multiple profiles and making victims work just to collect evidence. But it's like our readers took one look at the headline and decided to keep scrolling. *Zero* other publications have picked up the feature. And here I am again, questioning my journalistic skills and watching my career dwindle.

"How are the comments?" My boss asks. "Anything I should know about?"

"Oh, there's only been one. But it pretty much says everything." I unlock my phone and read him the message that was not Lydia. *"If women don't wanna get raped, they shouldn't go on an app."*

Randall's lip curls. "I'll get that deleted."

I shake my head. "Nope. I say we let it stand. The readers have spoken—there's no story here. Women are only victims on days that end in Y."

"You haven't had an email from Schneider himself?" he asks.

My stomach does an excruciating little twist, but I school my face. "Nothing, threatening or otherwise. Guess I missed the mark so badly even my main heckler doesn't think it's worth his time."

"None?" Randall's eyebrows confer on his forehead. "That seems . . . odd."

I wave a dismissive hand, turning my bluster up to ten. "The guy's probably just a coward. It's easy to send a girl dick pics and deliver rape threats anonymously. A bit more uncomfortable once she's told everyone who you are."

I say this to the wall behind his left ear, aiming for stoicism, but probably landing somewhere closer to neurotic. Every other time I've written about Unmatched, this guy was quick to send me slime. Anything to unsettle and make me uncomfortable. Now I've written directly about him, and . . . nothing.

The silence is so much worse.

Randall purses his lips under his mustache, but finally rises from the table. "Maybe. Just don't let down your guard."

I laugh, pushing my chair back and rousing Rufus from where he's snoring under the table. "Don't worry. I have my four-legged security detail."

Ugh. Another subject that feels like a minefield.

Rufus follows calmly on the way back to my desk. We haven't seen Drew or been to his facility in a week, and I'm ready for a lifetime subscription to never seeing each other again. I will never forget his icy stare when I called him out about supporting his brother. How he just stood there looking at me like I was *still* responsible for Kyle's choices.

I was so mad when I got home, I pulled up the piece I'd started writing after that awful scholarship ceremony. The one about Kyle that Randall's been pushing for. The one I wasn't sure I should write. It was a surprisingly decent first draft. I haven't told Randall about it. I'm not sure I ever will. But I've been reading, researching, and fine-tuning it all week.

Somehow, the only thing I've managed to get right in the last five days is keeping Rufus entertained and happy. At work, he's stayed busy under my desk with Kongs full of food. And as the weather has continued to warm, we've been doing obedience on lunch breaks and running every evening in the park. I even set up a makeshift agility course in my apartment. Which I'm grateful Drew will never see. But the dog seemed to appreciate it—leaping over a shoe rack from my closet, crawling through a tunnel made from a sheet draped over my barstools, walking up and across my decimated couch. I even cleared my coffee table so he could practice sitting and waiting five seconds.

If Rufus could have laughed at me, I'm sure he would have. But he hasn't been pacing or crying, and he hasn't stolen any of my shoes for several days. I even experimented with leaving him in his crate for a few minutes while I ran to the lobby to get the mail.

We both survived. And we did it without Drew.

After a soul-sucking few days replying to emails while researching kids' activities and events for our family entertainment section, Rufus and I are ready for the weekend. My Friday evening plan is to take him for another run in the park, order takeout, and curl up on what's left of my couch to binge Netflix all weekend.

The first part of my plan goes sideways as soon as we step

outside the *Observer* office. A strong wind whips both my ponytail and the hem of my skirt. I stop to study the sky, and Rufus's ears immediately flatten to a nervous position. We haven't had a major storm since the week of the scholarship ceremony, but I don't like the color of the clouds coming down from the mountains. When the dog issues a low whine and starts panting next to me, I give him a reassuring pat and head straight home.

The rain starts a block away from my building. Just a few drops at first, but it's steady by the time we dash through the front doors. There's a low rumble of thunder as we step into the elevator, mostly drowned out as the doors close, but the dog still squeezes his powerful body between me and the wall. I cross my fingers all the way to the fifth floor that this is one of those fast-moving storms that skips over Denver on its way to the eastern plains.

We have no such luck.

One hour later, I have loud big band music playing (the best I could do to drown out the thunder), and I've turned on every light in my apartment. Lightning flashes every few moments, and as I squeeze Rufus into the coat and leggings Drew left here, I make a mental note to order blackout curtains. The dog visibly flinches with each roll of thunder, so I turn up the music. He's refused to eat his dinner, refused every treat I've offered—even peanut butter. And I'm starting to feel like the few wins I thought I had with him this week were just surface and I have done *nothing* to actually help this dog.

The only thing that's even remotely better since the last storm is that he's standing up and pacing rather than squeezed under the frame of my couch—or at least it feels like an improvement. Until around ten o'clock, when I see him start to circle and position himself like he does when he's about to poop.

"No—*no*," I say, snatching my keys up with his leash. "Not again."

We're out the door and headed for the stairs before the next crash of thunder because the only place that might be worse to clean up diarrhea would have to be my building's elevator. I'm pretty sure going out into the black of night in this storm is a bad idea, but I don't know what else to do. We cling to the side of the building once we're outside, and almost immediately, the dog finds a patch of grass and squats. As the next flash of lightning lights up the sky, I cover my mouth and avert my eyes, hoping it rains hard enough to wash away what he's doing because there's no way that's solid enough to pick up.

Rufus repeats these motions a few more times until it seems less urgent and I'm able to focus on something besides him. The street we're on is empty—unsurprising because it is pouring—but it's so black out I doubt I'd see anyone if they were coming. Still, it's starting to feel eerie, standing out here in a thunderstorm alone.

As soon as the dog is done pooping, he turns right around, clearly anxious to get inside. But as we round the corner and head toward my building's entrance, the sky lights up again, illuminating a figure coming toward us in the dark.

A large and looming silhouette of a man.

I stop in my tracks, realizing we left my apartment so fast I didn't have time to grab my belt bag with its cache of personal protection options. It's just me and the dog.

I secure the leash in my hand and glance down at Rufus, who now stands alert and focused despite the storm, clearly watching the guy coming toward us. I'm not sure I could hear over the rain if he's growling. But why would he be? The guy is probably just another unfortunate pedestrian trying to get home in the rain. It only looks like he's coming straight for us.

Still, I take a defensive stance. Enough has gone sideways

for me this week; I'm not taking any chances. The man is between us and my building's entrance, but I eyeball it and decide to dash past him. I pull back on the leash, thinking the words *go get him* in my head just in case I need to say them out loud. If they would even work. At my side, Rufus stays rigid, laser-focused on the approaching threat.

Until suddenly he lunges. It all happens before I can stop it. One moment we're approaching the man, and the next— before I can give any command—Rufus launches himself at the shadowy form. I screech, heart pounding with the thunder, because either the dog is attacking an innocent person, or the person he's attacking is not innocent. But then a bolt of lightning illuminates the sky once more, and in that fleeting moment, with a surge of dread, I recognize the man.

CHAPTER
THIRTY

"What are you *doing* out here?" I yell over the storm.

"I could ask you the same thing." Drew Forbes's voice is also raised out of necessity, but I'm surprised when I detect no snarl.

"He—he had to go out. I didn't know what else to do."

Before Drew can answer, we're interrupted by a near-simultaneous flash and crash of lightning. I look down in time to see Rufus's ears pin down, tail wagging cut short as he slinks back to my side. Drew immediately drops down in front of him.

"Hey, everything's okay. I'm going to get you somewhere safe."

And I know he's not speaking to me, but I hadn't realized how hard I was shaking until he takes the leash from my hand and leads us to the door of my building.

We exit the elevator in silence. My pulse is so frenetic thinking about Drew entering my apartment again, I almost trip over an object in the hall in front of my door. The dog is already sniffing it, and I have to pull back on the leash before I can really register what I'm seeing.

A vase of roses. Dead ones.

All the air leaves my chest.

"What is this?" Drew asks.

My mouth is so dry I can't respond. Were these here before, when Rufus and I ran out? Or were they just delivered? Did I lock my door? I grip my keys instinctively, weaving them between my fingers as Drew picks up the flowers, giving them a slow inspection.

"There's no note."

I force a swallow. "Someone's idea of a joke."

Drew's brows draw together as he looks from me back to the shriveled bouquet, and then up and down the hall. And I hate to admit it, but as the walls of my building seem to close in, I am grateful not to be making this discovery alone.

"Would you—um," I try and fail to speak in an even tone. "There's a trash chute down the hall. Would you throw them away? Please?"

His gaze is searing through his glasses, green eyes bright and alert. He opens his mouth, then pauses, pressing it closed. Then he nods.

I take my phone out as soon as he turns away, pulling up the peephole camera app, waiting for the stupid thing to load. I have charged it diligently since the time my brother caught me slacking, and now there's no fucking way I'm entering my apartment without checking the footage first.

My pulse pounds—watching myself rushing to the stairwell with the dog—*not* tripping over anything or pausing to lock my fucking door. Then, only about a minute later, a hooded figure exits the elevator and comes down the hall. My veins turn to ice. They only pause long enough to deposit the delivery, and I let out a stilted breath when they don't try the knob. But they never once look into the camera, disappearing down the stairs a moment later.

"I peeked in there. Didn't see anyone," Drew says at my shoulder, making me jump. And everything inside me is so on edge, I actually step closer to him. "Do you . . . It's none of my business, but do you want to call someone?"

Rufus nudges my other hand, and I stroke his head gently, unsure if I'm reassuring him or he's reassuring me. But then I register a low rumble of thunder, and the last thirty minutes come spinning back to me as he trembles under my touch.

"We need to get Rufus safe," I say, pushing into my unlocked apartment.

Drew follows me inside without another word, taking note of the lights and music playing as I flip the deadbolt and secure the chain lock. My makeshift barstools and shoe rack obstacle course still litter my living space. I take a moment to right one of the chairs before realizing I'm literally dripping water all over the floor, and head for my closet instead. Rufus follows, walking at my heels like glue, which is okay with me. I stroke his head with one hand while shuffling through hangers with my other until I find a comfortable hoodie and shorts to change into. I glance over my shoulder, relieved to see Drew has shifted back into dog guru mode, opening his backpack and taking out a dry dog shirt and socks for Rufus. His own K9 Academy polo shirt clings soaking wet to his chest.

I hesitate a moment, then turn back to my closet and rummage deeper, only letting my eyes trace over the garment bag in the back because what I'm looking for is probably also in that stratosphere. And I'm right—I pull Kyle's soft black and gold CU Buffs sweatshirt off the hanger and hold it up. It was worn and frayed way before he gave it to me, and it's a little worse for wear considering I lived in it most of the time he was deployed. But it's the only thing I have that might remotely fit Drew.

"Here," I say, handing it to him and taking my own clothes to the bathroom. "I'm just going to . . . I'll be right out."

The steady, upbeat rhythm of "In The Mood" by Glenn

Miller and his Orchestra pulses through the door as I peel off my saturated clothes, trying not to think about Drew out there doing the same. If more thunder happens to be pounding outside, the trombones and bass do an excellent job of drowning it out. By the time I've dried off, changed, and pulled my damp hair into a braid, Drew has also outfitted himself and Rufus.

"Huh. That fits you better than it ever did Kyle," I observe, noting how well he fills out the sweatshirt.

"It . . . actually used to be mine," he says. "I think he stole it from me when I came home once freshman year."

My brows shoot up. "So, I've actually been wearing *your* sweatshirt all these years?"

His cheeks go a little pink. "Technically."

A clap of thunder rumbles under the music, and my gaze snaps to Rufus, who is decked out in a new, dry dog coat and leggings like the ones Drew left here last time. But unlike last time, he's sitting upright, panting. Not buried under the couch, and not drooling. I drop to my knees so I can rub the velvety fur on his nose.

"You're a good boy. You're being so brave." The dog lets out a light, pitiful whine, but then he sinks down, settling on the floor with his muzzle in my lap. I glance at Drew. "He's . . . he seems a little better?"

"He's still having a trauma response," Drew quips. "He might always with storms and similar things."

I bite my lip, worried I don't actually read him as well as I thought I did. What if I'm not doing enough and I can't even tell?

"I didn't want to take him outside. It was an emergency. But I did everything else I could think of—the lights and music like you did last time, I tried to talk to him—"

"He *is* doing better." Drew meets my gaze, and his eyes are a warm, earthy green. "You're doing a good job with him, Caprice."

"Oh." I hesitate, fidgeting with the dog's collar. "Thanks?"

"Look, I came here tonight because of the storm, and because I wanted to check on Rufus. But also . . ." He lets out a low breath. "I owe you an apology."

My stomach tightens at the question in his eyes. The softness of his voice. And suddenly I wish he'd just glare at me or make some criticism instead. "I don't need—"

"Yes, you do."

He lowers himself to the floor on the other side of the dog, much like we were in the last storm. And now I definitely don't want to hear whatever he's about to say. I wasn't expecting the word *apology* and I don't need it. I heard everything I needed to last week, and now I just want him to leave. But when he settles in front of me, gently stroking Rufus's ears, I press my lips together and force myself to listen.

"I was wrong for assuming anything that happened between you and Kyle. I'm sorry," he says. "The truth is, he hardly spoke to me before he died. You were always more of a family to him."

I twine my fingers together, a weight sinking in my chest.

"We'd always been close as kids. But things changed when I left for school," Drew says, laying a hand on Rufus's head in my lap. "He must've told you we raised assistance dogs growing up? We did basic training with puppies, took them places to get them used to different environments and people. It was our parents' idea at first. They said it would look good on college applications. But we loved it—it was life-changing, especially for Kyle."

I swallow down the growing lump in my throat. I know all these details, but somehow it feels new, hearing them from Drew's perspective.

"He just had a way with animals."

The reverence in his voice surprises me, as if he hadn't also been bestowed with the same gift? Rufus lets out a contented sigh between us, only panting a little at a low rumble of thunder. Overall, he seems far from the basket case who ate my couch just weeks ago. Mostly because of Drew.

"Seems like that runs in the family," I say.

The corner of his mouth tugs up, then drops again. "There was this yellow lab we raised. Her name was Boatie. I think I was about fifteen and Kyle was eight. She was a terror. She stole stuff off the kitchen counters; she would poop in her kennel and smear it everywhere. Never listened to anything. Our parents wanted to withdraw from the assistance puppy program just to get rid of her, but Kyle refused. He kept working with her patiently, every day for hours, and eventually he got through. He just . . . figured out what she needed."

My eyes burn. I nod. Kyle was really good at that.

"That was the first time he told our parents he didn't want to be a doctor. He wanted to train dogs." Drew's face is suddenly inscrutable. But he doesn't have to finish the story. I know what happened next. Their parents shamed Kyle, told him a career with animals was lowly and undeserving of respect. That the only path to esteem was the one they'd taken. Nothing else was acceptable—if he didn't become a doctor, he wasn't worthy of their love.

They had it so fucking backward.

A sour taste fills my mouth thinking about all this now. But I clear my throat and ask what feels like the hardest, most obvious question. "Do you think he would've been better off if he'd gone to med school?"

The expression on Drew's face tells me he gets my subtext: *If Kyle hadn't enlisted, if he hadn't had a TBI, maybe he'd still be alive.*

His big hands go still, buried next to mine in Rufus's fur. "We already discussed his depression . . . how it intensified after his injury."

Our eyes meet, and when he pins me with those desolate green eyes, it's like I'm being suffocated by Kyle's ghost—by the darkness and sorrow that always chased him, that he never got out from under. Then Drew pushes his glasses up his nose. And somehow, that simple gesture shifts the air between us, pushing oxygen back into my lungs.

"We did," I whisper.

"He struggled with it all his life. But Kyle always made his own choices," Drew says. "And I admired him for that."

Acid burns the back of my throat. That's possibly the most loaded statement I've ever heard. "You admired him? For fucking killing himself?"

"No—that's not what I meant." Drew goes pale and shakes his head. "What I admired was how he *lived*. He didn't compromise. He knew who he was and what he wanted. No one could force him into anything, especially not our parents. He chose his career. He chose to be with you. I was the older brother, I should've set that example, but . . . I couldn't."

I peer at him more closely, confused by his words. "I thought you wanted to be a doctor."

He doesn't say anything, and suddenly the room goes still.

"Drew?"

Finally, he raises his head, and the look in his eyes reminds me of one of the rare times Kyle spoke about his brother. All he'd said was, *Drew always does what he's told.*

My heartbeat slows. "I . . . think I understand."

His gaze drops to his lap.

"Well," I say, my voice thick. "That comes back to my point. Maybe if Kyle had followed your lead, he'd still be here."

"I doubt that," Drew says with finality. But then he looks at me a moment, tilting his head like he's conflicted. "Do you think . . . You made it clear how things ended. Would it be weird to tell me how you and Kyle started?"

This is so the last thing I expect him to ask, I nearly laugh. "I'm sorry, what?"

He shrugs, though I don't miss a flicker of a smile. "You

don't have to share. I was just curious. I know I missed out on a lot that was important to him."

I straighten, running my hand along Rufus's side. For a long time, Drew Forbes was a symbol of everything that had gone wrong. He was the last person I would've told anything about my first love. But sitting here, riding out another storm with him and Rufus, things have shifted. Right now, he feels like the only person in the world I want to talk to about Kyle.

"Um, it's been a while since I thought about this . . ." I close my eyes. "On some level, he was *always* there. Kyle and Theo were best friends. I'm not sure I stood out to him either for a long time." When I realize I'm grinning, I open my eyes. "I guess that changed sophomore year. Kyle and Theo showed up at one of my track meets, and of course Kyle had a very large 'puppy' with him." I stick out my tongue. "As you've pointed out, I've never been a huge dog fan, and that didn't improve when Kyle's dog got loose and chased me halfway around the track."

Drew covers his mouth with his hand, but his eyes dance.

"Eventually, his dumb black lab ran right in front of me. I nearly crashed, and I ended up losing the event for our team. So when I saw Kyle and his idiot dog waiting for me after the meet, I didn't hesitate to tell him exactly what I thought of his 'training skills.'"

Drew can no longer contain his laughter. "What did he have to say for himself?"

"He waited patiently until I'd run out of insults, then he asked me out." My heart does a light skip when I meet Drew's eyes.

He clears his throat. "Well, um . . . having been on the receiving end of similar criticism, I'm impressed he had the guts."

My smile broadens as the memory replays. Kyle was scrawnier then. His hair shaggier. But he had a double-dimple smile, a jaw that could cut glass, and enough charm in his little finger to make a team of cheerleaders swoon. "I lost the heat." I shrug. "But I won a *very* cute boyfriend."

"You were together a long time," Drew says quietly.

"Yeah. Eleven years." I clutch my chest as the ache seeps back in. "By the time we graduated from high school, I knew everything about him. His passions, his hobbies, his dreams . . ." I force a breath in and out. "But I still couldn't save him."

"I couldn't either, Caprice." His voice is somber. "I tried to make amends. I came to the wedding to show my support, to try and say I was sorry. But when I got there and thought you were leaving . . . I didn't know what to say to him. So I left. By the time I was ready to try again, he did the same thing to me that he did to you—he just pulled further away."

My pulse beats in my throat. "Sometimes I think if I'd just—"

"You did everything you could." Drew raises his head and holds my gaze. "Kyle's own thoughts were his worst enemy. It was never me, and it was never you."

My eyelids flutter closed. "I-I loved him so much."

"I know." His voice is raw. "I did too."

CHAPTER
THIRTY-ONE

When I open my eyes again, I realize we're touching. Just our fingertips brushing, woven into Rufus's golden fur. Something tender and a little broken flutters in my chest, but rather than pull away, I look up into Drew's face.

"I'm sorry," he whispers.

"For what?"

"That Kyle made you think you weren't enough."

I swallow, barely registering a low rumble of thunder as I slide my hand into his, giving his fingers a gentle squeeze. Our eyes meet with a question, but the answer is already there, reflecting at each of us through our grief. Shuddering through my chest into his. By the time it passes, our hands are grasping, clutching each other. And the next thing I know, we've risen to our knees above the dog—and my lips are on Drew's.

Somewhere in the back of my mind, Kyle's kisses linger, a sweet faded memory that will never be new again. For a moment I get scared, afraid I'm about to lose them—confuse them. Do something I'll regret. But while my chest vibrates with what's forbidden, my fears evaporate under Drew's lips. Soft and tender, echoing my hungry need. His clean, sandalwood scent takes over my senses, consuming my thoughts, suffocating everything else but this.

He pulls me closer with a strong arm, and I can't get close enough. We both pause, glancing down at the dog, now curled up peacefully on the rug, the way he usually sleeps.

"Is he . . . ?"

"He's okay," Drew murmurs, glancing out the window at the diminishing storm. "The worst is over."

With those words, we rise together, fingers still entwined. Afraid to let go, it seems, in case we break some kind of spell. Once we clear the sleeping dog, we navigate around the couch against each other's lips. My hands explore his solid arms and chest while his big palms curve over my waist and ass until we fall onto my duvet in a tangle of limbs. At least the beauty of a tiny apartment is that it's never far to the bed.

"Uh, my jeans are still kinda wet," he says with a glance at my linens.

"Then you should let me remove them," I say, burying my face in his neck, breathing him in.

His pants are on the floor moments later, soon joined by my hoodie. The freaking flagpole in his boxer briefs sets off all kinds of fireworks inside me as his mouth traces over my collarbone and down between my breasts.

"God, you're beautiful," he whispers against my flesh. "I knew you would be."

His glasses slide cool against my skin, making me shiver. He starts to take them off, but there's a tug in my gut and I reach down, stopping his wrist with my hand. "I like them."

His mouth pulls into an uncertain smile, but he leaves them on, making his way back up my chest and neck, laving my earlobe with his tongue until I am practically bucking my hips into his crotch. I slide my hands under the CU sweatshirt—his sweatshirt—and he raises his arms so I can slide it up and over his head. And then I'm running my fingers over the bare expanse of his unspeakably carved chest and stomach, as perfect and artful as the angles of his face.

I groan, my mouth watering just looking at him. Kyle and I may have done the long-distance thing, but even when it was virtual, he always took care of me. After our split, I upgraded my vibrator, but quickly got comfortable with casual sex. Probably on some level to soothe my anger, but also out of need. There is only so much you can get out of a toy before you're longing for the real thing. And since Rufus recently ate my vibrator *and* destroyed my dating life, there has been a near-steady ache between my legs.

"Take these fucking shorts off before I soak through them, please."

Drew moans briefly against my breast, but doesn't hesitate to peel the offending clothing down over my hips. I suppress an eye roll when he doesn't take my panties with them, only because I'm one hundred percent sure he's trying to be polite. Instead, I run a finger under the waistband of his black boxer briefs and give his straining cock a little squeeze.

"Condoms are in the bedside drawer," I say as he gasps.

By the time he's found one and turned back to me, my bra and panties have joined the rest of our attire on the floor. Something like dismay flits over Drew's face as he tracks the step I've skipped, but whatever frustration he might have had quickly shifts to lust as he drinks in my naked body.

"I'll hold that," I say, plucking the condom from his fingers so he can cup my breasts with both hands. He kneads them together, burying his face between them, rolling and teasing my nipples one at a time until the ache at my core is a full-on throb.

"My turn." My voice is raw and husky as I reach for his shorts, pulling them carefully down until his thick cock bounces free and points at me like a compass. I fist it in my hand, and we groan together when my fingertips don't even come close to touching around it. "Fuck. Yes, please."

But I'm a glutton for delayed gratification, so instead of rolling on the condom, the first thing I do is flatten my tongue and run it over his tip.

"Fuck," he hisses, and I savor a salty drop of promise as I run my tongue around the head to get him moist before closing my lips around him. This time, whatever words make it out of his mouth are unintelligible. I take this as verification that he likes what I'm doing, and keep up my ministrations. Opening my mouth wider, I slowly work him as far as I can manage into my throat.

He starts to move, and I relax my jaw, moving to his rhythm, letting the fire build between my legs, until suddenly he gasps and pulls out. He collects himself, then advances, tipping me back until I flop into the covers and he's caged me with his enormous, sculpted body. He looks me over like I'm something he's savoring, then grumbles under his breath.

"You are going to fucking kill me." He presses me into the covers with his kisses, then pulls back gently to look at me, trailing one hand down my body until his fingers slip between my legs, finding me wet and needy. "Ohh," he groans, sounding satisfied. "You are *ready* for me."

"Yes," I gasp. His fingers glide up and down along the length of my center, and I might combust if I don't get some relief. "Please."

Drew doesn't wait for clearer direction. He takes the foil packet from me, tearing it open and rolling it handily down his considerable length before positioning himself at my entrance.

"I'm . . . big. I'll try to ease in."

I rake my nails down his arms. "Just get inside me, Forbes."

So he does. With one short thrust and a flash of heat, I am deliciously filled, my ready channel expanding to accommodate him, except he *keeps* filling me. Pushing further, shaft stretching so far it feels like I have to exhale just to let him sink the rest of the way in.

"Did what you asked." He grunts.

"Yes." I gasp, wide-eyed, but *not* complaining. "Just uh—just need a sec."

He waits patiently, remaining still for the moments it takes to collect myself. Then I look straight up at him. "Oh, that's fantastic," I say. "Now, *please* move."

A smirk tugs at his lips, but he does what I ask, moving softly at first, stretching me further and making me pant each time his head nudges my cervix.

"Oh, fuck."

I'm not sure if that was me, or him, or both of us as I lose myself in his rhythm, savoring the friction he creates as he thrusts against my ache. I stretch my arms out, wrapping my legs around him as his movement intensifies. At some point he grabs my legs, pulling me up his thighs while he kneels. As soon as I'm in place, he reaches down and finds my nipples, rolling and squeezing them until my core is so tight I am bucking in his lap.

"What do you need?" he asks, voice quavering like it's going to break apart any moment.

"I-I—" There's no way I can speak, so I thrust my fingers between my legs, zeroing in on my clit as he keeps up his rhythm.

His face registers what I'm doing, but he bats my hand away, placing one of his big thumbs at my center instead without missing a single delicious thrust. "Allow me."

My eyes widen at the bold suggestion that he can balance his own pleasure with mine, but the look on his face is pure and confident lust, so I decide to let him try.

And I'm not too proud to admit when I am instantly impressed. He pumps his thick cock into me while somehow also maintaining the exact right amount of pressure in the exact right place to dial my pleasure through the roof. My body and mind can't handle the onslaught, and it takes roughly six seconds before I am literally screaming and convulsing with the best fucking orgasm I've had in two years. But Drew doesn't let up. He pummels his cock into me harder—never missing a beat with that clearly skilled thumb —until I climax a *second* time. At which point he emits a deep groan, and with one more great thrust, he comes along with me, his cock slowing its rhythm in time with my pulsing core.

We collapse together on our sides, and before I can speak, he pulls me with him under the covers. Only vaguely do I register Rufus's nose at the side of the bed, sniffing curiously at us until Drew mutters, "Ruf, she's okay."

I crack an eye open and laugh when I register the dog's uncertain face. I give him a small pat while fighting back a yawn. "Definitely okay. Quite a bit more than, I'd say."

Rufus looks back and forth between the two of us before making a bored snort and climbing back on his couch. Drew gathers me in his arms, and I press my face to his chest, breathing him in as he strokes my hair. Losing myself in his scent, his warmth, his skin. Vaguely, sometime just before I start to dream, the vase of wilted roses darts like an intruder through my mind, invading my peace. I'll have to speak with Randall about it tomorrow, try to figure out what it means. But for now, I clutch the sheets, burrowing closer to Drew. Sinking into a deeper, more secure sleep than I've had in months.

CHAPTER
THIRTY-TWO

I wake with a stretch, my limbs jutting into the cold, empty space beside me. Normally, my lonely bed is not somewhere I care to linger, but I'm reluctant to open my eyes and leave such wonderful dreams behind. The melancholy chorus of a Taylor Swift song flits through the back of my brain as I try to register what day it is—Sunday? I have an interview to prepare for about the rise in graffiti art downtown, I need to order groceries, and . . . something I'm forgetting. But when I blink my eyes open to find a shirtless, broody man staring out my window, I remember exactly what it is.

"Oh—"

I draw the sheets up over my naked form, going from zero to fully conscious as all the intimate details of last night flood back to my mind. The storm. Rufus. The dead bouquet. Drew. My cheeks warm as I study his tousled dark hair and glasses in the early morning light, and a pulse of desire echoes between my legs. I drag the sheets with me across the bed, needing to be in his arms again, wrapped up where I was warm and safe.

"Good morning," I say, leaning into his chest, breathing in the scent of bare skin and sex.

He doesn't speak, just cups the nape of my neck in one big hand, pulling me close. There's something urgent in the way he holds me, something careless, and I trail my fingers down his spine, relishing the way he shivers in response.

"Do you need to rush off, or can I convince you to stay?" I murmur.

He still doesn't answer. And now my senses are perking up, taking in the rigidness of his posture even while our skin feels ready to ignite. I wait a full minute, watching the light change on his face as the sun fades behind a cloud.

"Drew?"

"This was a mistake," he finally whispers.

A thick, familiar feeling creeps into my throat. I attempt to ignore it, sliding my hand down his torso. "I don't think that's a word I'd use to describe multiple orgasms. Maybe one more would change your—"

He closes a hand around my wrist—if I'm not mistaken, the one with the talented thumb. "This was wrong. We should never have done it."

I blink at his words, but now I'm the one who can't look him in the eye. "You . . . you didn't have a good time?"

He pulls back, his gaze raking over my body as if there's no sheet between us at all. "You know that's not what I'm talking about."

"No, actually, I don't." I step back, watching the lust fade from his eyes. And something fragments inside me. Because all I want to do is touch him again. "We're two consenting adults. We had fun together. What's wrong?"

"What's *wrong*," he says, dragging a hand over his face, "Is that I slept with my brother's fiancée."

His words hit me like a slap. Like I'm being accused of something.

"But Kyle—"

"Is dead." He glares at me. "So that makes it okay?"

"No, that's not what . . ." I trail off when I realize that even now, I crave his touch. I want him back inside me—I want that feeling. Like he'd made me whole again.

It was like I'd come home.

But now my throat goes dry. Because *is* it Drew I crave? Or have I been trying to channel a ghost?

Drew rakes his hand through his hair and steps away. Leaving me by the window, staring at the still-pink sky. He pulls on his jeans and the sweatshirt that was always his. When he speaks again, his voice comes out low and broken.

"I just wanted to ensure everything Kyle loved was cared for. He loved Rufus. He loved you. I didn't mean to—"

"You didn't mean to what?" I say sharply, folding my arms to protect myself from the pain in my chest. "It was just sex, Drew."

His face darkens. He crosses the room in three strides, coming so close I have to tilt my chin up to look at him. We aren't touching, but we will be if I so much as breathe. Then he leans down, eyes like embers as he whispers, "Was it, Caprice?"

I open my mouth.

But no sound comes.

He pulls away, and immediately the air cools. I watch as he jams his feet into his shoes, then picks up his backpack and keys. Rufus peeks his head over the couch, tail slapping against the ruined cushion when he sees us. Ready for breakfast and a walk.

I ball my fists.

"So, what does this mean?" I ask, voice low and controlled. "Because Kyle isn't here to love, we're all just supposed to suffer?"

Drew pauses on his way to the door, but doesn't answer. I look at the dog, staring at me with those golden eyes, like some window straight to my broken heart.

And what's left of it ices over.

"You know what?" I say, not giving myself time to think. "If that's the case, you'd better take the dog with you."

At this, Drew turns and looks at me. "I don't want—"

"No." I stop him. "We're not thinking about what we want, we're thinking about Kyle." I pick up the leash, the food bowl, and some random toys, piling them into Drew's arms. "Kyle clearly wanted to punish me. He knew I loved him, so he abandoned me. He knew I hated dogs, so he fucking willed me one. He probably knew I'd care about you, so—" My voice gives out as hot, fat tears break free down my cheeks.

"Caprice—"

I pull away, whispering. "Just take him. You got what you wanted, Drew."

Out the window in front of me, the mountains glow with golden morning light. I wish it were still dark and raining and less *dawn of a new day*, but I'd rather suffer the beauty than risk looking at the man or dog behind me. Drew says nothing, but after a moment I hear him moving around. My throat closes up when I recognize the rattle of Rufus's tags as he jumps off the couch. The light click of his leash being clipped to his collar. I squeeze my eyes shut at the sound of my door opening, two sets of feet passing through it. And finally, when it clicks closed, all the air is sucked out of my chest.

I turn to face my empty apartment, with its giant dog crate, half-eaten couch, and half-assembled obstacle course. And me, standing alone, clinging to a sheet still fresh with sex and longing.

I sink to the floor, wrapping my arms around my body, trying to hold myself together.

The pieces of my heart broken three times over.

CHAPTER
THIRTY-THREE

My mom hates when I drive my Vespa on the highway. Any time she finds out I've done it, she rails off horror stories and safety statistics, drawing a bleak picture of how dangerous it is and reminding me I'm the only daughter she has. But when I show up at her house Sunday afternoon, windblown, with snot and tears stuck to my face, she presses her lips together and makes me a cup of tea.

We sit at her kitchen table for over an hour. I don't have to say much. My mom has always been perceptive. By the time we've finished our second cups, I've used up half a box of tissues and she's clear on everything that matters.

"I just never thought I'd miss the damn dog," I say, clutching my hands in my lap because my inclination is to reach for the soft fuzz on his ears. I hate that my fingers actually ache from not being able to do this.

My mom reaches for me, squeezing my hand instead. "I'd be willing to bet you never thought you'd miss a Forbes again either."

I cut her a look, but her gaze is steady.

"I'll be right back. I need to get something," she says, letting go of my hand and slipping toward her bedroom.

She's probably getting out the home pedicure kit. Our go-to pampering when either of us is under stress. I stare at the bottom of my mug, waiting for her to bustle back carrying the Epsom salt and plug-in foot bath.

But when she glides back in, there's only one small item in her hand. An envelope that she places on the table in front of me.

I take a breath, staring at my name written in Kyle's straight, neat handwriting.

"I've held on to that long enough." She doesn't sit back down with me, but picks up her keys and crosses to the kitchen door. "I'm going to run some errands. Call if you need me."

When she's gone, I carry the envelope into the living room and wrap up in a blanket on the couch where Kyle and I first kissed—and did even more exploring. I bring the envelope to my face and inhale. It smells like paper, not like him. But I still savor that he touched it. That he wrote this and put it together with the same hands he touched me with.

Then I open his letter.

Caprice—my love,

I'm sure by now you're plenty pissed at me. Theo too. Your mom. Everyone else. For what it's worth, I'm mad at myself for not figuring this out sooner. I'm sorry.

You aren't going to want to hear this, but I want you to know I'm making this choice because I love you. Because while I was lying in bed, trying to imagine us at the church tomorrow, starting a life together, all I could think about was how much pain I'll cause you. How much I've already caused.

It's not just you moving across the country, away from your mom, your job, your friends—everything that enriches you. It's why you're doing it. Holding me up, keeping me going. The way you always have. You've literally made my life worth living the last ten years when no one else could. But what have I done for you except induce stress and worry? It's time I fight on my own.

I'm not an idiot. I know this is still going to hurt you. But only for a short time—not forever. I hope you'll understand one day. I hope you'll move on and find the things that bring you joy. It gives me peace thinking about the beautiful life you'll live. You'll always be the best thing that ever happened to me.

I love you,
Kyle

Monday, April 12, 20__, 5:16 AM

To: **Kyle.Forbes@mail.com**

From: **Caprice_Phipps@mail.com**

Subject: Re: Re: Re: Re: Re: Re: no subject

Dear Kyle,

Every day, for two years, I've wished that you'd stayed.

My life was never better without you—no one's was. For a while, I thought maybe you orchestrated everything on purpose, just to have the last laugh. But I bet it was hard—like everything else. Making your plan. Putting things in writing. Following through. All while you were suffering.

I wish you'd picked up the phone and called instead of slipping a note in my purse. I wish you'd answered my calls. Let me help. Let me love you. I wish you hadn't been in so much pain. You were always so burdened, but *you* were never a burden.

I've been so focused on what I might've done wrong, how I wasn't enough. But I think I understand now—I wasn't really the problem. It was that everything *else* was too much.

There's so much more I want to tell you, but I'll stick to what's most important—Rufus is good. I mean that in every sense of the word. He's a good dog. He clearly misses you, but he's going to be okay. Remember in high school when you swore you'd make a dog person out of me? Well, I just want you to know—I'm *still* not a dog person, but I love Rufus. And I'll always love you.

Love,
Caprice

DREW

It only took a couple of days for the dogs to work things out. Pudding and Blitz were never the issue. He'd introduced Rufus to the bulldog first, who welcomed him as a playmate, predictably, from the get-go. Blitz was more ambivalent, open to Rufus joining the pack as long as his existence didn't infringe on his own food or activities. But final approval fell to the shepherd. Drew knew Diesel would accept him eventually, though it was sort of like watching an old officer enduring a new recruit. Rufus came in bold and cocky, strutting around the house like he owned the place at first, until Diesel would get sick of him and put him in his place.

Rufus learned quickly, however, and before long his respect for the older dog was ironed out. Once the pecking order was established, they settled into a daily routine. Drew would bring Rufus with him to work, where he was, for the most part, a model of good training. They would take lunch breaks at home to engage with the other three. And most evenings, Drew would take the Malinois and the border collie for runs in the park.

They always looked for Caprice. They never once caught sight of her.

But they kept each other breathing.

The Sunday after he brought Kyle's military dog home to live with him, Drew decided to bring Rufus with him to family dinner. It wasn't a choice, exactly. There was a chance of thunderstorms, and he wasn't willing to risk leaving him, even in the companionship of the other dogs. Not for the sake of his mother's Cornish hens.

So he ended up ringing their doorbell with two of Kyle's favorites—a Belgian Malinois and a tub of rocky road.

"Drew, dear, if you wouldn't mind, I—" His mother's sentence cut off as she opened the door. She leaned outside, glancing up and down the street. "Did one of the neighbor's pets get out?"

"No, Mom," he said flatly. "This is Rufus. Kyle's dog."

He watched carefully as her lip twitched. "Why did you bring it here?"

"Because I'm here," he said, skipping the air kisses and breezing past her into his childhood home.

They entered the overly formal front hall with its black-and-white marble floors and curving staircase. His father descended from the landing, wearing a suit jacket and carrying a *pipe* of all things. Like he'd accessorized from a pinboard of pretentious male accessories. Drew would have laughed if his dad hadn't been frowning so hard in his direction.

"What's this, Andrew?"

Drew bristled. Either from being called by his formal name—his father's name—or maybe Rufus being referred to as *it* and *this* since they'd walked in the door.

"The dog was Kyle's," his mother said behind him. Over him.

He turned and handed her the fast-melting ice cream, giving her no choice but to take it and scurry off to the kitchen before it dripped and ruined the floor polish. His dad reached the bottom of the steps, and though they had been the same height for nearly two decades, Drew still felt small.

Rufus remained at his heel. A good dog.

"How have you been, son?" the man asked. Apparently there had been some quick, unspoken agreement with his wife to just pretend Rufus wasn't there.

This rankled Drew. They'd done the same thing to his brother.

He exhaled, trying to rein in his frustration. The real answer to Dr. W. Andrew Forbes's question was that he'd been terrible. He'd walked around like a zombie all week, nursing the giant sinkhole in his chest. After the first night listening to Rufus's mournful whining, he broke every rule in his own book and let the dog sleep in his bed. He'd hoped they might offer some comfort to each other, and on some base level, they did. Unfortunately, they also served as constant reminders that neither of them was Caprice.

But that wasn't the answer his father was interested in.

Drew aimed for the middle. As rebellious as he ever got.

"I've been really busy, actually." He ran a hand through his messy hair. "We've been getting a lot of referrals from one of the local doggie daycares."

Dr. Forbes's bushy eyebrows drew down. He exchanged a glance with his wife as she reentered the room. The air was so thick with disapproval that the barometric pressure might as well have dropped.

"Dinner is served," his mother said, taking her husband's arm and clicking her heels toward the formal dining room.

Drew made a study of his own feet as he shuffled behind them, grateful for the canine glued to his hip.

As his father pulled out his mother's chair, she cleared her throat and launched another assault. "I had a call with Dr. Rashida at Chapel Hill yesterday. They're still *very* interested in bringing you back whenever you're done with your little . . . project."

Drew's breath stuttered. He made a fist at his side and thought of Kyle. "You mean my business?"

She didn't wrinkle her nose, but he saw her effort not to. "Darling, we understood why you had to step away from the fellowship—"

"You understood?" he interrupted, surprising himself.

The two doctors looked at each other before she replied mildly, "Of course we did. You were upset about your brother."

She didn't speak his name.

Her husband took his seat at the head of the table spread with china, sterling silver, and high-flown birds. Drew made no move to join them. He laid a hand on Rufus's head, stroking the softest part of his ear. "Well then, maybe you'll understand why I'm not going back."

They straightened in unison, another silent conversation passing between them. And just like when he was growing up, all he could do was gird himself by petting the dog. But when he closed his eyes, he could almost feel Kyle at his shoulder.

"Now, let's not talk nonsense," his father said, taking a granite tone. "We know you struggled with your brother's loss, but in reality, that has only increased your responsibility to this family."

"My responsibility," Drew echoed.

"Correct," his father intoned. "You were always the eldest son. Now, unfortunately, you're our sole heir."

He raised his head. "What was our *responsibility* to Kyle?"

Another shared glance. That time, more uncomfortable. It reminded him of the dinners after Kyle turned thirteen when he'd started not-so-subtly informing them they were full of shit. They'd stared at him, told him what a disappointment he was for expressing his own opinions.

And what had Drew done about it?

Rufus pushed his nose into his hand.

"I don't want to be a doctor," Drew said, echoing his little brother's brave, tragic words. "I never did."

Dr. W. Andrew Forbes stood from the table, balling up his napkin. "All right, I'm done with this. We paid a lot of money for you to go to medical school."

"Do you want it back?" Drew said without so much as a flinch.

"I beg your pardon?" Dr. Forbes's voice was cold steel.

"I could pay it back." He shrugged, and it was like Kyle was standing there egging him on. "It might take a while, but if that's important to you . . ."

"Drew," his mother said, taking another tack. "You have too brilliant a mind—"

"To pursue the things *I* love?"

Their silence echoed through the room as he realized that's what this was really about. He'd spent most of his life putting these people first, meeting all their expectations and demands. But they'd never once done the same for him. And certainly never his brother.

What they called "love" was a condition.

Kyle had always understood that.

But Drew was certain now that as strong as his brother was, it had still eaten away at him.

And these people weren't worth it.

"You *are* a doctor," his father finally snapped.

Drew's mouth rose on one side as he gripped Rufus's leash. "I *was* a doctor. But now I'm not. And I never will be again." He took a deep gulp of air as soon as he said it, and it felt like his first breath. "Kyle had the right idea."

"Your brother is dead," his mother said, voice quavering like he'd just announced he was going to kill himself too. And then he realized that *was* how she saw it.

"He is. And *I'm* very much alive." He shrugged. "But I guess whether you lose both your sons is up to you."

"Is that a threat?" his father growled. And in a moment of pure poetry, Rufus looked at him and growled back.

"Get that animal out of here," Dr. Patricia Forbes hissed.

"Easy . . ." Drew whispered to Rufus. Then an idea occurred to him, and he gave another command.

The dog looked up at him, probably thinking he hadn't heard right.

Drew suppressed a smile and repeated himself.

Two seconds later, Rufus had sprung from the floor and was standing over the Cornish hens in the middle of the formal supper table. Drew ignored his parents' horrified gasps, carved some meat off a bird to reward the dog, then directed him back to the floor. In testament to his agile grace, not a single dish or crystal glass had broken. Not even Drew's own chipped dinner plate.

Drew didn't look back as he guided Rufus to the door. He wouldn't waste another second on these people. He'd made mistakes—years and years of them. And it was far too late for Kyle to forgive him. But maybe there was still hope for his heart.

CHAPTER
THIRTY-FOUR

THE DAY AFTER MY FIRST FEATURE IN A SERIES ABOUT CHRONIC depression and mental health runs in the *Mile High Observer*, Randall calls me into his office to celebrate. I'd given Kyle a pseudonym for the piece, but it was essentially a profile about him and his lifelong struggle. I cried when I finished writing it, while Randall assured me this was exactly the kind of story he knew I could produce. And apparently it resonated with people. A cluster of follows and shares led to a wider discussion of psychiatric and family support, and it was picked up pretty quickly by several national outlets.

One comment stuck with me in particular. A brief note from a mom whose son's life drew an eerie parallel with Kyle's—a head injury early on, which accelerated his already pervasive depression. But that young man was still here, still fighting, and she thanked me for bringing awareness to his unique situation and needs.

"I thought that would be the highlight of my day," I say, "until I got this."

I pass my phone to Randall, who trades me for a celebratory Hershey bar from his personal stash.

He scans the email pulled up on my screen, then looks up at me, grinning.

"A personal invite from the Features editor at *Denver Editorial*? Are you going to apply?"

I bite my lip. "Probably?"

He scoffs. "I mean, it's only *Denver Editorial*. You could hold out for *The New York Times* . . ."

I roll my eyes.

He chuckles and folds his arms. "You deserve it, Caprice. You've outgrown this place."

My eye catches on a forgotten dog toy sticking out from under his desk, and I frown. "Think of all the lattes I could create, though."

"Think of the cutthroat piece you could write about career baristas being a source of lost potential in the arts."

My jaw drops and he laughs. "It's almost five o'clock. Get out of here and go polish your CV."

Naturally, I go straight to the gym.

It *has* been blissful, easing back into a weight routine, getting to focus on toning and strength training rather than just cardio this past week. I've spent upward of ninety minutes every night catching up on lower body, upper body, and core exercises that were beyond the hand weights and yoga mat I squeezed into my tiny living room. Over the weekend, I even joined a kickboxing class.

What hasn't been blissful is going home to my quiet, empty apartment.

My phone rings as soon as I step out of the gym onto the sidewalk.

"Hi," I say, holding the device up so I can see Lydia's face.

"Ooh, I like your hair!" she says, peering at me. "Did you get it braided?"

"A couple days ago, yep." I turn my head so she can see

both sides. "Hadn't been to the salon in months. Needed a change."

"I love it." Lydia smiles. "God, I need to get a trim before I go into labor. I have, like, twice as much hair than before I was pregnant." She pushes her voluminous locks out of the way. "What are you up to? Anton said he saw you working out."

"He did," I say, playing along with her obvious surveillance. "He was doing hanging leg lifts, and I raised a threatening eyebrow at him from the bench press."

She grumbles. "I *asked* him to offer you a ride, but he insisted you'd say no. So, I thought we could just chat on your walk home."

"His guess was correct," I mutter, glancing up and down the sidewalk. "But just to set you at ease, there haven't been any new threatening messages, and no unusual activity on my camera since the flowers."

"Oh, I know. I've been checking it since you gave me the login," she says. "I think I know Darius and Todd's work schedules by heart. But doesn't it make you nervous *not* getting any messages? That seems . . . I don't know. Unlike him."

The "him," we're assuming, is Erik Schneider, the co-developer of Unmatched, who I profiled in my latest flop. And her instincts are dead-on—I'm more terrified *not* receiving garbage from him than when he was delivering regular notes. But there's no reason she needs to know that at more than eight months pregnant.

I check over my shoulder and shrug. "Don't worry, I'll be *fine*. I told you how seriously the police took my report. They're out there right now hunting down the dead-bouquet stalker."

She levels me with a stare.

"Wow, your fed-up mom face is legit," I say.

Instantly, she pales, and I feel a little guilty pinging her anxiety about motherhood . . . but not too much.

"Fine. Subject change," she says. "I loved your feature."

"Thanks." My tone softens. "This one seems like a home run."

"Because you're a star. And it's important." Her mouth presses into a sad smile. "Maybe since I knew him, it was obvious you were writing about Kyle. But when you described the isolation and despair he went through . . ." Her voice quavers. "Caprice, it was powerful."

I look away from the camera, checking up and down the street and wiping my eye as I turn a corner. "It felt important to tell his story. Though I'm not sure he'd approve."

"You know he would have," she says quietly, pulling her hair over one shoulder. "Giving a voice to the voiceless? He would have been proud of you."

My feet slap the sidewalk for five heartbeats before she takes another breath and speaks.

"Have you heard anything from—"

"No."

After the print issue dropped yesterday, I was worried Drew or his family would reach out to complain. Aside from using a pseudonym for Kyle, I didn't conceal much about who he was. If they read the article, they would know it was about him and probably be upset. But I have a seven-thousand-dollar dress in my closet that I wore, intending to marry him. It felt like I had the right to honor his memory. Still, it's probably best that they didn't read it.

"Okay, I'm entering my building," I say, flipping the camera around and turning in a slow circle for her inspection. "Nobody weird out here except the guys who are always vaping on the corner, and the lady walking by with the dyed pink poodle."

"Oh! She's a client!" Lydia waves and grins.

"Are you happy?"

"Nope," she says firmly. "Let's go for an elevator ride."

I sigh, following her orders, showing her every nook and cranny of my building's lobby and empty corridors until I'm standing in front of my apartment door.

"No creepy packages, envelopes, notes, or floral arrangements." I exhale, admittedly relieved.

"Great. Open the door and let me follow you inside," she says. "Do you have your pepper spray?"

"Have you been talking to Theo?"

She laughs me off and waits. I stand in the hall, clutching my stomach. Not because I'm scared—well, I am, as much as any harassed woman would be. But mostly I dread what I *know* is on the other side of the door. Or more precisely, what isn't.

"Okay, here goes."

It's remarkable how huge four hundred square feet can feel once it isn't being occupied by a sixty-pound animal. I do a quick tour for Lydia's sake, poking into the bathroom and closets, then circling back and making sure the front door is locked.

"We're going couch shopping this weekend," she says. It's not a question.

"Sure," I say, navigating around the now-empty living room space as if my destroyed piece of furniture is still there. "Okay, I have work to catch up on. I'm safe, I'm alive. I'm going to go."

"Great. I love you. Call me tomorrow!" she singsongs as we disconnect.

I set my things down on the kitchen counter next to a pretty glass bottle I repurposed as a bud vase. I spent the first five days vacuuming and Cloroxing every surface after Drew took Rufus. The downside now is there's nothing left to clean. My entire apartment is spotless.

"Fine, shower it is," I mutter, then close my eyes. I never used to talk to myself before I had the dog.

. . .

Once I've unwrapped my hair and snuggled up in my PJs, I work on my CV for an hour, then settle at the counter with a bowl of noodles and steel myself to open my email. I'm not *looking* to freak myself out. But I'd almost feel better if something unpleasant was waiting for me. Nothing too intense—a nasty note. Something criticizing my use of verbs. Maybe a comment about my name. A week of silence was not at all what I expected to follow a dead bouquet.

But when I open my inbox, what I find hits me harder than any nasty comment or threat.

There's an email from Kyle. Sent an hour ago.

Bile rises in my throat. If this is someone's idea of a sick joke, they're going to be so fucking sorry when I track them down. I click on the message, bracing myself for whatever they've written while trying to focus through a blur of tears.

Monday, April 12, 20__, 9:11 PM

To: Caprice_Phipps@mail.com

From: Kyle.Forbes@mail.com

Subject: Re: no subject

Caprice, this is Drew. Sorry—I hope this doesn't freak you out. I read your article

yesterday. It was *perfect*. Rufus and I have been sitting here, trying to figure out

the right thing to say. But then I opened up Kyle's laptop and . . . I hope you don't

mind. I read the emails you've been sending.

Can we talk?

-Drew

Below his reply is the long string of messages I've been sending Kyle over the past year, culminating in the long one I wrote after reading his letter, two years late. I close my eyes, thinking about Drew reading them—that message in particular. My lungs seize up, my entire body prickling with fear, with hope, possibility . . . and at least a hundred other things. I hop out of my chair. Then back into it immediately to send a reply.

Monday, April 12, 20__, 10:09 PM

To: Kyle.Forbes@mail.com

From: Caprice_Phipps@mail.com

Subject: Re: Re: no subject

Yes. I'd like that.

Could you bring Rufus here?

Caprice

I'm on my feet again a moment later, checking my face in the mirror. Brushing my teeth again. Looking around my weird, half-empty space, trying to find something to straighten. I put on music—downtempo, casual. Just something light to fill the air. My chest feels flooded, everything inside me loose and swirling. He *read* what I wrote about Kyle. He wants to talk.

Maybe what happened between us wasn't the mistake we both thought it was.

When the knock comes at my door, I don't register how fast it came. How it feels like hours, but I only replied minutes ago. All I can think is how much I want to see Drew, see Rufus—throw my arms around both of them.

But when I fling the door open, that's not who's waiting for me at all.

CHAPTER
THIRTY-FIVE

A TALL, NONDESCRIPT WHITE MAN SHOVES INSIDE MY APARTMENT before I can speak, closing and locking the door behind him with a sickening click. I reverse until my back hits a wall. My heart, which until this moment had been pounding with anticipation, immediately escalates into a more rapid, fearful rhythm.

"You—you're in the wrong place," I hear myself say. Stupidly. Passively. *Unlike* myself. I should be attacking this guy, shouting *Get the fuck out of my house.* Instead, my palms sweat. My feet and vocal cords refuse to work.

The guy tilts his head, looking me over with beady dark eyes. "You changed your hair."

And immediately, I know who this is.

Except I don't.

I've seen pictures of Marisol's ex, Erik Schneider, and this man is not him. His hair is too light. He's a little too gaunt. He doesn't have the same charming, boyish face. This man's eyes have a slight bulge over a receding chin.

"Wh-who are you?"

Something contemptuous flashes in his eyes, and I realize too late that this was the wrong question to ask.

He lunges forward. I land on the floor where my couch used to be, knocking the air out of my chest. I roll to one side, gasping, but he's on top of me, grabbing my arms before I can breathe. I open my mouth to scream, but only cough until finally I suck in a lungful of air and raise my knee into his groin.

He cries out, and I roll to the side, following some self-defense script I learned years ago. Or maybe I'm just improvising. I get to my feet, snatching my belt bag off the counter and plunging my hand through the zipper before he slams me into the wall.

"Get off me!" I screech over the music I'd put on for Drew. I close my fingers around the little Taser, trying to locate the switch. He grabs my arm and twists it painfully, and by the time I realize he's forcing the device back toward me, it's too late. I kick out just before the electricity jolts into my side, and then it's like my whole body is cramping up *while* being shot with lightning. My eyes widen, my arms and legs go rigid, and it is the single most terrifying, helpless moment of my life as I drop to the floor. My head cracks something on the way down, but I can't tell if it's that or the Taser that blurs my vision. I lay there for seconds, maybe minutes, eventually pulling myself into a whimpering ball, afraid to move.

Until somewhere far away, I hear a phone ringing.

Lydia's ringtone.

I close my eyes, slowly curling my fingers and toes to see how they respond.

My head now pounds in time with my heart, and there's something warm and wet sliding down my cheek. I don't know where the guy is. All I can hear is Lydia trying to reach me.

When I open my eyes and turn my head, I spot him by the door. He seems distracted, peering through the peephole, so I push myself away, trying to get to the kitchen. The phone stops ringing, and the music I put on earlier resumes, but the ringing starts up again almost immediately, and I keep moving toward it like a beacon. I get behind the breakfast bar, nearly vomit as I pull myself to my knees, and reach up to where I left it.

"No, you don't," says a nasally voice. And then I'm peering up into the man's empty face. My phone is in his hand, and he's turning up the music—cranking it until the drum and bass pound from my Bluetooth speaker.

I think I hear something over it, faintly. A light thumping? It's hard to tell with my head throbbing since I hit the floor.

The man comes around the counter into the kitchen, and my chest seizes as soon as there's no structure between us. I back into the fridge as he reaches out, fighting nausea as his fingers caress my braids.

"P-please," I whisper. "Whatever you want—"

But then the song transitions, and in the quiet, as the music fades, I hear the sound distinctly. Someone is knocking at my door.

"Hello?" I shout.

The man's hand whips from my hair to my mouth—my throat.

I panic, flailing my arms, grabbing for anything. My fingers wrap around the glass bottle by the sink, and I arc it through the air at his head. But instead of smashing and knocking him out, it lands with a thud against his shoulder and falls out of my hand, shattering on the counter as my phone rings again.

"Caprice?" a man calls through my apartment door. His voice is deep with commanding concern, and when I hear him, I want to cry.

I push out with my arms and legs until I have just enough leverage to sink down and bite hard into this douchebag's wrist. He shouts and lets go, and I urge my legs to get me past him. But he grabs my shirt as I round the counter. One of my barstools crashes to the ground as he yanks me against him, and I manage to scream.

"Drew!"

The knocking becomes a pounding—hard and clear now over the music—except my head is also pounding and I'm having trouble working my arms and legs. The angular fucker is dragging me to one side, and I'm so dizzy now I can hardly keep my feet under me when I see him picking up a piece of broken glass on the counter.

My lips feel numb. "Please, no—"

And then several things happen at once.

There's a loud *bang* somewhere in the room, followed by thunderous, powerful barking. Then a deep voice growls, "Go get him."

I see a blur of golden fur as I fall to the floor, and then a man is screaming.

"Ahh! Get it off me!"

There are snarls and thrashing. The room feels like it's underwater as I turn my head, but when I do, I see Rufus, his teeth tearing into my attacker's arm while the man lies on the floor shrieking.

My gaze traces to the large figure holding the leash, and my heart swells when I swear I see a blurry Superman. I squeeze my eyes shut, and when I open them it's even better. Drew stands over me, eyes burning into the man on the floor like all he has to do is take off his glasses to incinerate him. But then he registers me looking at him, and his green eyes immediately soften.

"God, I was so—" He kneels, placing himself between me and the chaos of snarls and screams. "You're safe now."

"I . . ." My throat is tight. My head swims.

"Caprice! Oh my God, girl."

I blink, registering for the first time that there are more people here. Gentle hands roll me over, touch my wrist, and I'm staring up into my neighbor Darius's gentle eyes.

"Todd, is that ambulance on its way?"

"Five minutes," his boyfriend responds from the hall.

Suddenly, thankfully, the too-loud music cuts off, and for a second all we hear are the bitten man's wails.

"Hey, uh, maybe you should call him off before the cops get here?" Darius suggests.

Drew frowns, then utters a command, and Rufus, the best boy ever, releases his bite, returning obediently to his trainer's side. The man moans on the floor. I hope Rufus bit him in the groin.

My phone rings again, and somehow the pulse in my head pounds harder. I try to sit up, but the room spins, and Darius stills me with one hand.

"Could someone just—tell her I'm okay?"

"I got it," Drew says, rising and picking up the phone. "Hi, this is Drew Forbes."

As he attempts to reassure my best friend, something cold and wet nudges my arm. I pry my eyes open to find Rufus beside me, golden eyes dark with concern. He issues a low whine and licks my hand as a group of voices moves toward us down the hall. I reach up to stroke the softest part of his ears and whisper, "My hero."

The next moment, a slew of first responders troop in, and we're inundated with people and questions. Drew tucks Rufus into his crate where he's safe before returning to my side and taking my hand.

"Hey guys," Darius says, slipping further into nurse mode. "Assault victim over here—multiple witnesses present, including myself. Laceration to the head and a likely concussion, possible broken ribs. Also pretty sure she was tased. Alleged perpetrator is over there with a dog bite, but that motherfucker can wait."

There's a *lot* of back and forth from there, between police, firefighters, and paramedics. I doubt this many people have ever crammed into my apartment. Someone takes my pulse.

Blood pressure. Shines a light into my eyes, which is excruciating. I'm asked questions. Drew answers others. But he stays by my side the entire time.

The next thing I know, I'm on a gurney, covering my face to escape the awful glare of overhead lights as I'm wheeled toward the door.

"Wait—what about Rufus?" I ask.

"Don't worry," Darius says. "Todd and I will be collecting Rufus kisses until your girlfriend gets here."

Drew squeezes my hand. "She's on her way now."

I let out a breath, fingers trembling in his as my adrenaline drops. As it slowly sinks in that I'm okay now. I'm safe. "Thank you, guys. For everything."

"Don't thank me." Darius grins. "Nothing was going to keep this perfect ten of yours from getting in here. Or your pooch. When Todd and I saw what was going on, we mostly just called for help."

My lids flutter closed again, a tear trickling from the corner of my eye as the whole ordeal flashes through my mind. From the first terrifying moment after I opened the door, to the time it finally ended with Rufus and Drew barreling in. I rest my throbbing head back on the gurney as I'm wheeled to the elevator, fingers entwined with Drew's. And I think maybe Kyle got something right after all. Maybe somehow he did protect me.

CHAPTER
THIRTY-SIX

THE FIRST THING I SEE WHEN I OPEN MY EYES IS A LARGE, BLURRY shape crammed into an uncomfortable-looking chair. I blink, and a handsome, sleeping man comes into focus in a pair of dark jeans and an unreasonably snug Henley. His glasses sit next to him on a hospital tray table, and just for a moment, asleep like that, he looks so much like Kyle.

Except . . . he doesn't. Now that I'm really looking, all I see anymore is Drew.

"Oh, good, you're awake. How are you feeling?" a nurse says, slipping into the dim room as I sit up. She glances at the hunk of masculine beauty in the chair and gives me a knowing smile. "This guy's pretty devoted."

My mouth twitches. "Has he been here all night?"

"We were supposed to kick him out, but . . ." She rolls her eyes. "I'm a softie for a good dog story."

My gaze flickers back to Drew, and this time warm green eyes blink back at me. He reaches over, slipping his glasses back onto his face, and my heart does a soft little skip.

"I'll be back to change your fluids in a bit," the nurse says, stepping out as quickly as she came. Before the door even closes, Drew has the chair right up next to the bed, and my pulse starts dancing.

"How's your head?" he asks.

I reach up instinctively, fingers tracing over the gauze still taped to my temple. I received nine stitches, a CT scan, and a cocktail of IV drugs before landing here for observation. It felt like some kind of torture getting through all the questions, tests, and pokes with my head ready to explode. But the IV helped a lot, and I was grateful to come out of this ordeal with "only" a moderate concussion and a few bruised ribs.

"Much better." I roll awkwardly toward him, trying to get closer without tangling my wires and tubes. "And Rufus . . . ?"

"Is with your friend Lydia, I can confirm." He hands me his phone with a lopsided smile. On the screen is a selfie of Lydia and Rufus—she's grinning at the camera while he drags his long tongue up the side of her face.

"What's that on his neck?" I ask.

Drew's eyes darken. "He needed a couple of stitches where that asshole cut him when he attacked."

"He what?" I zoom in on the photo, and sure enough, a patch of his golden fur is shaved around a stitched, crooked wound. My heartbeat pulses under my skin. "He got *hurt*?"

"It wasn't deep. He'll be okay," Drew says gently. "He did exactly what he was trained to do."

"I just . . ." I swallow, trying to put my feelings into words, but all I choke out is, "That damn dog means so much."

Drew takes my hands in his and waits until I meet his gaze. "You both do."

We sit there a minute, holding onto each other. Until finally, I clear my throat. "Listen, Drew—"

A muffled ruckus cuts through the air, and it's a second before I recognize the familiar notes of *Scooby Doo*. I sit up, scanning the room for my phone as Drew hops out of the chair, pulling my device from his jeans pocket.

He hands it to me, then steps toward the door. "I'll just give you some—"

"No," I say too quickly. My face warms at the intensity in my voice and the flutter in my chest. If there's anything I'm certain of, it's that I don't want Drew to leave. I tap the screen to answer, then look at him and mouth *Would you stay?*

He sits again almost immediately.

I take a deep breath and put the call on speaker. "This is Caprice."

"Okay, you *are* alive. That's a positive." My brother's voice comes over the line thick but surprisingly clear. "Some Forbes answered your phone last night, and I wasn't sure whether I should believe him."

I raise my eyebrows, wincing when I forget my stitches. "Very much alive. Are you stateside?" He must be if he's calling from his cell.

"Yeah. I'm in . . . Delaware," he says. "Trying to get my ass on a flight so I can bust some balls in Denver." He hesitates, then asks softly, "Are you okay?"

My cheek twitches. I don't know how much Drew told him, and honestly, I don't know how to answer his question yet. "You do *not* need to fly here and do anything." I let out a low breath. "I'm okay, Theo. Thanks in part to that smelly dog you gave me."

The corner of Drew's mouth curves into a smile.

"Okay, *see?*" Theo's voice rises. "I told you—"

"Blah blah blah, I'm grateful for Rufus. I'm keeping him. End of conversation." I sink happily into our usual banter.

"Well, I'm glad that's settled." A barely audible chuckle comes over the line before my brother ruins our playful facade. "Reece, if I'd been there—I—I'm so sorry—"

My throat closes. I don't know if he's really in Delaware. If he's really somewhere safe. But I can't listen to Theo beat himself up because he thinks he failed me.

"The guy's in jail. I'm okay." I squeeze Drew's hand,

letting out a shaky breath my brother can't hear. "The police are still investigating, but they think it was the same guy sending me shit this whole time."

"The one from Unmatched?" Theo growls.

"Not the guy I originally thought, but yeah. He was on there. Apparently, I'm not the first woman this asshole has stalked." I swallow. "And before you say anything, I know this wouldn't have happened if I hadn't written about that app, but I didn't become a journalist to write about shit that doesn't matter."

There's a long pause, and I gird myself for a lecture. Something about safety and not drawing attention to myself. But when he speaks again, my badass little brother is clearly holding back emotion.

"I hope you know I've only ever given you shit about your job because I love you and I want you safe. I *never* meant to imply you were responsible for any man's behavior." He takes a breath and continues. "Your work exposing that app has been important—admirable. And when I read your piece about Kyle this week . . ." He hesitates, voice quavering. "It was beautiful, Reece. You honored his life, but you also shed light on his struggle. I think it'll help people. I think he'd be proud."

I press my lips together, unsure what to say. Then I glance at Drew in the chair where he spent half the night. And the shine in his eyes is everything.

"If I haven't already said so," my brother goes on. "I admire you. You're a damn good writer. A talented journalist. And you're fucking brave."

"Thanks, Theo," I whisper.

He clears his throat. "I'm gonna have to run. I-I just needed to hear your voice. I *will* be checking to make sure that motherfucker who came after you gets what he deserves, but mostly . . . I just needed to say I love you."

I wipe the corners of my eyes. "I love you too."

"Oh, and Mom's on her way up from Castle Rock right now. Sorry."

"You didn't . . ." I bring my hand to my face, but he's already ended the call.

I set the phone next to me on the bed, staring at my fingers still curled around Drew's. He pivots toward me and clears his throat. "You know, your brother was right."

I tilt my head, afraid to look straight at him until I've fought back my tears. "About what?"

"What you wrote about Kyle. His depression. Not just after his TBI—his lifelong battle." Drew's voice is thick, but his words are unflinching. "I could tell how much you loved him just from what you wrote. How hard you must've tried to make his existence easier."

My throat tightens.

He squeezes both my hands, catching my eye again. "But Theo's right. The most powerful part of your article, the part that's going to help people heal, is your forgiveness. Of Kyle, but also yourself. Acknowledging that while you did everything you possibly could to help him, ultimately the choice he made was never about you."

A tear splashes onto our joined hands. Mine.

"Or you," I whisper.

He reaches up to my cheek, wiping the next tear before it falls. And then he's out of the chair, squeezing gently into the hospital bed until he's pulled me into his arms.

"Since my brother died, I've been so focused on doing right by him—at first through Rufus. But then I started trying to do the same thing with you."

He strokes my face, taking care to give my stitches a wide berth.

"But last night, when I heard you scream, when I didn't know what was happening inside your apartment . . ." His voice breaks. "Kyle hardly crossed my mind, Caprice. I was just desperate to get to you."

I lean into his big body then, wrapping my arms around his warm, too-firm chest. Getting as close to him as possible.

"I know you said what happened before was just sex," he says so low it's barely a whisper. "But I—"

"I love you," I say.

We each pause a heartbeat, listening as those words hit the air.

"Whatever I said before was bullshit. I felt everything you felt. I still do. And I will *never* forget the way you made me come. But more than that, you're not the person I thought you were, and it's been magic realizing I was wrong. You make me feel safe. You love my dog." My vision hazes again as we stare at each other. "And I love you."

His lips are on mine before I can breathe. My hands twist in his hair, knocking his glasses askew. There are too many IVs and wires and beeps, and pretty soon, there's a nurse in here yelling at me. But I don't even care. All I hear is Drew uttering my words back to me, into my skin.

"I love you, Caprice. You are everything to me."

EPILOGUE

ONE MONTH LATER

THE FRONT DOOR SWINGS OPEN, AND DREW DRAWS ME INSIDE and into his arms before I even get my key in the lock. When our lips meet, his hand cups the back of my neck, and almost everything about the last eight hours ceases to feel important. Until he kisses along my cheek and whispers in my ear.

"At least five of us are dying to hear about your first day."

Just as he says this, a big furry body presses against my thigh. I look down to find Rufus wedged between Drew's jeans and my black crepe skirt, wagging his tail with delight. As he stands there, beaming up at me, Pudding, the bulldog, shoves between *his* legs until they resemble some kind of mashed-up mythical creature. Drew's German shepherd and border collie also circle us, albeit with a more respectful energy.

"*You* are the reasons I've had to invest in a lifetime supply of pet hair rollers," I say, carefully slipping out of my brand new Louboutins and sinking down to greet the dogs.

Rufus licks my face in reply, which still makes me cringe, but I let him. He goes straight for the fading line where the stitches used to be at my temple, and I instinctively run my

310

fingers over the shaved spot on his chest. Both of us are healed, but we check in on each other's scars.

"Can't blame them for missing you." Drew's eyes twinkle as he extends a hand and pulls me back to my feet. "Now, how did it go?"

I bite my lip, releasing a satisfied sigh. "Well . . . it was flipping amazing."

He doesn't say anything, just breaks into a grin. An expression I'm still getting used to, but quickly coming to adore.

"It was completely overwhelming, but I loved every single second," I say as he picks up my heels, stowing them in a dog-proof cabinet. "I had to start in HR and do all the new employee stuff. They have really tight security policies, so I appreciate that. Next, they gave me a tour of the entire building before introducing me to my department, which comprised about as many people as the entire staff at the *Observer*. And then I was shown to *my office*"—I can't help giggling, saying it is still a thrill—"which, okay, isn't truly mine. I share it with another reporter. But it has a door and a window, and four entire more walls than I used to have around my desk. And Drew, my *name* is on the door."

"Already my favorite room in the building." He smirks. "Who's your officemate?"

"Her name is Jessica. We hit it off right away and even compared notes on some future projects. We're both interested in a couple of recent disappearances near Fort Collins." I bite my lip. "I also had a meeting with Monique King."

"Ooh, the new Randall?" He leads me toward the big, cushy sofa. "How'd that go?"

He pauses to toss a ball to Rufus, who has clearly made himself at home. We worked out a custody agreement of sorts after what happened with my psycho stalker. Rufus stays with me every night, but once the job offer came in from *Denver Editorial*, we decided he should spend his weekdays with Drew. As we've spent more time together over the last month, though, the custody lines have started to blur.

"It was actually a great conversation, and she was super welcoming." I make a face. "But she still scares the crap out of me."

"I'm pretty sure she knows how lucky she is to have you." He pulls us down to the couch and me into his lap. "She's probably anxious to secure awards for the *Editorial* with the Colorado Press Club."

My cheeks warm. "It was just a nomination. There's no guarantee I'll win."

He folds his arms the way I've coached him to recently in his dog training videos—which instantly makes my throat go dry—then pins me with one of his adorable Clark Kent gazes. "There's no guarantee you won't."

I cover my face with my hands, emitting an excited screech. "Agh, Drew! It's just everything I used to imagine being a journalist would be like back in high school and college. It's like I finally got my dream job."

He tugs my hands away from my face, eyes crinkling as he draws me closer. "I think I know what that feels like."

When our lips meet, he tastes like home—warm, and sweet, and safe. His hand starts politely on my knee, but as our kisses grow more heated, he begins exploring the length of my thigh. I sink into him, losing myself in the stroke of his hands and the warmth of his lips until a distinct ringtone cuts through the air.

We pause, staring into each other's eyes.

Drew quirks an amused brow. "You better go see what's happening."

I plant one more big, wet kiss on his lips, then hustle across the room to where I set my phone down by the door.

"Is it time?" I ask before Lydia can say anything.

"No. I wish." She pouts. "I can't take much more of this. I feel like the Goodyear blimp."

"You look gorgeous," I tell her, and I mean it. She must have her phone propped up in her kitchen. Her belly fills most of the screen, and she's wearing one of two dresses she claims are the only things that fit anymore, but she radiates health and beauty like she's some kind of fertility goddess. I guess this is how the human race manages to keep going.

"Thank you," she says. "But I didn't call fishing for compliments. I need to hear about your big day!"

Drew hops up to feed the dogs. Blitz and Rufus are circling at his heels, and the other two are close behind. So I settle into the warm spot he left on the couch and tell Lydia everything about being *Denver Editorial's* newest feature writer.

"I'm so happy for you," she squeals. "This job sounds like a dream."

"It basically is. I still miss Randall, and maybe even Jana a little bit. And my commute. But I can't complain about not having to see Brian's smug face anymore."

"Oh yeah, how are the new wheels?"

I shrug. *Denver Editorial* is too far downtown for me to walk, and since Rufus is now a permanent fixture in my life, I conceded to Theo and Drew's urges and bought a modest used car. "I'll admit, it was nice having air conditioning on the way home."

She laughs. "Well, I hope the rest of the week is just as smooth, and I can't wait to read your first feature. If I *still* haven't gone into labor by next weekend, you and Drew should come over for Sunday dinner. I'm going to need people to distract me."

It surprises me how quickly she's accepted my boyfriend. Honestly, I'm still getting used to it. But she had been like a sister to Kyle in college, and once she and Drew started talking dogs, he was pretty much granted an all-access pass to our inner circle.

"You're not due until tomorrow, right?"

"*Today*," she says, moaning at the ceiling.

"Oh . . ." I clear my throat. "Well, why isn't anything happening? Maybe you should eat a pineapple or something?"

"That's an old wives' tale. And I've already tried it. And eggplant parmesan. And Mexican food—"

"Have you had sex?"

She glares at me through the screen. But the way her face turns an immediate tomato red tells me they've checked that box too.

"Well, unless your family expands more than your waistline this week, we would be happy to join you for Sunday dinner."

Drew settles back in beside me and peeks into the frame, his expression hard to discern. Maybe a little surprised? But then he smiles and gives me a squeeze. "That would be incredible. Thanks, Lydia."

She beams at us through the camera, then mutters something about a glass of orange juice, and we say goodbye.

Drew nuzzles my ear with a light sigh, his gaze tracking across the room to his framed photo of Kyle and me. Suddenly, I understand what's on his mind.

"Your parents used to do family dinners."

He nods, leaning his head against mine. I don't know all the details of what went down between Drew and his parents, but I guess he said some things on behalf of himself and Kyle, and now he's blocked their numbers from his cell. It's clearly been hard for him, but he also seems more at peace.

I place my hand over his.

"You want to order in tonight?" he whispers, laying spare little kisses along my neck until I shiver.

"Yes. If we can get something . . . spicy." I walk my fingers down to his waist.

He catches my eye, one brow arching over his glasses. "Again?"

I hold his gaze, challenging him to suggest he's not interested. My hand slides to the front of his pants, where it's clear that's not the case. "It's a great way to start—and end—the day."

He answers wordlessly, lips soft and warm against mine, cupping his hand where my hair is still gathered in a low chignon. I take the urgent exploration of his tongue as an invitation to climb on top of him. Which seems welcome enough when his big, warm hands find their way under my skirt. I shiver as he traces my legs beneath the fabric, hands hot against my flesh. He groans at my response, keeping his hands moving until they've rounded the contour of my hips and he's grabbed two fistfuls of my silk panties.

I groan, closing my eyes and losing myself as I trace my lips and tongue over his stubbled jaw.

His voice is husky in my ear. "Stay here tonight?"

My mouth tugs to one side, his breath sending tingles over my skin. I still land back at my apartment here and there, but it hasn't felt the same since the night of the attack. I won't even enter the building without Rufus by my side, and even then, I seem to jump at every noise. Without my truly realizing it, half my work wardrobe and a toothbrush have already ended up over here. Drew has even started buying my favorite coffee creamer.

"Hmm, I don't know . . . hard decision," I whisper.

In response, he thrusts his rock-hard cock against my center through our clothes. I gasp, arching against him.

Until a cold, wet feeling against my thigh makes me shriek.

I look down to see Rufus wagging his tail next to the couch, gazing up at me with his golden eyes. He's dropped a soggy tennis ball into the limited space between us and seems to think this is a good time to play.

"Ew, dog!" I fling the ball to the floor, wiping at the drool on my skirt. "You are seriously lucky I love you."

Drew chuckles and sits up, pulling me with him toward the edge of the couch as Rufus retrieves the ball. "Maybe we should move somewhere less crowded."

He wraps my legs around his waist and powers to his feet, cupping his hands under my ass to hold me up. I gasp at his strength as he carries me down the short hall leading to his bedroom, stopping to press me into every stretch of bare wall along the way, kissing and grinding into me while discarding layers of clothing.

By the time he drops me gently onto the bed, he's lost his shoes, his chest is bare, and I'm down to my skirt and bra. My panties are so soaked, they've left a wet mark on his pants.

"A little privacy, please," Drew says, swinging the door closed between us and Rufus. This never would have been possible a month or so ago, but the other dogs have had a calming effect on him. We hear a shuffle of paws, followed by a swish of the dog door, and then through the window, we can hear Rufus and Blitz running through the backyard agility course.

"Now, where was I?" Drew asks, crouching down and lifting the edge of my skirt. "Oh, right—under here."

Cool air hits my hot-and-ready center as he slides my panties off and out of the way. For just a moment, my flesh is exposed and aching, but the space between my legs is soon invaded by his warm and eager tongue.

I buck so fiercely the first time his lips lock over my clit, my ass rises right off the bed. He reaches up with one of his long-fingered hands, somehow freeing my breast from its straining bra cup, and gives my nipple a subtle pinch.

"*Oh.*"

You might think he'd drop his pants and just go for it at this point, but to my benefit and possibly also my detriment, the man is some kind of cunnilingus champion. He actually pulls back until he's only stroking my clit with the tip of his tongue. Which you wouldn't think would do much until you remember the ten-thousand-plus nerve endings in that magic little nub. And when he emulates the same tiny strokes with his fingers against my nipple, I am already strung so tight it takes about forty-five seconds for him to finish plucking me like a violin.

Open windows be damned—I scream.

But my body has gotten to know this man intimately over the past month, and my core pulses as I come down, knowing he's just warming up.

He makes his way up between my legs, casting aside our remaining clothing until it's just our two naked bodies, my skin smooth and brown against his pale tan. He lays kisses in a line from my belly button up to my throat, whispering that I'm beautiful as he kneads my breasts in his hands.

His cock rests thick and heavy against my entrance, and I might actually die of anticipation if I wasn't *sure* this was worth the wait. We got testing and birth control discussions out of the way the second night I stayed over. So when he finally slides his impressive length inside me, bare and slick with my juices, it is almost enough for me to come right away.

I have to actively bite my lip, holding myself back as he starts to move. And he quickly finds an intoxicating rhythm made especially for my body, squeezing my breasts together and toying with my nipples as he rocks his hips.

When I am almost incoherent from trying to hold myself together, he gazes down at me between thrusts and says, "Rufus got you a present."

"He—what?"

I open my eyes, confused about why he's mentioning the dog now. But the sight of this carved Superman hovering over me, *filling* me, is so intoxicating. I run my hands over the relief of his deltoids, pectorals, and ab muscles, and almost can't believe he's real.

He smirks and leans to one side of the bed—crucially,

without pulling out—and straightens back up, holding a purple silicone vibrator. But it isn't just any purple vibe; it's my favorite. The *exact* one Rufus destroyed however many weeks ago.

My jaw drops. "How did—"

"A little dog told me," he says, thrusting his cock deep as he flicks the switch on the vibe, bringing it humming to life. I didn't think my core could actually ache this way *while* being fucked, but here we are. I gulp as he nudges the purple toy against my clit.

"*Unfair*," is all I manage to gasp.

"Oh, you don't want it?" he asks, turning it back off.

"Hand it over, Forbes," I snap. "You know I want all your dicks."

He snorts, but obeys. And a few delicious moments later, Drew's thick length is stroking in and out of me, and I have the tip of my *second*-favorite cock vibrating against my clit. The sensation is too good, and I come so hard, I am certain I'm going to launch off the bed. Maybe I would if I weren't pinned in place by Drew's magnificent cock, pushed inside me to the hilt. He grunts and pulses through his orgasm right with me until finally we collapse in a tangle of skin and sweat and satisfaction.

When I open my eyes a couple of hours later, the house is quiet and dim. Drew must've gotten up because the dogs are in here, all sacked out in their respective beds—except Rufus, who is squeezed into a ball at my feet.

The familiar scent of my favorite Thai food wafts down the hall. I close my eyes and inhale, then slip Drew's discarded Henley over my head.

I find him in the kitchen, shirtless, in a pair of low-slung joggers. There's a plastic bag on the counter that is the obvious source of the deliciously spicy smell, but his attention is on an open cardboard box next to it.

I clear my throat as I enter, trying not to startle him. He turns his head, eyes shadowed, and reaches for my hand.

"I was moving some dog supplies around when the food arrived. I'd forgotten I had this . . ." He swallows, squeezing my hand. "There was almost nothing in his apartment the last time I was there. The shelves and drawers were nearly empty, nothing on the walls. It was—it was like he'd already stopped living."

I move closer to Drew, curling my arm around him as we look at the box.

"It's mostly papers. His diploma. Ranger tab. A few books. He'd rented the place furnished. But the last time I saw him, the time I told him about the business and begged him to come back with me—" His voice breaks. "He had this with him."

Somehow, I know what it is before he takes the photo out of the box. It's a little dusty, in a modest frame that matches the one I used to have. We picked them out together, just before he left to join the army. I lean into Drew as I run my fingers over the glass, over our smiles and embracing bodies. For a long time, I couldn't look at the photo at all. Not without just aching for the people in it. The boy with the sorrow and the girl who wanted to save him from it.

The same ache throbs through me now. But as it does, I close my eyes and allow myself to also feel grateful. For the memory. For the boy who loved me with his whole heart, even if he didn't know how to love himself.

"I'm glad you kept it," I whisper.

Drew pulls me to him. Neither of us speaks. We just stand there, holding one another. Holding each other up.

Eventually, he murmurs in a wavering voice, "Would you feel weird if I put it out . . . here? To look at?"

I turn to look at him. "Would *you* feel weird?"

His eyes are a gray-green when they meet mine. "A picture of two people I love?" He shakes his head and pulls me closer. "I think I'd like to look at it every day."

Thank you for reading!
If you enjoyed this book, you can get more of Caprice and other characters in:
Love Unmatched **&** *Love Mismatched*

WANT A FREE STORY?

Receive *In The Making*, the exclusive free prequel to The Unmatched Series, and stay up to date on new releases and events when you sign up for Emilia Reed's newsletter:

SIGN UP HERE:
emiliareed.com / newsletter

ALSO BY EMILIA REED

THE UNMATCHED SERIES

Love Unmatched

Love Mismatched

Love In Training

Love Rematched (TBA)

Love Bombed (TBA)

BONUS CONTENT

FREE when you sign up at: emiliareed.com/newsletter

In The Making - series prequel

Forty Weeks - *Love Mismatched* bonus epilogue

ABOUT THE AUTHOR

Emilia Reed was raised in Upstate New York until she fell in love and fled its gray skies for the sunny Rocky Mountains. When she is not attempting to substitute couples therapy with romance novels, she spends her time obsessing over dogs and searching for the perfect coffee and ice cream pairing. Emilia lives in Colorado with her family.

You can find out what's new with Emilia Reed and sign up for free bonus content at emiliareed.com

www.ingramcontent.com/pod-product-compliance
Lightning Source LLC
Chambersburg PA
CBHW020249010826
48973CB00006B/1715